Freemen Shall Stand

Frank Becker

9/14/2016 Frank

Greenbush Press
Spring, TX

Published simultaneously worldwide.

Becker, Frank
Series: "The Chronicles of CC"

Book Three
Freemen Shall Stand / Frank Becker

ISBN:
Trade paperback, 978-0-9836460-4-4
Electronic book, 978-0-9836460-9-9

Library of Congress PCN 2014938459

Printed in the United States of America

8/16

Freemen Shall Stand

is for my good friend and colleague,

Senator Stephen R. Wise
and his wife Kathy

The Star Spangled Banner
Francis Scott Key, 1814

Oh, say can you see by the dawn's early light
What so proudly we hailed at the twilight's last gleaming?
Whose broad stripes and bright stars thru the perilous fight,
O'er the ramparts we watched were so gallantly streaming?
And the rocket's red glare, the bombs bursting in air,
Gave proof through the night that our flag was still there.
Oh, say does that star-spangled banner yet wave
O'er the land of the free and the home of the brave?

On the shore, dimly seen through the mists of the deep,
Where the foe's haughty host in dread silence reposes,
What is that which the breeze, o'er the towering steep,
As it fitfully blows, half conceals, half discloses?
Now it catches the gleam of the morning's first beam,
In full glory reflected now shines in the stream:
'Tis the star-spangled banner! Oh long may it wave
O'er the land of the free and the home of the brave!

And where is that band who so vauntingly swore
That the havoc of war and the battle's confusion,
A home and a country should leave us no more!
Their blood has washed out their foul footsteps' pollution.
No refuge could save the hireling and slave
From the terror of flight, or the gloom of the grave:
And the star-spangled banner in triumph doth wave
O'er the land of the free and the home of the brave!

Oh! thus be it ever, when freemen shall stand
Between their loved home and the war's desolation!
Blest with victory and peace, may the heav'n rescued land
Praise the Power that hath made and preserved us a nation.
Then conquer we must, when our cause it is just,
And this be our motto: "In God is our trust."
And the star-spangled banner in triumph shall wave
O'er the land of the free and the home of the brave!

"...and this desire on my part, exempt from all vanity of authorship, had for its only object and hope that it might be useful to others as a lesson of morality, patience, courage, perseverance, and Christian submission to the will of God."

—Johann Wyss, 1812
Author, "The Swiss Family Robinson"

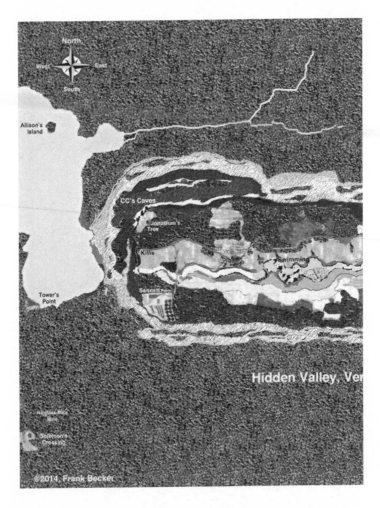

West End, Hidden Valley

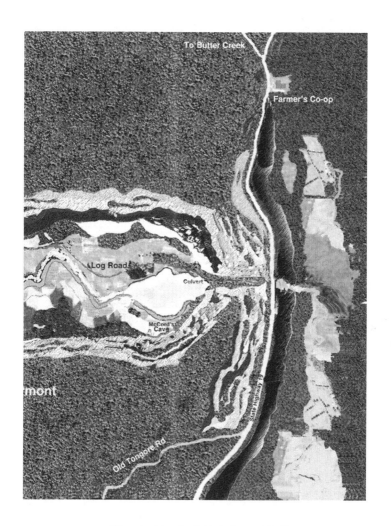

East End, Hidden Valley

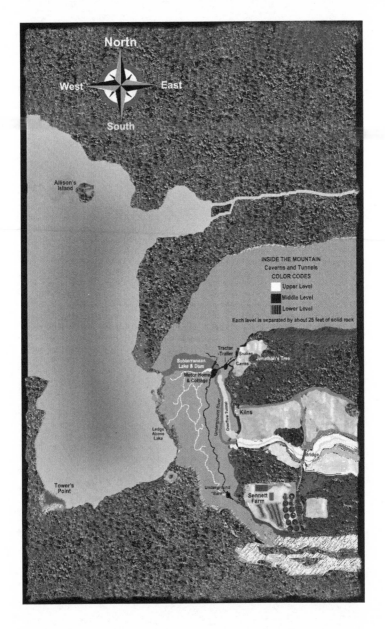

Caverns to Allison Lake, West end of Hidden Valley

Return to Hidden Valley

Old Tongore Road
Central Vermont
June 18th, 7:30a.m.

J ust moments before, while under fire from the air, CC had
watched in amazement as a teenager with a small game rifle
had suddenly appeared in the back of his pickup truck and shot
down the attacking airplane. Now the burning remnants of
that plane and its two man crew was strewn among the trees
along that mountain road, and CC and the boy were in the cab
of the truck racing away from the scene.

CC had been driving that old pickup truck along a winding forest road when he suddenly found himself under fire from
a small plane. The plane had suddenly appeared from the east,
diving out of the early morning sun, and spraying the area in
front of the truck with an automatic weapon.

Skidding to a stop, CC had taken cover behind a rock out-
cropping, and futilely emptied his pistol at the plane. He
thought he might leave his precious cargo behind and try to escape through the forest, but when the pilot started setting the
plane down on the dirt road, CC realized he might have only
minutes to live.

His life had been saved by the teenager who was now sitting beside him. The boy had stowed away in the back of CC's
pickup truck by hiding beneath the canvas tarpaulin that CC
had used to cover his load. When CC skidded to a stop to seek
shelter from the unexpected attack, the lad had suddenly
slashed his way through the canvas and brought down the
plane with one amazing shot from his small-game rifle.

But it was not merely the wrecked airplane and its dead crew that spurred CC to race away up the dirt road. It was the specter of vengeful pursuers who would not hesitate to murder both he and the boy. America had been at war for only a short time, but its Chinese invaders were now in control of much of New England. CC had monitored the airwaves, and had heard ham radio enthusiasts warn that the invaders were attempting to bring all American survivors under submission. Failing that, they planned to either imprison or eliminate them. CC now believed these reports, for without any opportunity for a hearing, he had very nearly been murdered by the crew of that airplane.

Why would the Chinese want to kill me? he wondered. *I can't imagine that I am of any importance. I don't even know my own name.*

As he fought to keep the old truck moving up the winding road, he glanced at the boy who had just saved his life. Recognizing that their prospects for survival were small, he pressed the gas pedal to the floor, pushing the old truck to its limits.

With the truck's engine clattering and his own body pumping adrenalin, it seemed to take forever to get up the mountain road, though it was probably no more than ten minutes. The dirt road unexpectedly ended where it intersected Vermont Route 19, and he slid around the corner onto the blacktop without slowing for the faded stop sign. The engine was beginning to knock, and steam curled from under the hood as the decrepit truck heaved itself around the last curve before starting the climb to the crest of the mountain.

The kid was shouting at him above the sound of the wind and the engine. "Mister, did you see the markings on that old plane? A big star and four small ones. Those guys must have been Russians."

"Russians?" CC turned to look at the boy. "The Russians have a single red star. Those markings were Chinese. Don't they teach you anything in school?"

"Yeah, sure," was the sarcastic response. "School was great." CC regretted his caustic question.

"It could have been the Russians," the boy persisted.

"There are no Russians; only Chinese."

"I heard that the Russians invaded Canada, and are on their way toward Boston."

"I hadn't heard that," CC admitted, now regretting even more that he'd mocked the boy. He was silent for a moment, then in a conciliatory voice, "The Chinese flag has yellow stars on a red field."

"The markings might have been Chinese," the boy countered, "but those guys in the cockpit weren't. They were Americans!" He started to cry again. "I killed Americans."

CC realized that he sounded callous when he responded, "So what?" He was not insensitive to the boy's pain, but those two men had sold out to the invaders, and they had been trying to kill them.

He seemed to grind out the words. "An enemy is an enemy, and it doesn't matter what country issues him a passport." The boy might have nodded his head in agreement, but CC was focused on the rumors he'd heard over the radio, wondering whether they were true. He had just seen evidence that the Chinese had invaded America, and it stood to reason that the boy was right — the Russians were coming too. And there was even one report that a large body of well-armed Islamic invaders were moving up through the United States from Mexico.

Dear God, I hope that's not true. But even so, America is a lot of country to conquer, and many of the Americans who have survived are showing themselves to be pretty tough customers. He smiled grimly. *Maybe taking over the USA won't be as easy as her invaders assumed.*

He turned to the boy. "The Chinese have been preparing for war for decades. They had plenty of money, the world's largest army, and a technologically advanced navy and air force. They stole every military secret and weapons system from us that they could, and if it couldn't be stolen and wasn't for sale, then they found traitors in government and industry who would provide those secrets."

The boy nodded in agreement, then revealed his surprise when CC added, "In spite of all those advantages, they still may have bitten off more than they could chew."

"What do you mean?"

They probably invaded a number of countries. It's my opinion that— in spite of their stealing many of our military and industrial secrets, and in spite of traitors in government and industry and government giving or selling them a lot more, it's my opinion that, when push came to shove, some of our military still gave them a bad time."

The kid merely stared at him.

"The point is," CC said patiently, "that maybe the Chinese won't be able to supply enough troops and equipment to pacify all the countries they've invaded. Unless, of course, they can blackmail, brainwash, intimidate, and bribe the local populations to work for them."

"Maybe so," the boy responded, "but they sure did '...blackmail, brainwash, intimidate, or bribe..' the two guys in that plane."

"Yes, they certainly did," CC agreed. "And that's why you must not feel guilty about defending yourself against them."

The truck was rolling down a short steep grade, and CC pulled the wheel gently to guide the old truck around the broad turn. When he'd cleared the crest and was completing the short distance to his turnoff, CC drew to a stop and put the truck in neutral to let the wind cool the idling engine.

He pulled a dark stocking cap from his pack on the seat and said to the boy, "Put this on." The lad seemed reluctant, and CC repeated himself. This time the boy obeyed him, pulling the knit hat down to his hair line. CC told him to pull it down over his eyes so that he couldn't see. The kid looked at him in distrust, but again he obeyed.

"Put your hands on the dashboard and brace yourself," CC commanded. The boy shrugged, then stretched out one arm to grasp the molded contour of the dashboard, used the other to grasp the armrest of the door, and spread his feet on the floor, his legs straddling a carton of canned goods.

CC did not see anyone on the road or in the air, but he waited until he'd reached his turn before braking violently and sliding the battered vehicle across the highway and between two trees on the edge of the highway. They bounced heavily across the swale, for he was intent on vanishing quickly, whatever the cost to the truck and generator trailer. His speed was almost his undoing, for the trailer bounced from wheel to wheel, almost flipping over.

He had pulled into the mouth of a hanging valley. No one would suspect the valley's existence because its very narrow entrance was carved as though by a sharp knife in the face of the tall cliff that ran along one edge of the highway, and that edge of the road was heavily overgrown with trees. He pulled well in among those trees, then slipped the transmission into neutral, set the brake, and told the boy to stay put while he ran back to scuff out any tracks. He took particular pains to hide any sign of his passing because he was sure that pursuit was inevitable, and he feared that his new enemies would somehow discover the hidden entrance.

CC didn't want to think about the burned bodies in the plane's wreckage, but he couldn't help hoping that the pilot had been so sure of himself that he hadn't bothered calling in a report their contact with him, and that any search party would assume the plane had crashed as a result of a malfunction.

As he swept the ground with an evergreen bough, CC thanked God that there had been no rain, and that the leaves were dry. He left no evidence of his passing but for a small tree that he'd sideswiped in passing, leaving a splintered branch with a white scar, almost invisible to a searching eye. He rubbed the raw wood with soil, dropped the evergreen bough, and took a can of black pepper from his pocket and sprinkled the contents over the area. That should slow down any hounds they might put on our scent, he thought.

Just as he returned to the safety of the trees, he heard a roar. He looked out across the valley to see a low-flying helicopter, the five red stars unmistakable on its fuselage, heading across the mountain toward the cloud of smoke which rose from the downed plane's wreckage. The copter was gone before its potential malice registered on him. These people certainly appear to have the necessary ordinance to subdue a stricken and passive society.

Once again, he slid behind the wheel, knowing the truck wasn't going much further, and began to plead with God to keep it running just a little longer. He had been destroying a lot of motor vehicles lately. About a hundred yards up the trail, they reached a small lake and he again stopped the truck under the trees.

He told the boy to remove the knit cap that served as a mask, then got down to try to pour water into the cooling system. He had left the radiator cap loose so that it wouldn't build up pressure and scald him when he needed to remove it again. The engine had almost died, but when he poured water in, and poured more over the radiator, it began to cool the engine and it slowed its frightening clatter.

The boy just sat there staring through the windshield of the truck. He seemed to be stunned by the mystery of the canyon. CC wondered whether he was held in the thrall of its beauty, or traumatized by the occurrences of the past twenty minutes. Still worried about pursuit, CC ran back toward the highway to see whether they had been followed. He was standing well back from the road when a state police car, its siren wailing, roared up the hill and disappeared in the direction of the plane crash.

Another Foundling

The Bottleneck
Hidden Valley
June 18th, about 7:55 a.m.

W hen CC walked back through the bottleneck, he didn't hear the engine's clatter, and he wondered whether the old truck had breathed its last. If so, he'd have to find another way to drag the trailer-mounted electrical generator the entire length of the valley. When he was several yards from the truck, however, he saw the teen leaning under the hood, and he stepped quietly to the side to see what he was up to.

The boy was using the screwdriver blade on a Swiss Army Knife to tighten a radiator hose clamp. CC watched as he gave one final twist to the screw, and as he snapped the knife closed the boy's lips twisted in a hint of a smile, as though expressing his satisfaction. Then he began to slowly refill the cooling system with water from the lake.

CC was impressed with the teen's initiative, but in spite of his thoughtful labor, he wondered if it would be safe to turn his back on him. There had been a lot of killing during the weeks since the war began. Many had been committed by marauders intent on stealing whatever they could from any refugees they could easily victimize. Some was done by innocents, in self-defense. And some by people driven nearly insane by their circumstances.

Some people had responded heroically, almost nobly, to the crisis, while many who discovered themselves free of society's restraints and its accepted norms of behavior, found that freedom to be too great a burden. Liberty had given way to license, and a great deal of savagery had erupted in the now unrestrained society.

CC turned to the boy. "Son, I've got a lot of questions that I need answered, but right now I've got one important one: 'What in the world am I going to do with you?'"

Tears began to slip from the lad's eyes, and when he tried to speak, he lost control. It was as though a dam had broken. His chin dropped to his chest, he hunched his shoulders, and began to weep uncontrollably. The sobs with which he was wracked provided ample response to CC's rhetorical question.

He waited for the boy to speak. In his mind, he'd somehow confused this insecure and frightened teenager with a mature man. That was probably because the boy had just saved his life. Now CC realized that this young man still had a lot of boy left in him. And he was actually happy to discover that the teen was so sensitive.

After a minute or two, the teen made his way to the pond's edge and knelt down so that he could splash his face with water. CC took his elbow and helped him to his feet. They walked back toward the truck together, and he handed the boy a bottle of water. The drink helped him regain control.

The boy looked up into CC's eyes. "Mister, I don't have anyone left. No family. No home. I can do a lot of things pretty well, and I've always been a fast learner." He spread his hands wide, his voice timorous. "The problem is, they took everything I owned — gun, ammunition, and food — and I don't have anywhere to go."

He took a deep breath. "I was wondering, please, can I stay here?" His hands spread out to engulf the valley that lay before them. There was desperation in his eyes as he stammered on. "I wouldn't bother you." The boy looked out across the lake, then back at CC, and the man could see hope warring with despair.

"This is a big place. You wouldn't even have to know I was here. And I could make out. Honest. I could build a little place, do some hunting, live off the land. Please mister?" Hope seemed to surge in the boy as he built his argument for remaining nearby. "Please let me stay here. I'll do whatever you say. Honest!"

CC put his hand on the boy's shoulder. "Never promise to do something without knowing what that something is," he cautioned. "Rash promises like that are just crying out to be tested, and they often need to be broken." The boy studied him carefully, but merely nodded.

He's enumerating my qualities and potential liabilities just as I'm weighing his, CC realized. To the boy's credit, he stood unflinching beneath his examination. It occurred to CC that the teen was attempting to appear transparent, trying to avoid any appearance of guile, as the boy licked his lips and forced a self-conscious smile to cover his nervousness.

A bullfrog roared at the edge of the lake and they both jumped, startled by the racket. Then they laughed self-consciously, knit together in a common bond, their humanity exposed. Strange that a small embarrassment, a mutual exposure to meaningless stimuli, could affect two people just as much as near-death at the hands of an air-borne killer with a machine gun.

For that is what they had been threatened with. A small propellor-driven plane had swooped down out of the rising sun, and someone in the passenger seat had fired on them with an automatic weapon. If this boy hadn't fired his old rifle, wounding the pilot, they'd both be dead.

CC studied the lad more closely. He was lean, stretched somewhere between adolescence and manhood, with the calloused hands of the rare working teenager. He had pronounced cheek bones, a lantern jaw, and eyes which were alert but not haunted. The boy was slightly shorter than CC, and little more than half his weight, with a shock of unkempt brown curls overgrowing the greasy collar of his worn flannel shirt.

There were a few freckles sprayed across the bridge of a finely cut, but not effeminate nose. He had a wide mouth, good even teeth, and brown eyes, with a sparkle not quite burned away by the pain and sorrow of the past weeks. He had an altogether unthreatening appearance for a young man who had just shot an airplane out of the sky with a 22-caliber rifle.

CC said, "That was quite a shot, one in a million."

The boy was silent for a moment.

"I knew I only had the one shot, so I prayed."

"You prayed?" CC smiled at him in amazement. "You mean that you think God helped you shoot that plane down?"

The boy looked defensive, and wondered whether he was being mocked. Then his jaw firmed. "That's exactly what I mean. I think we'd both be dead if God hadn't guided my hands, just like he guided David in his battle with Goliath."

"So, you think that you're a David?"

"No. Of course not!" The boy acted as though he considered the question absurd.

"I just meant that God helps those individuals who love and trust him to defeat evil." The boy seemed surprised. "You just said that it was a one in a million shot. This is only a 22 rifle. Just hitting the windshield was a one in a million shot, but it could have bounced right off the glass, and certainly shouldn't have done any real damage."

"Why do you say it could have bounced off?"

"Because those windshields are coated with a tough plastic material to cut UV and IR radiation."

"How do you know that obscure fact?"

"I took flying lessons for a while, until I became involved with computers."

CC realized he had been attempting to evaluate the lad's inner being by studying his outward appearance.

God doesn't do that with us, he knew, *and I'm going to have to trust in God. After all, the boy's explanation really does cover it all.*

He also realized that he had been trying to probe something deeper than a combination of the teenager's genes and chromosomes, and even deeper than the evidence of his child-rearing. He was trying to look into the boy's soul — to somehow weigh, and measure him, for CC realized that his life might again one day depend upon this boy. He sensed something beyond the lad's impulsiveness, beyond even his creativity or marksmanship, a quality that he believed existed within the lad that would cause him to make the right choice at a critical moment.

Will I take a chance on this lad, and risk everything I have, he asked himself, *trusting God to make up the difference if he should fail me?*

And then CC realized that it was not the boy's essence he was seeking at all, but his own. It was suddenly obvious.

I can't know whether I will always be able to rely on the boy. The real issue lies with me. Do I have the quality of character to do what I must do for both him and for Sarah? Then he realized, *What's important is that we both build trust and grow to understand that we can rely on one another.*

He smiled wryly. All these questions, these arguments, were futile. The die was already cast. He had no choice. It wasn't just the realization that he himself might have a wife or child drifting hopelessly somewhere, needing help just as this boy needed help. Nor was it merely a matter of people helping one another in the hope that someone else would some day reciprocate in a similar emergency.

CC understood that he must help this boy because it was the right thing to do. More than that, he needed to help the boy because, if he did not, he would shrivel as a man, and would lose something of his own reason for existence. On the other hand, if he helped the boy, he might just grow a little as well.

The boy was saying something that failed to penetrate his musings, and he tried to recall his words. "Mister, I know you don't have a lot of food here, but could you spare some? Just a little, enough to keep me for a week, or even a day or so, until I can kind of get set up."

An offbeat sense of humor began to exert itself. CC looked at the lad, his mouth hinting at a smile, but when he answered the boy, there was just a little quirky twist to his lips, and his response was heavy with gravity. "I'm sorry son. I can't do that. I have a family to support."

The boy was taken aback, for his response seemed to clash with CC's earlier kindness, but his obvious disappointment was overcome by his curiosity.

"You have a family?"

"I have a little girl. Not my own, but a little girl I am caring for."

The boy's voice took on a tone of guarded interest. "You take care of kids?"

"No. She was all alone, and I didn't have any choice."

"Oh, you mean you don't really care about her."

"Oh, I care, but I haven't been looking for people." This sounded inane even to CC's ears. "I mean I haven't been actually searching for people that I might help, nor for people to join me here."

He wondered how he'd allowed himself to become enveloped in this ridiculous conversation. He'd just wanted to banter a little, but realized the issue was one of life and death to the boy, and nothing to joke about.

The boy was again pawing the ground with that toe. CC now realized it was a characteristic pose, and it almost made him laugh aloud. That would certainly be inappropriate, especially since the lad, unaware of CC's amusement, persisted.

"Maybe you could just spare a can or two of food?" He sounded near tears. "I mean, we're out in the middle of nowhere, and I'm not asking much."

Yes, CC thought, *and you did, after all, save my life by shooting down a plane whose co-pilot was trying to machine gun me to death.* CC knew he had to bring this to a close, but couldn't seem to terminate his perverse attempt at humor. So he found himself denying the request.

"I don't think so. I'm going to need everything I have here to feed the kids I'm caring for."

"Oh," the boy said, obviously crushed. Then he evidently processed CC's words, and curiosity replaced his frown. He challenged CC. "I thought you said you just had a little girl."

CC put his arm around the boy's shoulders. "That was before I met you."

He turned the boy so that they were looking into one another's eyes.

"That little girl's name is Sarah, and she would be very upset if I didn't bring you home with me."

The boy stood there, put off balance by this strange turn of events, not knowing whether the man was serious, or perhaps a little bit mad.

But then CC patted him on the back and said, "It's the least I can do for the boy who saved my life."

"You really mean it?" Tears began to stream down his cheeks again, and CC felt ashamed of having teased the boy, for the lad was so shaken, so uncertain, that he again asked for confirmation.

"I can stay with you?"

"Yes, I mean it, but stop your crying. I don't want a teen-age boy around Sarah who cries all the time."

"Oh, yes sir. I mean, no sir!" He gulped, then he laughed, but the tears continued to stream down his cheeks in spite of his next words. "I won't cry any more."

He began to grin from ear to ear, as he again asked, "You really mean it? I can really go with you?"

The revelation of this boy's starvation for companionship struck a chord in CC, and he realized that taking the lad home with him was one of the wisest decisions he'd ever make. He reached over, swept the boy into his arms and gave him a hug so that the lad couldn't see his own tears.

They climbed into the cab, and CC got the tired old engine to heave itself over one more time, and then he looked up the valley, the rising sun reminding him that it was time to get back to his little girl, and back to his work. He reached out his hand in way of introduction. "Call me, CC."

"My name is Jonathan," the boy responded eagerly, firmly grasping his hand. "Jonathan Whitkowski. I'm from New York, near Kingston. Lake Katrine to be exact. My dad..." he faltered,

"...my dad and my mom...they died in the war. He swallowed hard. Anyway," he added, "I guess I can tell you all about that later." And then, again uncertain and almost in a whisper, "I can, can't I?"

"Sure, you can." CC started to let the clutch out, then changed his mind. Feet braced on the peddles, he turned toward the boy. "I'm going to make one rule right now."

The boy looked at him, eagerness mingled with anxiety, as CC charged him with the most important concern he had. "You must promise never to leave this valley without my express permission. Is that agreed?"

The boy responded dutifully, "I will never leave this place without your permission."

And with that, CC let the clutch out, and the truck jerked a little as the trailer broke loose and started up the track for home.

The spring snow melt had ended, but the stream was still boiling and crashing beside the trail. CC glanced at Jonathan. It was obvious that the teen was as totally captivated by the strange and wonderful shapes of the rocks in this amazing place as he had been when he first arrived. And then CC realized that, while the trip into town had been nearly fatal, he'd found something far more valuable than a mere piece of electrical equipment.

He drove slowly up the rough valley track, dust rising knee-high behind the truck. There was no point in waiting until night. As they drove up the ravine, they were occasionally sheltered by the limbs of trees that overhung the road, but CC wasn't enjoying the view. Until they were safely home, he could not enjoy the beauty of the day.

If the enemy's search activities were currently in the area of the crash, he might just get the truck into his cavern before they widened their search to fly over this valley. He just had to hope that none of the clones the Chinese People's Army were rumored to have brought to America might be flying over this valley at this moment.

The exhausting labor of the next two days did not permit time or energy for an extended discussion of the boy's history. CC assumed that he would be able to determine more about his character by working shoulder to shoulder than by having him verbally showcase his own thoughts, and indeed little bits and pieces came out as Sarah continuously probed for information.

Sarah had been delighted at CC's return, but ecstatic to meet someone much closer to her own age. CC was, in fact, a bit hurt that his reception was not warmer, and surprised to discover in himself a hint of jealousy at the way she immediately warmed to Jonathan. At the same time, he worried a lot less about Jonathan because she immediately accepted him as an older brother, and CC had come to realize that she had a keen intuitive sense about her.

The three of them ate a light snack to ward off their hunger, then began preparation of a grand feast to inaugurate their new family. Hours later, they sat around a camp fire that CC had laid just inside the cave mouth. They talked and laughed while the fire burned down to coals. Jonathan kept marveling about the place. He'd been an amateur spelunker, or, as he explained it to Sarah, an explorer of caves, and he compared this favorably with caverns he had visited. And little Sarah, who wouldn't admit she'd been frightened during CC's absence, acted the part of the subterranean sophisticate, poohing his comments, and making arch assertions about her lengthy experience and knowledge of the caverns.

When it was well past her bedtime, CC scooped the laughing little pixie up and started to carry her to her bed, but she would have none of being treated like a little child in front of her new brother. After all, she'd survived here while taking care of her sick grandmother, hadn't she? So she reached up to pound CC playfully on the chest to protest his manhandling. She would dress herself, she insisted, and tuck herself in, but they could come over and say "good night" when she was ready.

After the child was asleep, CC threw another log on the fire, and he and the boy sat sharing a comradely silence until it was time for them to sleep.

Do It Yourself
Hidden Valley
July 6th, 8:15 a.m.

J onathan and CC spent a lot of time going back and forth between the cave and the farm to repair fences, sharpen tools, plant and cultivate crops, and care for the animals.

Jonathan was not merely a willing helper. The boy who'd once spent hours every day staring at his computer seemed to relish the physical labor. CC jokingly told him that he was cut out for the life of a farmer, and the teenager agreed.

CC had no idea if or when the soldiers who had burned the farm house across the valley might return, but he decided to take advantage of the time to rescue the rich heritage the Sennetts had left their granddaughter. "Who would have ever thought," he asked Jonathan, "that a few hundred pounds of heritage vegetable seeds would become priceless?"

"Priceless? Why's that?" the boy asked. "Don't hybrid seeds produce better vegetables? Why wouldn't you want them?"

CC was obviously working out his answer. "I'm not a botanist, but my understanding is that hybrid seeds are produced by cross-pollinating two specific varieties of a fruit or vegetable in order to produce in the new seed the best characteristics of both."

"Sounds good to me," the boy quipped. "What's the problem?

"As a rule, when you harvest a hybrid fruit or vegetable, the seeds you get from them generally won't reproduce."

"Huh?"

"In other words, you're at the end of the line. You can't get a new plant from the hybrid output."

"Oh, wow!" There was only the sound of their footsteps as they headed back toward the barn. The boy broke the silence.

"So, the heritage seeds are like original, and not hybrid?"

"Right."

"And even though they might not have all the best characteristics of a hybrid, I could use the seeds they produce to make a new crop?"

"Exactly."

"And the Sennetts gathered a lot of these heritage seeds?"

"Hundreds of pounds of various plants and vegetables, mostly grain."

"Wow," he repeated. "We're pretty lucky, aren't we?"

"I wouldn't call it luck," CC answered. "I'd say that the Lord is looking down on us."

Jonathan laughed, and CC looked at him sharply.

"You find that funny?" he asked.

Jonathan took his meaning.

"Oh, no."

"Well?"

"I was just thinking that once those apples are ripe, every time I eat one, you'll have me saving the seeds."

"That's almost true," he responded to the boy's surprise. "Do you remember that carton of small blank envelopes we found in the barn?"

"Yeah."

"Whenever we make apple sauce or cider, we'll wash and dry the seeds, and pack them in those envelopes."

"Really? Why?"

CC ignored his question. "We'll label the envelopes with the name of the seeds, the date we harvest them, and the quantity."

"What would we want with all those seeds?"

"We'll plant some. Apple trees, for example, live a long time, but not forever."

"And the rest?"

"One day, when this war is over, maybe we'll be able to support ourselves by selling the apples, the seeds, and even some of the saplings, and help our neighbors start over."

The boy thought that over.

"So we could also help people and pay our bills by selling vegetable seeds and berry cuttings too."

"Exactly."

Over the next few days, they drove the old pickup back and forth to the farm, not only to remove the heritage seeds, but to remove the large metal storage bins full of feed and seed.

They decided to leave most of the burned farmstead untouched, but there were certain things they believed were worth doing, regardless of the risk. Saving the fruit trees was at the top of the list. While they were cutting weeds and cultivating around the trees in the orchard, Jonathan noticed several bee hives.

They consulted a book on bee husbandry, and immediately located and sterilized the processing equipment in the barn. They found two empty hives, cleaned them thoroughly, and moved them to their own side of the valley. He reasoned that, if the hives at the Sennett farm were discovered, perhaps the new ones near their caves would survive.

Then, suffering just a few stings, they were able to remove over fifty pounds of the precious sweetener from the existing hives. They processed some, storing it in sterilized bottles, and placed some of the comb and honey in each of the new hives near their caves. Late the next afternoon, the bees at the Sennett farm divided into swarms with some remaining behind and others moving across the valley to the new hives.

Such discoveries were mixed blessings because each one burdened them with additional work. For example, Jonathan was dumping a wheelbarrow load of weeds and dead branches when he found that a large area of what he'd considered weeds were actually patches of blueberry and raspberry bushes.

The three of them spread out and began walking across the farm from one side to the other. In a sunny field to the east of the farm, they found a large plot of strawberries, and on a rocky knoll, they discovered blueberries.

They wound up picking fruit for two days, then spent an additional two days converting them to jellies and jams.

In their clumsy attempts to learn new skills, they wasted a good deal of the fruit they'd picked, but finally succeeded in canning about twenty quarts of the berries by using the supplies and equipment the Sennetts had kept stored in the barn.

They would have failed completely if little Sarah hadn't taken things in hand, and shown them a couple of tricks that she'd learned from her grandma, particularly about the need for absolute cleanliness in every step of the process. Jonathan had to stifle a laugh as Sarah stood, fists on hips, and declared, "Don't forget, cleanliness is next to godliness!"

Jonathan joked that the jars of fruit and honey that they stored on shelves in their cave would last them several years, but the humor went over CC's head, and he simply remarked that the cave would make an ideal root cellar.

During this period of adjustment, it was necessary for CC to share the twin beds in the motor home with Jonathan, while Sarah slept on the bunk above the driver's compartment.

CC wasn't comfortable with this arrangement, simply because he felt they both needed more privacy and a place to spend time alone with the Lord. In addition, he was concerned that the motor home would not meet their needs during the coming winter because there was no way to heat it. There wasn't room to safely install a wood stove, and even if there had been, there would be no efficient way to vent the smoke. They couldn't use the built-in gas heater because they lacked a supply of the LP gas that would be required, but even if they had it, the gas would be dangerous.

When CC had awakened with amnesia in that X-ray room in Deep River Junction, and found himself the only living soul in that hospital, he'd begun preparing lists of items he'd require to survive if and when the radiation levels dropped to a survivable level.

When CC finally left the hospital sixteen days later, he discovered a new tractor-trailer in a dealer's parking lot, and had driven it to a home improvement warehouse where he then loaded everything he thought he might need to survive in the forested wilderness of central Vermont. He had decided on an underpopulated area because of the reports he had heard from the few remaining radio stations, reports to the effect that mobs were pillaging as they moved from one community to another.

Included among the items he loaded on the trailer were the strapped-together prefabricated pieces of a wood-framed, two-car garage which he planned to convert into a small cottage.

Now that he had two young people to care for, he realized that it was time to begin assembling that garage and converting it into the small home he'd envisioned. He laughed aloud when he realized that he'd never imagined assembling that little twenty-four foot square structure within the confines of a giant cavern.

It would be a conventional wood structure, but since the cave was dry, there would be no need to shingle the roof to protect it from rain or snow. The cottage would, on the other hand, be insulated. The beauty of the situation was that the year-round temperature in the cave was fifty degrees, so they would only have to raise the temperature in the cottage about twenty degrees in order to remain comfortable.

And if they were able to find a way to route electricity to their little house, they would be able to use an electric heater to sustain that temperature in what Jonathan had begun to refer to as, "The Manor House." If, however, they had to burn firewood, they'd need to find a means to exhaust the smoke.

One of the first things CC had noticed when he moved into the cavern was that the cave that had been enlarged by the miners had a stone fire ring in an out-of-the-way-cove near the entry tunnel. In the ceiling above it was a smoke-darkened hole in the rock. As an experiment, he set fire to some old newspapers, and the smoke was drawn straight up into that hole.

He put some damp papers on the fire to produce thicker smoke, then ran out into the meadow to see if he could spot it rising above the cliffs. He could not, and concluded that it was funneled through caverns far up inside the mountain and somehow dissipated. It was obvious to him that the original cave had been used as a shelter for a long time, perhaps thousands of years, because it was dry and had this old fire ring.

Propping his extension ladder up against the edge of the vent hole in the cave's roof, he dropped a plumb line to the cave floor to determine where he would position his wood stove so that he could run the stove pipe vertically up into the natural chimney in the cave's roof. The position of the wood stove would then dictate the position of their living room, and the placement of the living room would determine the layout of the other rooms in the house. Once he calculated that, he would use a measuring tape and a can of spray paint to mark the perimeter of the cottage on the cave floor.

Foul Footings Fall

The Main Cavern
July 6th, 8:35 a.m.

S arah awoke early, but she found that CC was already at work on the cave floor, preparing the foundation. Rubbing the sleep from her eyes, she stretched her limbs with the easy luxury of the young. She brushed the back of her hand across the tip of her nose, while peering at CC through the glare of the bulbs that were strung above the subterranean work area.

She shouted to be heard above the throb of the small generator that was providing power for the lights. The air was slightly foul from the exhaust, but most of the fumes were being swept away by natural ventilation.

"What are you doing?" she shouted. She gestured at the trench he was scraping in the tunnel floor. "And why are you digging that hole?" She looked around. "And where's Jonathan? Are we going to have breakfast soon?"

He turned to her, glad for any excuse to stop work. "Whoa there! Which question should I answer first?" He smiled, leaning on the handle of his shovel. Even in the chill of the cavern, he'd managed to work up a good sweat. "Let's see... Jonathan's gone to the farm to bring back concrete blocks."

"Well, why aren't you helping him? Those blocks are awfully heavy, and I am sure he can only carry one at a time all that long way."

"No, Sarah. Jonathan's bringing the blocks back with the pickup."

"Oh," she responded cheerily, totally nonplussed.

"Well then," he asked — "question two?"

"When are we going to eat breakfast?"

"As soon as Jonathan gets back. After all, you're concerned about his being overworked. You don't want to neglect his nutrition, do you?"

"Of course not!" Her response was indignant.

"Well then, question three?"

"Question three? Question three... Oh, yes. Why are you digging right here, for I might step out of the door, and trip, and fall in that hole, and hurt myself."

"These are the footings for our new house. With Jonathan here, there is not enough room for us all to fit comfortably in the motor home."

CC stepped over to one side, and pointed at a mark he'd painted on the floor. "This is where we will put the wood stove. These ditches I'm digging in the cave floor are where we will raise the walls of the main room. Over there will be a small bedroom for Jonathan and another for me. And your room will be on the other side."

"Whew. It looks like a lot of work."

"It will be, but it's worth it. We're going to have a nice warm solid home."

"Why do you have to dig those ditches?"

"We call these 'footings.' We will fill them with concrete to make a level place to lay the framing for the floor. These footings will keep the walls from sagging or cracking."

"I thought you said the floor of the cave is made of stone."

"You're right, honey, but I have to scrape down to the solid rock, then make the building level by pouring a concrete foundation. We need to have a perfectly level surface so that the walls stay level."

"Oh," she answered, smiling. "You're not a crooked little man, and we don't want a crooked little house, do we?"

He laughed.

"Why do they call it a footing?"

"Now that's question number five, and I have to go back to work right after I answer it, okay?" Without waiting for her reply, he resumed scraping the bottom of the ditch. He spoke over his shoulder as he worked.

"I suppose it's called a footing because it's wider than the wall that will stand on it, just like your foot sticks out under your leg. That way, the weight is spread out over a larger area."

They were working on the house because they had given up on the generator, stymied by their inability to locate a passage to move it from their cave to the dam. It was also too big and heavy for them to move it through the long, narrow and twisting tunnels from the farm. And even if they could get it to the dam, it would be useless unless they found a way to run cable back to their cave.

Even with Sarah's help, they hadn't been able to discover the route by which the cement workers had removed the limestone to the kilns at the end of the valley. Perhaps that tunnel had caved in.

At any rate, for the time being, they were working on newer, larger quarters. During construction, they were lighting the work area with a string of bulbs powered by one of the portable generators he'd brought along. They would soon run out of fuel for the generator, and then he would be forced to light the area with gasoline lanterns.

With Sarah's curiosity momentarily satisfied, CC returned to his work. He was standing in a shallow ditch, scraping out loose sand and eroded rock, attempting to scrape clean the surface of the bedrock for the simple twelve-inch-wide forms into which he would pour the concrete for the footings.

He was watching Sarah as he absent-mindedly chipped at a lump of limestone with the tip of his shovel. He pressed down hard beneath the edge of the lump, put the weight of his foot on the blade, and pried and twisted, trying to work it loose. Unable to free it, he hammered his foot down on the shovel blade.

Quite suddenly the stone gave way, and the blade sank its entire length into the cave floor. Since CC was leaning forward and pushing down on the shovel handle, his foot followed the blade as it slipped down through what he thought was solid rock. A feeling of unreality was instantly replaced with a sense of shocked terror. The shovel handle followed the blade down through the hole, and he found himself falling forward, the end of the handle still loosely gripped in one hand.

CC let go of the shovel and spread both hands to arrest his fall. When his hands struck the cave floor, his upper body was supported as though he was doing pushups, his hands resting firmly on the dirt on the sides of the trench, but the ground on which his feet had come to rest had began to shift and slide toward the place where his shovel blade had disappeared.

In what seemed a mere instant, the shovel handle had dropped from sight, swallowed by the earth. CC's feet were still in the shallow depression, but the small hole that had opened in front of him was now located between his knees and was rapidly growing larger as loose dirt broke free and disappeared beneath him.

CC tried to jerk his feet apart, to get one of them up onto what he hoped was solid rock, but they were sliding down the trench, and his toes were inexorably slipping toward the rapidly enlarging cavity. It was as though the ground were being ripped open like a piece of paper, and he was suspended over the crack. As he looked down toward his knees, he could see a conical hole rapidly widening. It now looked like an earthen funnel beneath him, already a couple of feet deep. The opening at the bottom of the funnel was a black void.

It seemed impossible. The earth had opened beneath him and was threatening to swallow him alive. It was like something out of the Bible. He had a momentary vision of the ground opening and swallowing up Korah and his fellow renegades as the Old Testament described it. And it was happening so fast that he had virtually no time to react.

A sense of the unreal, coupled with the fear of being buried alive in the earth, suddenly overwhelmed him with a certainty of doom. *I must have punched through to a sink hole!* he thought. As he determined to resist this unexpected danger, he thought of the child.

"Sarah, get back...get away," he gasped. He tried to throw himself to one side, releasing his left hand from its uncertain position, but it was hopeless. It left him on his right side, but the earth continued to fall away with a rush, and the width of the cone-shaped cavity, now at least two feet wide at its base, was just inches forward of his feet.

He was annoyed to feel his shoes filling with the gritty sand, then realized that it was the least of his problems as they slid relentlessly down into the growing opening, his hands scrabbling as he lost his grip, his fingertips scraping futilely across the earth.

It was stunning. One moment he had been working in the lighted cave, the next he was falling into midnight darkness. His arms windmilled wildly, but he felt nothing but the falling dirt that surrounded him. He was conscious of a chill dampness. Strange how one's senses can register such things in the rush of danger.

He wondered how long it would be before he smashed to the floor of the cavity, but in that same instant his feet landed on a mound of soft, loosely packed earth that had collected beneath the hole. CC slid down its side, sinking into its softness, and was startled to feel icy water filling his boots. He threw himself toward the pile of dirt, but it had already become a heap of muck that was quickly dissolving in the fast-flowing current.

A small quantity of dirt and rock continued to fall from above, filling his eyes and ears and threatening to suffocate him in a smothering blanket. Beneath him, the falling earth was being turned into a sucking mud which was relentlessly dragging him under. He was choking and gasping, his responses totally involuntary and automatic, fighting for breath and life.

As the fall of dirt slowed, the water whipped the residue away. It was a mixed blessing, clearing his eyes and ears of the filth, but dragging him relentlessly down stream. He found himself trying to swim against the strong current. In his frenzy, his feet struck the rocky bottom, but when he tried to stand, his legs were swept from beneath him.

After a moment, the water cleared his eyes, and he could perceive a dim glow filtering down through the dust produced by his breakthrough. That dusky light from the cave above became his polar star. He fought to return to the place of his fall, to reach the spot directly beneath the hole from which the light emanated.

Leaning into the current, he found that the cleats of his boots gripped the bottom loosely, but when he attempted to move against the flow, his feet were again swept from beneath him. He was totally disoriented as he tumbled in the darkness, choking and spluttering.

Regaining his footing several feet downstream from the hole, he was afraid to move. He was even afraid to turn his head to see what danger might lurk behind him, for his slightest movement threatened his equilibrium.

Sarah's screams reached him above the din of the water's flow and his own panicked breathing, and his clearing eyes began to pick up the finer nuances of light and shade, depth and height.

He shouted toward the hole, but shortness of breath made his voice come out in a croak. "Sarah, get back."

Something dropped through the hole and slapped the water just upstream from him. It was a rope, and CC caught the end of it as the current snaked it toward him.

"Wait," he heard her shout. He looked up toward the hole, and to his horror, saw her hanging head-first through the opening. She was looking down, her face hidden in the shadows.

"Sarah, get back! Get away." It was a terrible effort to try to scream to her, but he didn't seem able to vary his voice in any appreciable way. Why wouldn't she listen? His foot slipped, he slid beneath the surface, and his mouth filled with water. He literally crawled against the wash, pushing himself up and forward, trying not to pull on the rope, fearing she was holding on to the end of it.

Sarah was yelling down at him.

"CC, I tied the rope to the bumper. Hang on. I'm going for Jonathan."

"Wait," he screamed, waving his arms, and was dragged beneath the waves as a result of his effort, but she was already gone. He realized it was probably for the best. At least she was away from that accursed hole, and he'd already discounted her help. It could easily be an hour before she returned with Jonathan, if she found him at all.

He pulled tentatively on the rope, expecting it to drop down through the hole. It didn't. Then he yanked on it. Perhaps her childish granny knot would hold. He spun himself around so that the rope wrapped around his waist, then, grasping it tightly in his hands, he hung from it for a moment, trying to think. The cold was rapidly draining his reserves, and he was already finding it more difficult to reason.

He became aware that the cave into which he had fallen was receiving more illumination than the dim glow which penetrated the hole above him. *Perhaps there's an opening through which sunlight's shining,* he thought.

Then he realized that he was seeing several spots of light through the thick mist. They seemed to be glowing well above the torrent, and he reasoned that his double vision was a result of the dirt and water in his eyes. Then he realized that there really were several lights. It took him a moment to comprehend where he was — to orient himself.

It can't be, he thought. *I've fallen into the pool beneath the dam.*

He could make out the big water wheel off to his right, turning relentlessly in its ceaseless production of electricity. He recalled that the channel was fairly narrow below the dam. That meant the shelf of rock — the walkway — had to be just to his right. The old rusty stanchions and stair rails had to be no more than ten or fifteen feet upstream.

With difficulty, because his hands were stiff with cold, he gripped Sarah's life-saving rope and stood on his toes. Hanging onto the rope, he sort of bounced himself in an arc across the channel away from the shelf he wanted to reach. When he'd gone as far as he could get without being dragged sideways, he took a deep breath, grasped the rope as high as he could reach, jerked his body as far out of the water as he could, and used his weight to swing him across the channel in the opposite direction and toward the ledge, like a child on a rope swing.

He didn't make it. In fact, he didn't get very far at all before he was dragged to a stop. When he could sense his movement slowing, he allowed himself to slip down the rope, splashing back into the stream, trying to grip the bottom with the soles of his feet. He threw his right hand out, and it struck the ledge. The blow to his near-frozen fingers was very painful, but since he was losing his endurance, he saw this as his only chance, and forced himself to ignore the pain.

He pivoted toward the bank, lunged with both hands, and caught the edge beneath his elbows, but the water threatened to sweep him away. His arms were being dragged off the surface of the ledge, and he was almost weeping with the effort to hold on, when his right hand slapped against the base of a stanchion that supported the railing. He locked his fingers around the pipe in a death grip.

Pulling himself toward it with every bit of strength remaining, and no longer concerned about bruises or pain, he dragged his upper body onto the ledge. He drew his right leg up and over, and, after a moment, pulled himself out of the water.

The rope was now a hindrance, threatening to drag him back into the stream. He struggled to disengage his sore left hand, his sprained thumb now wooden from the cold. Then he pulled himself all the way onto the cold, wet walkway and lay there gasping for breath.

All's Well That Ends Well

Below the main cavern
July 6th, 9:05 a.m.

C C rolled onto his side, and stared down from the ledge into the pool. He could see that the level of the water was lower than when he'd first discovered the dam. If it had been just an inch or two deeper, he'd never have been able to hold his chin above water while anchoring his feet on the bottom. If it had been any shallower, he might not have been able to pull himself up onto the shelf. And he realized that if he'd been dragged a few feet further downstream, he'd have been caught in the whirlpool. *Too many coincidences,* he reasoned, *to be mere coincidences.*

As his eyes swept the area, he also realized that this was an incredible discovery, though he didn't feel that the path to knowledge should have to be strewn with so many painful and life-threatening experiences.

Pulling himself into the fetal position to limit heat loss, he realized that he had to get out of this tunnel and back to the motor home before he died from exposure. It was then that the kids' voices penetrated his thoughts.

He looked up toward the hole. Now that his eyes were adjusting to the murk, he noticed that the roof of the cave had been eroded by water over eons of time, gouging a long groove in the rock that passed over the dam and the pool into which he'd fallen. The hole he'd dropped through was centered in that groove. His shovel work had broken through a soft thin area. With a certain amount of irony, he took note of the fact that he'd need to rethink his construction plans.

As he looked up toward the hole, he could see that Jonathan had laid a couple of planks across the opening, and was now straddling them. Holding a floodlight in his hand, he was shining it down toward him.

"CC," he shouted, "are you okay?"

CC dragged himself to his knees as Jonathan turned the light full on him. He could hear the boy reassuring Sarah.

"He's all right, Sarah. He's on a ledge." Then, "Wow...that's neat. We could build a staircase down there and have a great escape hatch."

Kids! I could be lying here dead, and they'd be building sand castles in their imaginations. Still..., he grudgingly acknowledged, *it's not a bad idea. It's only about four or five yards from the top of the dam to the hole where Jonathan's lying.*

He shouted. "Jonathan, get Sarah away from that hole. It's not safe for either of you."

"I have her sitting on the step of the motor home," he answered. She'll be okay."

"Good! Now get me some dry clothes and something hot to drink. Then meet me at the farm. I've got to get out of here before I freeze to death."

"Wait a minute," he yelled back. "I'll tie the thermos to a cord, and lower you some of the breakfast coffee."

He was back in little more than a minute. Swinging the thermos back and forth, he managed to get it above the ledge where CC could catch it. Although it was bitter, it was also hot. In the meantime, Jonathan was busy lowering a bundle of dry clothing through the hole, while at the same time providing Sarah with a blow-by-blow description of the situation.

"Look," he exclaimed, "he's found a shortcut to the dam!"

CC could hear her excited response. "Let me see! Let me see!"

CC felt that he didn't need any additional problems, so he took a deep breath and bellowed toward the opening. "Jonathan, get Sarah away! Make her stay inside the motor home."

To his horror, her head appeared over the edge of the opening. "Do you want me, CC? Can I do anything more for you?"

Instead of appreciating her quick wit in tying off the rope and dropping the end down to him to save his life, he hollered back, "Get into the motor home right now."

She moved away without a word, and Jonathan, lying on the opposite edge of the hole, might have been wearing a look of contempt.

CC was shaking so from the cold that he had trouble rubbing himself down and pulling on the dry clothes, and while he was preoccupied with that chore, Jonathan disappeared.

Dressed in dry clothes, he had begun climbing the stone staircase to the top of the dam when Jonathan dropped the weighted end of the rope through the hole. Jonathan began swinging it back and forth in pendulum fashion until CC was able to reach out over the railing at the top of the dam and catch hold of it.

Jonathan then suggested that he tie the rope off to the base of the railing, as he was going to lower something down to him. Before CC could question him about his intentions, the boy began lowering some sort of metal device through the hole. As it slid into the light, CC recognized it as the bottom of their aluminum extension ladder.

"What are you doing?" CC demanded.

"I've extended the ladder to eighteen feet, and roped the rungs together so that the two sections can't telescope together. Then I fastened a length of rope to the top rung, and tied the end of the rope to the bumper on the motor home, so that the top of the ladder can't slide down through the hole."

Then he added a comment CC considered unnecessary. "I tied it to the bumper just like Sarah tied the rope when she saved your life," he added accusatively.

The next thing CC knew, the end of the extension ladder was slipping down through the hole at about a thirty-degree angle, its base guided by the rope he held. He drew the lower end so that it came to rest on the ledge at his feet.

Then he looked up. Satisfied that the ladder was sufficiently extended and that the top couldn't drop down through the hole, he wiggled it until one of the legs was against the base of the railing that ended about ten feet uphill from the end of the dam. When he was satisfied that the two legs were squarely seated on the rocky floor, he tied the base of the ladder against the stanchion. As he finished tying the knot, he felt the ladder shake, and looked up to discover that Jonathan was already halfway down, a bundle nested in one arm. He'd brought down a sandwich and fresh coffee. Real luxury.

"That's from Sarah," he declared flatly.

CC was aware that his newly acquired children had saved his life. Tipping his head back, he hollered, "Thank you, Sarah!"

"You're welcome!" came back the answer, but he could tell she'd been crying. Even so, he was happy that he did not see her head reappear over the edge of the hole.

Jonathan looked at the almost-ideal angle the ladder took, and suggested that it would be just fine to leave it sitting there as a means of getting from the new house to the dam. The number of rungs exposed on the ladder made it clear that it was only about sixteen feet from the top of the dam to the floor of the cave above them. He estimated that it was an additional fifteen feet down to the surface of the water below the dam. In other words, CC had fallen over thirty feet.

Jonathan was much more confident in climbing over that torrent than CC, so the teen steadied the ladder for him while he climbed shivering back up to the motor home.

Some hero I am, he thought. *Afraid of heights. And that kid is really something! That short climb saved me an hour's walk through the tunnels to the farm and back again across the valley. He's one smart teenager.*

Back at last in the privacy of the motor home, CC stripped and toweled himself dry, then lowered himself onto the bed. After he'd eaten the hot soup the children brought him, and they covered him with enough blankets to almost smother him, he fell into a fitful sleep.

The Generator

The Main Cavern
July 7th, 8:15 a.m.

J onathan was right. CC's terrifying trip down through what they now jokingly called "Alice's Rabbit Hole" had turned out to be heaven-sent. Not only had they located the dam, but it was immediately below the cave in which they already made their home.

The advantages were enormous. The hole in the floor should permit access for installing and maintaining the generator, and the distance they would have had to run electrical cable would be reduced from up to a mile to about a hundred feet.

Additionally, it provided them an alternative exit from the cavern, a rabbit hole, for escape purposes. It seemed to him that falling through the floor was one of those divine events, an *"all things work together for good to them that love God, to them who are the called according to his purpose"* moments.

CC was bruised and tired after his fall, and he spent the remainder of the day resting and thinking of how they might take advantage of this incredible discovery. In the back of his mind, however, was the concern that the entire floor of the main cave might collapse into the cavern below.

To put those fears to rest, they spent the next day surveying the cave from above and below. The ladder came in handy as they climbed down from the main cave to examine the rock that formed the ceiling above the dam and the floor beneath their proposed cottage. They were soon satisfied that the rock was essentially sound.

CC came to the conclusion that the there was a layer of solid rock between six-and eight-feet thick separating most of the upper and lower caves. The exception was where he'd actually fallen through. Evidently, the hole he'd dropped through had once been a natural drain for water flowing from the upper cave down into the cavern below. Over the years, it had evidently been plugged with rock and soil. Because of that hole, CC was afraid to build anything on the cave floor above it, much less risk leaving the motor home and all their supplies and equipment nearby.

Jonathan had other ideas, for he'd watched his own father successfully reinforce a cave floor.

"Look, CC," he said, pointing at the hole. "The floor where you parked the motor home is very thick, and most of it is not even suspended over the cavern below. It's on bedrock that forms the outer walls of the lower cave. All we need to do right here is build several steel-reinforced concrete beams to bridge the thin part of the floor and to form a box around the hole. Those beams will handle a lot of weight."

CC was about to deride the idea when he remembered the boy's background. He decided to give him the benefit of the doubt and at least hear him out.

"How would we do that?"

"The actual hole is an oval, roughly three feet wide by six feet long at its widest points. We'll just build forms using long pieces of twelve-inch-wide framing lumber, lay them about four feet apart around the edges of the hole, set steel rebar in them as reinforcement, and fill them with concrete. Most of their length will be over the thicker parts of the roof, and the beams will be extremely strong. Once we've crossed those thin places in the floor with a few of those beams, we can build right on top of them, and even if a little more of the floor beneath them were to drop into the pool below, everything would still be fine."

CC pursed his lips. They were both reasonably confident that all of the soft and loose rock had already fallen. For their purposes, Jonathan's idea might work.

It was also Jonathan who seized upon the idea that they might erect a framework to lower the generator through the pothole to the dam below. "Once the generator is down below," he added, "we could support one corner of the house on those same reinforced concrete beams, using them as footings. That would serve," he also argued, "to hide both the hole and the ladder, while protecting us from the noise, dampness and cold of the underground river."

When CC realized the genius of the boy's idea, he added his own thought that, once the generator was in place below, they'd replace the ladder with a hidden stairway that would run from a closet in the cottage down to the top of the dam.

It took two days to build the forms and pour the concrete for the crisscrossed concrete beams that lay above the pothole. They'd found an entire pallet of ready-to-mix concrete in Sennett's barn, more than enough to complete the task, and CC had bought a couple dozen lengths of rebar with him in the tractor-trailer. After they'd poured the reinforced beams, they allowed several days for the concrete to cure.

On the fourth day, they mounted a heavy wooden gallows atop the new beams, and used a system of blocks and tackle to slowly lower the generator to the ledge at the base of the dam. The fact that the ledge where the water wheel was mounted was located nearly thirty feet below the pothole did not represent a great problem. The fact that it was not a vertical drop from the hole to the ledge, and that the the pothole was actually above the pool, did. The pothole was nearly six feet off-center from the stone shelf, and it would be necessary to fasten another block and tackle to the base of the water wheel in order to drag the heavy generator sideways as they lowered it down to the ledge.

CC was grateful for whatever impulse had caused him to load all the tools and equipment in the tractor-trailer months before. As he started swelling with pride, he was immediately convicted, reminded that the impulse had come from the Holy Spirit.

He had just enough strength to lower the generator an inch at a time using the heavy-duty cable hoist, while Jonathan, working from the ledge far below, took up the slack and dragged it toward the water wheel using a similar block and tackle combination. Since the generator was being lowered at an angle, Jonathan had to pull harder with every foot the machine was lowered.

CC listened as the pall clinked into place with each movement, and kept one eye on the sagging wooden framework that was groaning under the weight. It was too late to raise the generator back up to the cave floor, too late to reinforce the framework. If the framework they had erected collapsed now, the chain hoist would go with it, and the generator would be lost in the pool below.

The two of them spoke back and forth over a set of walkie-talkies. It was a novelty to use electronic communications for the project, and as long as CC remained above the hole, the line-of-sight radios worked fine.

When the generator's weight became almost too great for Jonathan, CC had to climb down the ladder, then down the slimy stone stairs beside the dam, and join him on his block and tackle as they dragged the generator a few more inches toward the ledge. Then they both climbed back to the upper chain hoist, and lowered it a few inches more. They had to repeat that process about a dozen times, in ever-smaller increments, until they were barely able to drag the generator onto the ledge next to the water wheel.

Exhausted, they rested on Sunday. After breakfast they spent a half-hour reading the Bible and praying. Then they took a walk in the woods, kicked a soccer ball around outside the cave entrance, ate dinner in mid-afternoon, and after Sarah's nap, sat around the campfire. Between songs, Jonathan and CC discussed how the seemingly unrelated events of the past few months, when taken in perspective, made it clear that God had poured out his blessings on them. There was no other explanation for what the world would merely call "good luck."

On Monday morning they returned to work. Building the stairway was, in many ways, as great a challenge as lowering the generator. When they were finished with the last tread, they stepped up through the hole into the upper cave where Sarah applauded them. Then, before they could catch her, she slipped around them and padded down the stairs to the cave below.

Jonathan went down and held her hand as she climbed back up, and when she'd reached safety, CC threatened to lock her up if she did anything so foolish again.

Now that they finally had the stairway properly positioned, they used short lengths of angle iron and lag bolts to secure it top and bottom.

CC was amazed that it took another full day to nail risers to the back of each tread, and to build railings that he considered solid enough to be safe. When they were finished, he felt far less concerned about Sarah running up and down. Building even a crude staircase is a real science, he realized, but they now had a reliable shortcut to the dam. It took three more days to secure the generator to the ledge, attach it to the water wheel, and run 4-o electrical cables to the top of the dam, up the side of the stairway, and into a circuit box in the cave above.

It took yet another day to make the final connections to the circuit load center and to check the circuits for faults. Then Jonathan shouted, "Let there be light," Sarah threw the switch, and they all cheered as the area around the motor home was suddenly flooded with bright artificial light.

CC relocated the walls of the proposed house so that one corner would rest over the pot hole, completely enclosing it, while shifting the floor plan so that the wood stove would be positioned beneath the ancient smoke hole in the cave's ceiling. Even though they would now have electric heat, the idea of being able to look at a wood fire on a cold winter night was very appealing. As planned, the upper end of the staircase would ultimately be secreted in the bottom of a corner closet.

Using a power saw and a nail gun, the construction of the cottage went quickly. They had run the heavy electrical cable up the outside of one stringer on the staircase, and on the other side, they ran a three-quarter-inch plastic pipe through which they drew water from the reservoir above the dam. A small quarter-horse water pump lifted the water to a pressure tank they installed next to the cottage.

An electric water heater installed next to the cottage provided hot water to both the motor home and the new cottage. They used a reverse osmosis system to purify their drinking water, but as far as CC could tell, the water in the cave below was pure. It had, after all, been running for miles underground through limestone.

Getting rid of waste water was equally important, and they ran a sewer line out of the cave and into the meadow, where they built a dry well to serve as a septic tank.

When the little cottage was finally finished, they had a housewarming party. After giving thanks, they sat down to a somewhat elaborate meal, discussed what should be their next project, and began planning how to best take advantage of their new power supply. They even talked about hooking up the closed-circuit TV equipment that CC had brought along in the tractor-trailer. Like the Sennetts before them, they might monitor the entrance to the valley as well as the immediate approaches to the caverns.

Harvest Time

Hidden Valley, Vermont
August to September

Time seemed to fly by, and their lives fell into a regular routine. They were faithfully thanking God for their meals and their relatively luxurious and secure home. Even

Sarah was increasingly conscious of the incredible providence that had come their way. She would run to either CC or Jonathan, and reach out to be hugged, seizing the love and security she'd lost in the passing of her grandparents and the wanton destruction of her home. Their good fortune was increasingly evident as each day they'd rise, bathe in hot water, dress in clean clothes, and enjoy a breakfast of pancakes with maple syrup, oatmeal and homemade toast, or bacon and eggs.

Clothes washing was possible because they had both an automatic washer and electric dryer. These were Sarah's responsibility, but the kitchen was her pride and joy, and while they were off with their men's work, she worked hard to keep it clean. She tried to prepare at least one of the meals every day, even if it was simply peanut butter and jelly sandwiches. That seemed simple enough until they remembered that Sarah was kneading and baking the bread. Her little hands and shoulders were no match for the stiffening dough, and Jonathan would make it a point to stop by and help her with that chore.

They all shared housekeeping responsibilities, including cooking and washing up.

The three of them were remarkably free from illness. CC attributed that to the fact that they were following Sarah's oft-repeated adage that "cleanliness is next to godliness." They stuck fairly close to the dietary practices of the Old Testament, not because they considered themselves to be under The Law, but because they believed the practices made sense. They ate simply, but well, and the fact that they had been able to avoid contact with outsiders kept them free of communicable diseases.

They did however experience a couple of scary moments when, for example, Jonathan was splitting firewood and bounced the axe blade off the stump they were using as a cutting block, driving the sharp edge through his jeans and cutting his leg. Fortunately, he didn't damage the muscle or sever an artery, and a queasy CC had been able to clean and close the wound with a half-dozen stitches. Then Sarah got wet while playing outside, caught cold, and gave them a couple of bad days. CC thanked God each day for their health, realizing that the kids in particular would be in serious trouble without an adult around. Indeed, they'd all come to depend upon one another.

Each morning they tried to be up by five, simply because the cow needed to be milked and the other livestock cared for. They had talked about using a horse and wagon to carry things back and forth to visit the farm, but CC finally vetoed the idea because they wouldn't be able to hide if a plane flew over. The pickup was also out of consideration for the same reason, but also because they were conserving what little fuel they had left. CC had treated the gasoline with a special chemical that would extend its life by a year or so.

So they carried their lunches to the farm, and carried back fruit and produce in their backpacks. At the same time, they were slowly but surely planting garden patches and moving livestock to their side of the valley.

When it was a particularly hot day, they would take a picnic down to the swimming hole. Sarah would shriek with laughter as they enjoyed an hour or so dropping into the water from a rope that was tied to the limb of a huge old tree that leaned out over the pool. After they had shared their lunch, they might take a nature hike, identifying plants and animals by searching through various books. At other times, they would just lie on a boulder in the shade and enjoy the vagrant breezes.

When the unusually warm fall weather arrived, they were busier than ever, laying up hay, straw, and field corn for the animals, and harvesting wheat and oats.

They picked vegetables and carried them back to their cave where they canned and stored them. They had to revert to ancient methods for threshing the wheat and oats. They cleaned and scrubbed the smooth concrete floor of the Sennetts' barn. Then, with each of them wearing a nuisance dust mask, they took bundles of the stalks and banged them on the floor until the kernels dropped free. Sweeping them into heaps, and shoveling them into sacks, they loaded them on the truck and raced across the valley, where they stored them in the now nearly empty bins. The straw would serve to bed the animals during the long winter days.

They would later grind both wheat and oats into flour to make bread or cereal, but the livestock would eat most of the oats and field corn. CC was again thankful that Sennett had stock-piled and used heirloom, non-hybrid seeds.

As they harvested the crops, they were careful to prepare and store enough seed for multiple plantings, not simply for their own future use, but in anticipation of one day giving or bartering the surplus to others.

Apart from their field crops, they were harvesting apples, peaches, plums, cherries, and pears for baking, drying, and canning. They even canned pumpkins and squash. The dozens of cases of bottles, lids, and paraffin that the Sennetts had on hand no longer seemed excessive.

They buried the potatoes and carrots in a bin of dried sand that Sennett had set aside for the purpose, and hung onions along the ceiling of their cottage. One Sunday afternoon, they wandered through the woods, searching for any walnuts and hickory nuts the squirrels had missed.

The kids had never enjoyed a healthier diet. Everything was organic. Nothing was treated with hormones, antibiotics, or artificial additives, and their diets were rich in fruits and vegetables. They had put on muscle, and were rosy-cheeked.

Although they were in excellent health, there was no question that the intense routine was wearing thin on all of them, and CC had an itch to get out of the valley. It seemed to him as though he'd never worked harder. With the completion of the fall harvest, as they stood together staring at the hundreds of jars of fruits and vegetables, they all shared an enormous sense of accomplishment. At the same time, they all felt a bit let down. Worse, the children sensed the disquiet in CC, and were frustrated because they couldn't seem to help him shake his malaise.

Fatal Attraction

The Main Cavern
December 24th, 6:15 a.m.

C C leaned into the motor home kitchen where Jonathan was preparing hot chocolate.

"Where's Sarah?"

"She went to bed about a half-hour ago."

"I'm going into town."

Jonathan had been expecting something unusual, but this particular statement took him by surprise, and his face revealed his shock. He had become deeply concerned because CC appeared increasingly morose and had not spoken much lately.

"Are you sure that's a good idea?" the boy asked evenly, trying to hide his dismay.

"Why shouldn't it be?" CC snapped back.

"I don't know, but you keep telling us that we should never leave the valley because someone might follow us back."

"Well," CC stammered, "you're just kids. Nobody will follow me."

"Suppose they see you before you see them, and they hide from you?"

"That isn't going to happen," he retorted. "It's important that I check out what's going on around us." He hadn't really meant to say that, and saying it didn't make it any more true. Worse, he realized that he was ignoring an internal warning signal. But, having said it to the boy, it somehow became important that he make it true.

He threw a little food and a few emergency items into a backpack, explaining to Jonathan that he wouldn't head down the valley until after nightfall and that he'd be sure to keep an eye out for anyone coming into the valley. His words sounded hollow even to his own ears.

He gave Jonathan a pair of binoculars so that he could keep watch, and told him not to worry if he didn't return that night.

He explained that he planned to skirt the village of Butter Creek and nose around a little.

He could tell that the idea frightened Jonathan, and the teen didn't hesitate to condemn it. "This is stupid, CC. What if something happens to you?" Even as the words were leaving his mouth, he too realized that he had made a mistake.

CC bridled at being rebuked by the teen, not the least because his plan was characterized as stupid, even though he knew in his heart that the teen was probably right.

"Is that all you think about," he retorted, "you and Sarah?" He knew that he was being unfair, even childish, and understood the children's fear about being left alone, but argued to himself that he had the right to pursue a little personal time. So he had closed his mind to the potential risks.

The boy, however, persisted. "You'll leave tracks the length of the valley."

"No. I'll stay beneath the evergreens, on the pine needles where the snow's melted off. When I am far enough down the valley, it won't matter so much."

To forestall further argument, he hastened on. "Besides, I think it might snow again tomorrow, and that will cover any tracks." Without another word, Jonathan turned and left the room, slamming the door behind him.

CC started to follow him, then turned back, shrugged into his backpack, and left the cottage.

He told himself that he simply couldn't stand to remain in the cavern one more night. The possibility of seeing other human beings was like a siren song, and Jonathan had neither a ship's crew to bind him to a figurative mast nor wax to plug his ears. The boy's words were like babble, and the more he spoke, the stronger CC's rebellious determination became.

When CC stepped down from the motor home, Sarah came out of the cottage rubbing her eyes. She had been awakened by the shouting, and was clearly disturbed. And CC was seething because he assumed that Jonathan had awakened her. She rushed over and threw her arms around his legs.

"Please, CC, don't go."

He extricated himself from her from her arms with some difficulty, then picked her up, and tried to assure her that everything would be all right. Then he gave her a kiss and set her back down on the cave floor. She stood there snuffling while he walked toward the camouflaged door that he'd installed to hide the outer cave from the network of caverns in which they dwelt.

"Now you listen to Jonathan," he called back to her. There was no reply, and when he turned back, she had disappeared. Shrugging his shoulders in pretended indifference, he made his way to the outer cavern where he found Jonathan waiting. "You told her?" he asked, without preamble.

"No," the boy answered. "I've been waiting right here."

"Then how did she know?"

"I assume she heard us shouting," the boy responded with sarcasm.

CC nodded his head, realizing that this was the first time they'd ever argued, but he didn't apologize.

The boy surprised him by clasping him desperately to himself and whispering, "Come back, CC We can't do without you."

Deeply touched, he nearly relented, but something seemed to compel him to go on, and he responded with like fervency, "I'll be back, Jonathan."

It was an empty promise.

"I can't do without you two characters either."

The truth.

Then he caught hold of the handlebars of the electric bike that leaned against the cave wall just inside the secret door, and lifted the front wheel to get it over the high sill.

Jonathan opened his mouth to repeat his warning that the tracks would be seen, but decided that any further argument was futile. He followed CC through the door and stood silently at the portal of the cave, watching while CC pushed the bike across the meadow.

Just before CC disappeared into the trees, Jonathan shouted, "CC! Did you pray about this?"

The man shortened his step, then squared his shoulders and went on without responding. *God will understand,* he argued to himself.

And then he was on his way down the log road, but the joyful abandon he had anticipated was somehow spoiled by his sense of having fallen short.

As promised, he tried to stay to the clear patches of ground. He wasn't aware that someone was keenly following his progress from atop a ledge on the far side of the valley.

Butter Creek Tavern

North of Green Mountain Feed and Grain
December 24th, 8:30 p.m.

The sun set early in the vale during the winter, and Butter Creek Tavern was quiet. If it had not been snowing, a few of the more hardy souls might have stopped by to quaff the dark home-brewed beer and swap local gossip. Indeed one or two might arrive later, after caring for their livestock and completing their chores, but few were willing to risk a long walk home through drifting snow.

The few farmers who had survived the war and the deprivations of the invaders were forced to work late this Thursday evening, for they no longer enjoyed the benefit of machinery powered by gasoline or electricity. With the grid down across the eastern United States, farmers were forced to return to methods forsaken nearly a century before. They were milking their few cows by hand by the light of kerosene lanterns, and using horse-drawn equipment. Even before the war there weren't many draft horses, and now the few surviving animals had become incredibly valuable.

Just a few weeks earlier, the farmers would have remained at home anyway, not just because of the snow, but because of political realities. They had been required to be at home before dark in obedience to the curfew instituted by the new order, but like most of the people in what had once been the state of Vermont, the majority of people in this little backwater hamlet had decided to co-operate with the new authorities, and were therefore enjoying a slightly greater degree of freedom than the more recalcitrant New Englanders

Most of the communities in Vermont had proven as tractable as the residents of Butter Creek. The people of the Green Mountain State were nothing like their fiercely independent forefathers, those patriots who stood up to the mightiest nation on earth during America's almost-forgotten "War for Independence."

Nor did it matter that it was Christmas Eve. The phrase, "Happy Holidays," had long since replaced "Merry Christmas" as the acceptable greeting, and even prior to the commencement of hostilities, the celebration of the Advent had become pretty much irrelevant in American culture. In fact, all Christian holidays had been labeled politically incorrect, and public celebrations were ultimately outlawed by an increasingly godless government.

Then, following the invasions, all Christian practices — public or private — had been outlawed by the two groups fighting for control of New England. Few Americans even noted the irony associated with the fact that both the atheistic Chinese Communist army, and their adversaries, a theocratic group calling itself the *Muslims of the Book,* shared the primary goal of wiping out Christianity.

The *Muslims of the Book* considered themselves the true heirs of the Prophet, the only faithful adherents to the *Holy Koran,* and the true servants of Allah. They were in fact as brutal and murderous to those of their own faith — whose beliefs seemed to fall short of their own, — as they were to citizens of that Great Satan — America.

In fact, they had secured their grip over all who followed Islam by exercising terror and torture. Those who might have once been considered moderate Muslims quickly came to understand that they would either adhere enthusiastically to the rules of the fanatics, or they and their families would be executed. It was a very effective means of winning converts.

The Chinese Communists were equally efficient in their own way, though they invested themselves somewhat more heavily in propaganda than in threats and violence to achieve their ends.

CC knew little of Butter Creek nor of the current political situation. He had seen the owner's name crudely carved into an old plank next to the front door, "Henry Burton, Proprietor," but had no idea of his leanings.

As he sat in the far corner of the near-freezing dining room, he wrapped his coat tightly about himself, collar turned up against the mountain cold that invaded the pre-revolutionary walls. His initial concerns were not with the politics of the owners, but with the bitter drafts that seeped through the cracks in the sagging and soiled leaded-glass windows.

In recent years this out-of-the-way tavern had been bypassed by tourists who'd moved on to the more charming and historic villages of Vermont. In order to make ends meet, the owners had cheapened the quality of their food and drink, had become even more lax about cleanliness, and had even raised prices. Yet the owners couldn't understand why they experienced a declining local patronage.

The takeover of this part of the state by the Chinese had changed the proprietor's fortunes for the better. Whether it was because the Burtons passed out free drinks to those in authority, or because they informed on their neighbors, they had become very successful in ingratiating themselves with the powers that be.

The new Chinese military government had proven a boon to the tavern keepers, not because they offered better fare, but because they had bent over backwards to co-operate with those in authority. As a result, their only competitor had been closed down, and they now had a virtual monopoly in Butter Creek.

In spite of this, business hadn't improved. In truth, the Burtons had traded whatever little community loyalty and patronage they'd formerly enjoyed for the iron-fisted support of the Chinese military. And while the Chinese appeared to be solidly entrenched, the truth was that there was not only a force of opposing Jihadists rumored to be operating within a hundred miles, but also a small but growing restiveness on the part of the Americans in the area. Maybe the activities of the Americans could not yet be characterized as an insurgency, but the Burtons could sense a rebellious spirit that the winds of injustice and abuse might soon fan into a conflagration.

The Burtons had come to realize that they might have allied themselves with the wrong invaders. "Suppose," he had asked his wife, "the Muslims defeat the Chinese? Or that the Americans somehow throw them all out? Where would that leave us?" It was a rhetorical question with profound implications for these two opportunists who now realized that they were "none of the above."

The Burtons sensed that they'd risked everything on their decision, and were no longer happy that they had tied their futures to the success of any of the invaders, but it hardly mattered. The die was cast. They were therefore determined to do anything and everything they could to assure the success of the Chinese, and thus secure their own futures.

CC had been blithely unaware of any political undercurrents when he'd walked through the front door of the inn, but his ignorance was rapidly being dispelled. In spite of the fact that he seemed oblivious to his surroundings, his eyes were busy.

A comely serving girl was busily arranging a half-dozen colorful mugs along the back bar, while the pear-shaped proprietor, with his bulbous red nose, was perched on a stool behind his ancient stained bar, chiding her for her laxity. His role as owner-manager provided an excuse to keep both eyes riveted on her as she moved back and forth. It was clearly no game to her, and she was trying futilely to avoid making any movements that might excite his lecherous advances.

It angered her that the Burtons criticized her for laxness because, like an indentured servant, she worked long hours every day while constantly dodging his groping hands, merely to earn her room and board. She shook her head. *It's difficult to characterize the cold, barren room they provide me, and the garbage they feed me as room and board.*

Apart from her being forced to do the work of two people, the Burtons benefited even more because her sweet spirit attracted customers that would otherwise never set foot in the tavern.

The flames in the fireplace, whipped and stretched by the wind that was whistling down the chimney, occasionally accented CC's darkened silhouette. The fire was simmering and guttering — snapping and snarling like a pack of mad dogs caught in a flaming maelstrom, playing a vicious game of tag among the charred logs and crimson coals.

The icy wind whipped sleet against the glass, but all was dark outside, lost in the twilight of the storm. Icy drafts crept through countless seams, and a blanket of cold dropped continually from the windows, chilling his legs, but the disquiet he felt was not the child of physical discomfort.

CC's forehead rested on an open palm. He was observing the innkeeper's activities from beneath hooded brows while wrapped in his own thoughts. And his thoughts were heavy ones. He realized that he should never have succumbed to his loneliness and come to this place.

He was sitting on a rickety old captain's chair whose seat had known the buffing of countless random garments and whose loose arms were hand-rubbed by generations of men at their ease. Hewn beams hung close above his head. Plastered walls—darkened by the smoke of endless wood fires and candles guttering raggedly in the drafts—gave mute testimony to a long and checkered history.

This was true Americana, a visible representation of the rich traditions once sought after by countless tourists. Now it served to remind him that he was out of place. A year earlier, the old tavern might have been a somewhat popular half-way house for skiers on their journeys to and from the northern New England slopes, but now it seemed sinister and dangerous.

He realized that memories of the near past would not seem fond to the proprietor. He was obviously bitter for what once was and could never again be. That man who sat ogling his serving girl as she stretched to reach a glass, had become as stale and moldy as the bread he served. Even as he was seating CC, he had cursed the world that he considered responsible for his misfortune, then boasted of the favor that he was receiving from the new order because of his outstanding co-operation. CC pegged him as a man who would promptly sell his own mother to the devil for any meager advantage.

When the host was showing CC to the table near the fireplace, he'd asked, "What did you say your name was again?"

CC had pretended he didn't hear. "Have you got any soft drinks?"

"Mister, you ought to know that all our phosphates have been confiscated." He leaned over the table to study CC's face, as though cataloging it for future reference. "You can have some cold home brew or hot coffee." He rubbed his hands together, his face twisted in a venial smile. "We've still got some real coffee, but it would really cost you."

He looked CC up and down, a frown on his greasy corpulent face. "By the looks of you, you'll settle for a cup of chicory. We make a real good cup from our own acorns. It'll save you money." As he moved back toward the bar, he threw back over his shoulder, "Take your choice. It's all the same to me."

Later, when the man stopped by his table again, CC revealed his surprise at the availability of real coffee. The man gave him a penetrating look, then grudgingly explained as though to a backward child, "We who are smart enough to co-operate with the authorities enjoy many advantages."

He walked away muttering to himself. He had nearly reached his perch behind the bar when he turned to stare at a poster on the wall. It was then that CC sensed that he might be in trouble. The man's exaggerated effort to avoid staring openly at what looked like a wanted poster, then pretending to survey the room while actually trying to compare him with the photo, was ludicrous.

While this was playing out, the serving girl brought CC a bowl of watery stew, some stale bread, and a cup of thin coffee. She tried to start a conversation, but grew discouraged when he used the arrival of his food as an excuse to avoid speaking.

She was probably not quite as lovely as she looked, but his total separation from any female over the age of seven had left something of an edge on his appreciation. His unwillingness to converse resulted from a combination of being tongue-tied with the first woman he'd met since he awoke in the hospital months before, plus the uncertainty of any commitment he might have to an unknown wife. Apart from that, he was experiencing a newly discovered diffidence about speaking to anyone, complicated by a very real fear that he might already be in a great deal of trouble.

It seemed clear that the girl was simply trying to be friendly. And judging from her employer's behavior, she really needed a friend. But she had not sensed any response from CC, and had reacted to his aloofness by following the rule to which the best servers adhere when faced with patrons seeking solitude — she offered efficient service, but didn't volunteer any further conversation.

For CC's part, starved as he was for contact and mesmerized though he was by her movements, his attraction to her was more of a platonic nature than that of a fantasized lover. He too was starved for the fellowship of a kindred spirit. Dried out as he was by too much time alone in the wilds, and in spite of his easy relationship with Jonathan and Sarah, he was now afraid to reach out to adults.

Afraid? Why? Because I might be rebuffed or scorned? The fact is that I am frightened of facing a changing world. And right now I have to face the reality that I seem to have blundered into a very bad situation.

He had a real fear that someone in this tiny village might report him to the authorities, and he would find himself jailed on some contrived charge.

He shivered, but when he drew his coat more tightly about himself, he felt no warmer. He thought of dragging his chair closer to the fire, but preferred the security of the shadows to the bright warmth of the hearth. Several times he determined to go to the bar to strike up a conversation, but each time he drew back further into his chair.

He hadn't been in the place more than fifteen minutes, and he'd already overheard the innkeeper openly criticize a number of the village's citizens. Worse, he kept staring at him. CC was certain that the man had already appraised him, and had conveniently pigeonholed him in one of a half-dozen slots he probably used to classify every human being he'd ever met.

CC's journey into town in pursuit of human contact had brought him only disappointment. This was not at all what he had hoped for. He now realized that if he engaged in conversation with anyone here, he'd expose himself to additional danger.

He had been justifiably frightened of interaction outside his own valley. The suspicion and greed exposed by the war were tragic, but real, and his fear of the new regime had clearly not been unrealistic or overly exaggerated.

He was glad that he'd left the motorized bicycle hidden in a stand of evergreens, and had instead walked into the hamlet. Now he felt a compulsion to get up and leave, willing even to brave the danger of the near-blizzard conditions, and the dangerous trip back up the mountain, but for some reason he was afraid to move.

CC understood that he had been drawn to the tavern by a craving for adult fellowship, but now realized this had become a world where the possibility of such fellowship was both limited and dangerous. He recognized that he was starved for the presence of others, and particularly stirred by the sound of this woman's steps as she crossed the floor, and utterly charmed by the grace of her movements.

He stared unseeing at the greasy bowl which had contained the slop the landlord called "supper." He lifted his cup and swallowed the last of the flat, lukewarm brew. In spite of the fact that he'd opted for the inn's far more costly offering, it was not nearly as good as his own fresh-ground coffee, and he wondered what the proprietor might do if he were ever to learn that CC possessed over two hundred pounds of prime organic beans.

His thoughts were no longer on the food or the server. Sensory perceptions had taken on a new dimension. Vision, hearing, the senses of smell and taste, had all become exaggerated. He seemed to feel with all of his senses, as though he were actually touching objects across the room. They were palpable realities. And he was inexplicably afraid of the unknown in what should have been a relaxed environment.

His mind wandered back through the months to the beginning of this new life. He braced his elbows on the table to rest his chin on his hands, wondering whether his face displayed his inner turmoil as he relived the most challenging period of his life. While everyone in this inn could undoubtedly remember events back to their own childhoods, all that he had was barely one year of memories, a year fraught with enormous challenges.

It had started when he'd awakened in an x-ray room in the hospital with no memory of who he was. He soon discovered that he was alone on the basement floor, and a radio he discovered playing in the cafeteria revealed that America was under attack. Following the advice of the commentator, he'd found himself well-prepared to sit out the two-week minimum that might see radioactivity drop sufficiently to go outdoors.

During those two weeks, he took advantage of the hospital's library and computer system to learn all that he could about surviving in a post-nuclear environment. When the two weeks were up, and he was able to venture outside, he found no one alive. He located a new tractor-trailer, and loaded it with tools and materials to build himself a little shelter in some remote forest in Vermont. Then he visited a variety of stores and warehouses from which he gathered many of the things he would require to survive. Finally, he'd driven north from Deep River Junction, and discovered "Hidden Valley."

Throughout that entire year, however, he'd learned nothing more about his own background. All he had to identify himself was the wedding ring he found laying on a chair in the room where he'd regained consciousness, and a poem he'd either written or copied onto a paper napkin. There were two sets of initials engraved on the inside of that ring. He chose the first set for himself, "C.C." He had no idea whether his wife had survived, nor where he might find her. His goal in the short-term was simply to survive.

The innkeeper's movements interrupted his reverie. A beer stein he was holding had become a prism, capturing the candlelight, and splashing a spectrum of color across his face. Their eyes met across the room, and the proprietor immediately looked away. His furtive glances were not reassuring. His face, made sinister in the glow of the dancing flames, was wreathed in shadow. CC held his head down, glancing up from beneath his brows to see the glint of the innkeeper's eyes as he surreptitiously studied him in return.

The various posters on the wall made it unmistakably clear why any stranger would find himself being examined. Large rewards were being offered for various individuals. CC grudgingly admitted that Jonathan had been right. He had made a stupid mistake in coming here. He had not imagined the extent of the conspiracy that had overtaken America.

One poster in particular made him appreciate the potential danger. He did not need to take a second look. "Up to 1,000 Yuan Reward (or equivalent food and/or clothing) for any information leading to the arrest and imprisonment of persons lacking official identification papers." And in smaller print, "Contact your local magistrate or any member of the Home Guard."

On the wall beside the poster, some wag had used lipstick to scribble some graffiti, and it had bled through the paint with which someone had tried unsuccessfully to cover it: "If you're a traitor, I've got a yen for you."

Somehow it didn't seem at all humorous to him.

A second poster was lost in the gloom, and he hadn't noticed it until after the serving girl had brought his stew and coffee. If he'd known what it said, he'd never have entered the tavern.

> This establishment accepts only Chinese currency. Bartering, or the use of other mediums of exchange, is punishable by a fine, jail sentence, or both. U.S. currency may be exchanged only at licensed facilities.

CC had never so much as seen a Chinese yuan, much less possessed one. It was clear that he could not use the five-dollar bill in his pocket to pay his bill.

He resumed examining the innkeeper, and saw his eyes caress the serving girl as she carried a carafe of coffee to CC's table. The man suddenly jerked to attention when a reproving voice called sharply from the kitchen.

"Henry!"

He appeared to ignore the woman's voice, instead carefully wiping a clear glass ash tray with a soiled bar towel, then holding it up to the light, pretending to check it for cleanliness while actually using it as a mirror to locate where she was standing.

"Henry!" she repeated.

He took another swipe with the towel as she continued to whine at him.

"Henry. Things are slow tonight, so I'm going home. See that you wrap the bread before you close up."

She moved up behind him, and tapped his shoulder to make sure she had his attention. She was a harridan of a woman, worthy all the most unpleasant adjectives — dumpy, frowsy, brassy, unkempt, dirty, and bossy — and she seemed to stare right through her husband.

"And you keep your mind on your work," she almost spat, as she stared pointedly at the girl who was pouring CC's coffee. Then she returned to the kitchen.

Just as he believed her gone, she stuck her head back around the corner.

"Henry, you get on with your work! You've spent a lot of time polishing that bar since we took that little tart in." She spoke loudly enough for everyone to hear, and CC could see the girl flush in embarrassment, though she pretended to ignore the comment and continued moving from table to table, thoroughly wiping the surfaces and rearranging the chairs. She was obviously avoiding her return to the kitchen for as long as possible.

The innkeeper mumbled aloud as he continued to polish beer mugs with the same soiled rag he'd used on the ash tray.

"If I defend myself, I must be guilty. After all, 'Where there's smoke, there's fire,' she'd say. If I don't defend myself, she assumes my guilt. And if I criticize the girl, she swoops like a hawk to the kill, ready to get rid of her." And that would mean more work for me." He slammed the ash tray to the floor, where it shattered, its pieces scattering around the bar.

CC watched him as he backed through the open kitchen door. He was removing his soiled undershirt, exposing a pigeon chest above a swollen belly, his sweaty torso gleaming in the light. His pants strained, like a girdle, below his massive stomach, surrendering to his hairy girth, and slipping down almost to his groin. A strip of soiled underwear showed grayly above the greasy waistband of his slacks, well below his navel.

The dirty building attested to its owners slovenly habits. Even from this distance, CC could smell the sour odor of the man's unwashed body clashing with the odor of crusty, freshly baked bread.

He watched as the proprietor set a tray of the hot loaves on the surface of the bar, then poked his index finger up his nostril to the first knuckle and worked it around, pinching the flesh with his thumbnail. He extracted his quarry, examined the specimen for a moment, then rubbed his fingers on his pants.

His wife appeared beside him again, snorting in disgust. He laughed. Long experience had taught him how to handle this shrewish woman. He looked across the room to stare boldly at the girl, then picked up a loaf of bread in his right hand, pressed it against his sweat streaked belly, and slipped it into the paper bag he shook open with the other.

He whispered to the woman. "That guy's still sitting over there," he observed, thinking he could turn her anger away, as a fencer turns a foil.

"What's he doing?" she asked, making no effort to lower her voice or to hide her sarcasm. "Ogling her too?"

He cursed under his breath, angry that he'd given her another excuse to return to the subject of the girl.

"I thought you were going home."

"I was, but I changed my mind. I can't trust you," and she pointed across the room toward the girl. Although she had successfully refused the bait her husband had set before her to distract her from the girl's presence, she had nevertheless become intrigued with the possibilities represented by a stranger in their tavern.

She was staring at CC as though he were a piece of meat on a butcher's cabinet. In his turn, CC imagined the woman calculating what pecuniary advantage she might gain from him. The innkeeper dipped his head to whisper in her ear. As he spoke, he nodded slightly toward CC, then tipped his head toward the poster. She smiled, and turned to walk back through the kitchen door.

An Unexpected Ally

Butter Creek Tavern
December 24th, 9:15 p.m.

T he young woman picked up the coffee pot and returned to CC's table. She held the carafe in one hand, while wiping his table with the other.

To make conversation, he asked, "Why no Christmas ornaments?"

"You don't know why?"

"Should I?"

She set the coffee pot down, and began to fastidiously wipe the table while examining him out of the corner of her eye.

"Yes, you should! Christmas decorations, and indeed any symbols related to Christianity, are forbidden." She continued to rub the table top vigorously. "I won't ask you why you don't know that."

He realized that he'd really put his foot into it. He should never have spoken. Now he mumbled some feeble excuse about having forgotten, but she obviously wasn't fooled.

Scarcely moving her lips, she muttered, "You've got to get out of here."

He turned to stare at the fire, trying not to look surprised.

"What do you mean?"

"They're suspicious. They think you're the man pictured on one of those wanted posters. They have a working phone in the kitchen, and she's gone to call the Home Guard."

He was shocked. It had to be a case of mistaken identity. Nagging at his memory, however, was the fact Sarah's grandmother had claimed to recognize him. He had originally assumed that, since she was already *in extremis,* she couldn't see him well in the darkness of the cave, and that she was hallucinating, but then he remembered that he'd held the light so that she could see him clearly.

And now these people also seemed to think that I'm somehow notable.

He would later regret his failure to ask the girl to check the name of the person on the wanted poster. Instead, he asked, "Why are you warning me?"

She didn't answer. Instead, she stepped to the fire, bent over to pick up the tongs that lay on the hearth, and knocked the logs apart, causing the flames to die, and making that part of the room appreciably darker. Then she walked back toward the bar, again passing close by his table, presumably to avoid bumping into a chair. Without looking down, she hissed, "Leave, now. Run for your life!"

Then she moved on to the kitchen.

If she hadn't spoken so calmly, he would have concluded that she was being overdramatic, and was perhaps emotionally unstable, but after a moment's thought, he decided to take her advice. He stood, and was turning to walk to the door when the owner moved out from behind the bar to block his path.

Watching him from lowered brows, CC turned to stand before the fireplace. He didn't have to pretend to be trying to warm his hands; it was so cold that he almost regretted the fact that the serving girl had knocked the fire apart.

Suddenly the landlord was standing beside him, moving very quickly for such a heavy man. CC turned as though to return to his table.

"That's all right, sir. You don't have to move. I was just going to stir up the fire to give you some more heat." He looked toward the kitchen where the young woman had disappeared. "That girl doesn't know a thing about laying a fire," he smirked, "but I'll bet she can do other things, eh?" He elbowed him in the side, delighted with his own wit.

CC ignored him and simply said, "Thanks, but don't burn any extra wood on my account. I was just getting ready to leave."

"Don't rush off." He pulled a chair up. "Here, sit yourself down right here by the fire. Besides, where could you possibly go in a storm like this? Why, I known everyone who lives around here. I've lived here myself for more than forty years."

His voice became insinuating. "I've lived here for over forty years," he repeated, "and I know you don't belong here. So you'd just better sit down, and wait the storm out."

"I heard your wife say that you're getting ready to close."

"Oh, I wouldn't be putting you out on a night like this."

Yes, CC thought, *you're a regular good Samaritan.*

He instead said, "That's very kind of you."

"So while we have a few hours to kill, why don't you tell me a little about yourself."

"There's not really a lot to tell."

"Ah, you're much too modest. I'm sure you are a very interesting man. Why not start with what you're doing here?"

The direct question frightened CC. This man did not seem afraid to go right for the jugular.

I should have pushed my way out of the place when the girl warned me. There's no help for it now. I'll have to try to bluff my way through.

"I'm visiting in the area."

"Really?" The question had a mocking ring. "And who would you be visiting? And from where, if I might ask?" He almost sneered. "I mean, it's very difficult to get a travel permit."

CC decided that it would not be prudent to remind him that it was none of his business. For one thing, under this new government, it might very well be his business. On the other hand, the man's curiosity was causing warning bells to ring. CC remembered a name he'd seen on a mailbox on the edge of the village, and decided to take a chance.

"I'm staying with the Burtons, down on the edge of town."

"Oh, the Burtons, is it? That's good. That's very good. The Burtons love visitors. And are you a relative?"

CC decided to bluff it out.

"Why, yes. I'm a cousin from New York. A few years ago, they came to visit my family, but with the way things are in the city, it seemed prudent to come here for a long visit."

"That's very interesting. The Burtons, h'm?"

"Something wrong?"

"Well, perhaps not. How long have you been staying with them?"

"Just a few days. This is the first time I could gracefully leave to visit your inn."

"I'm surprised. I surely am. Seeing as how the Burtons spend most of their time right here at this inn."

Something cold gripped CC's stomach as the man went relentlessly on.

"I'm surprised you are visiting the Burtons, seeing as how my name is Burton, and we're the only Burtons in the village, and neither my wife or me has any relatives in New York."

CC stood so quickly that he knocked his chair over backward. *Be sure your sins will find you out,* he thought with bitter irony. He tried one more time to bluff it out. "I'm sure there's some mistake here. I, uh..."

"Don't even think about it!" The innkeeper's voice had become a snarl, and in the darkness of the room CC noticed the gleam of the pistol in his hand.

At that moment, the beams from an automobile's headlamps swept across the windows at the front of the inn, for an instant lighting up the grime on the wall above the fireplace. As the innkeeper's eyes were drawn toward the light, CC was tempted to try to slap the gun aside, but he hesitated too long, and the opportunity was lost.

The innkeeper backed away from CC, but kept his pistol carefully trained on him. In the meantime, unseen by those inside the inn, a big suburban had followed another vehicle into the parking lot and stopped in front of the entrance. The driver of the SUV stepped down, adjusted his coat collar against the blowing snow, and turned back to shout above the gale.

"Stay in the truck. I'll leave the engine running so that you'll be warm. Don't try anything stupid!"

The three in the back seat remained silent, though a little boy was intensely interested in everything occurring around him. "Mommy, what's happening?"

"Shh, honey! Be quiet."

"That's right, kid" the driver warned. "You kids be quiet as church mice and it will go better for you."

At the same moment, the three men who stepped out of the other vehicle were laughing and joking as they entered the inn. As they came through the door, CC was slightly comforted to see that they looked like local people, definitely not orientals, and hoped that in the confusion of their arrival he might slip between them and make his escape.

He turned toward them, hoping that the landlord would not dare shoot for fear of hitting the wrong person, but when he looked at their faces, he realized that he had made another mistake. Their drunken revelry had obviously been a ruse intended to keep him off guard, for now their expressions were stone cold sober and they were all holding guns that were pointed at him.

One man offered a smile filled with contempt as he stepped forward. He didn't mince words.

"You're under arrest as an enemy of the state."

"I don't understand," CC replied.

"You will," he responded curtly. Turning to the others, he gave a few quick instructions. He was obviously experienced at this work, but from their conversation CC couldn't decide whether they considered him a significant catch, or just a run-of-the-mill refugee. Finally awakening to the fact that his identity might actually be printed on the poster beside him, he turned to look at it, but one of the men was standing in the way and when CC tried to step back to get a clear look, he was thrust forward toward the door.

When they walked out into the blowing snow, they were caught in the headlights of the SUV.

The little boy in the back seat noticed them, and gasped.

"Look Mommy!"

The urgency in his voice penetrated his mother's dark musings, and she turned to look out the window just as the captive's face was caught full in the high beams. Then her daughter started to exclaim, "Mommy, it's.....," but her mother's arms had been wrapped around the two children to comfort them, and her hands now covered their mouths and cut off their exclamations. Startled, and seeing the tears pouring down her cheeks, they were both struck dumb.

The little girl lowered her voice so that she couldn't be heard above the noise of the roaring defrosters in the front seat. "Mommy, why are you crying? Isn't that Daddy?"

"I'm crying because I'm so happy, honey. Now we know that your daddy is still alive."

"Can't we go see him?"

"Not now darling. We need to pray for your daddy."

"But Mommy..."

"And one more thing," she whispered, "no matter what happens, you must not tell anyone that you've seen your father. Do you understand?"

They stared at her for a moment, trying to understand her meaning, then dutifully answered, "Yes, Mommy."

Who's Who?

Butter Creek Tavern
December 24nd, 9:25 p.m.

While the tableau of the stranger's arrest continued in the dark and the cold, the serving girl, a dish cloth still gripped tightly in her hand, had slipped back into a dark corner of the kitchen. She would have remained hidden in that corner after they'd half-dragged, half-pushed the man out the door, but old man Burton had been keeping his eye cocked for her.

"Girl," he called, his voice reaching out like a slimy tentacle, "get over here!"

"Yes, Mr. Burton," she replied, infusing the words with what she hoped was sufficient subservience to override the contempt, bitterness, and fear welling up within her. She positioned herself on the customer side of the bar to avoid his inevitable pawing.

His face impassive, he told her, "You won't be going home with Mrs. Burton tonight." Something in his voice caught at her.

The two locals sitting at the bar seemed to sense something too, for both their faces turned toward him as he addressed her, and something passed between them in the glances they exchanged. These were decent men. Both were farmers, but one was a lay preacher — one of those rare and extraordinary servants of God who took no pay, but used every spare moment to study God's word and to assist in every meaningful way the people of his little community. Both of these men had been experiencing increasing difficulty with submitting to the new order, and did so only to protect their own families. They were meeting here tonight to discuss more overt ways to resist their oppressors.

Rachel hadn't replied to Burton's insinuating statement, but waited for a hint of what he might have in mind. She didn't have long to wait.

Burton turned to the two men seated at the bar.

"Closing time, gentlemen."

Their coffee cups were still nearly full, and one said, "You told that guy that you were staying open all night because of the storm."

"Well, what of it? I changed my mind."

"It's too far for us to walk back to our farms in this blizzard," the older of the two replied.

"That's just too bad, Reverend." He made no attempt to hide his contempt for the preacher, sneering as he drew out the title. "You shouldn't have come out here with the weather like this. Besides, you're only drinking coffee."

"You were only too glad to take our money for the coffee," the younger man replied.

"It's no matter," Burton smirked, glancing at the girl. "I'm closing now."

The preacher pointed at the sign thumbtacked over the back bar.

"Closing time is eleven p.m."

"Well, there's a blizzard," Burton retorted. "No customers, and I'm closing up."

"We're customers, and you're not closing up until we've finished our drinks," the younger of the two men said, a threat implicit in his words. "And we probably won't finish until long after closing time."

"I told you that it's closing time now," he shouted, making his growing frustration evident. Burton stared toward the door, as though invoking it to open. Then he made his threat. "When those guys get back in here, I'll have them clear you out."

"No you won't," the younger of the two answered, a thin smile on his face.

"How do you intend to stop me?" he challenged, a sly smile on his face.

"First, I'll offer them a round of drinks."

"They'll take your drinks and then throw you out," he replied.

"No, I don't think so."

"Why not?"

"Because there will be the offer of a second drink."

"And when you run out of money?" Burton asked, daring to challenge him, but unable to hide the uncertainty in his voice.

"I don't think it will be necessary to buy them more than one drink," the preacher interrupted. "I'll just tell them how you've been shorting them on the taxes you collect for them."

"How do you...," he started to ask, but his voice sounding strangled, a thief caught with his hand in the cash register.

He knew that even the miserable scum that were in the Home Guard would believe this man. His word was gold to the local community, and the fact that the pastor had pioneered his little church in this economically depressed area and that he supported himself and his wife from his little farm, gave his word even more credence. If the younger man had been bluffing about spending his hard-earned money to buy drinks for the members of the Home Guard, Pastor Kenzy's response left no doubt in his mind. But they weren't finished.

"And then," the other farmer added with an almost nasty smile, "I'll tell them you want all of us out of here so that you can be alone with this young lady. And you know how they'll respond to that." He left the sentence hanging.

Yes, I know, Burton thought, bitter frustration welling within him. *They will take what I want.* He tried to hide his disappointment.

"You don't frighten me," he blustered.

"And I have little doubt that one of them will mention your little tete-a-tete to your wife," the farmer added.

"All right," he surrendered, "eleven o'clock, and not a minute longer."

The girl watched all this with a fatal fascination. They were talking about her, and she was understandably frightened. It seemed obvious that the two farmers were on her side, but they too were walking a tightrope here.

Then there was the matter of the other man. While they'd been talking, she'd gazed at the poster. Her eyes passed over the name of the suspect unseeing, but there was no doubt in her mind that he was the man pictured in the photo. And below it were the words, "Wanted for Rape, Robbery, and Murder. $5000 reward."

How can that be? she wondered. She'd only spoken to him briefly, but she had been impressed somehow that he was a decent man. One thing was clear. He'd treated her with polite respect. He hadn't even ogled her, nor had he said anything out of line.

After thinking about it for a moment, she decided, *If I had to choose between Burton, those three guys in the Home Guard, and even these two farmers, I'd bet my life on the "rapist, robber, and murderer" on the poster.*

A Trip to the Woodshed
Butter Creek Tavern
December 24th, 9:20 p.m.

Two of the men grabbed CC by his upper arms and pushed him out into the blowing snow, holding him upright when he stumbled in the rising drifts, half-pulling, half-carrying him. They were about a hundred feet behind the inn when they came to a stout little shack. Without any discussion they pushed CC through the entry, knocking him to the ground, then threw something in after him, and slammed the door.

He heard them secure the latch, but did not move until he was certain that they had sufficient time to return to the inn.

I doubt very much that one of them is standing outside this door in this blizzard to guard me, he reasoned. But he nevertheless went to the door and shouted to see if anyone would answer.

He'd read somewhere that the best timeframe for escape is during that brief period immediately following capture. Though his prospects might already seem dim, conditions were not likely to improve. His current jailers were amateurs, obviously undisciplined, operating in some confusion and with limited guidance. The fact that they had returned to the comforts of the inn without posting a guard, and were trusting this shed to secure him, revealed their unprofessionalism.

He knew he must try to escape immediately, before they could decide what to do with him, and before they could get someone more experienced and authoritative here. In that respect, this savage storm was on his side. Even if such a person were willing to leave the comforts they were enjoying, it would take some time to travel here.

He knew that he needed to try to escape before he was more effectively secured, and before he was debilitated by cold, hunger, and physical abuse. If he became broken down physically, it would be increasingly difficult to concentrate on prayer and to trust the Lord. At some point, most prisoners begin to feel helpless and submit to their plight. He also knew that the prisoner who had faith in God faired best.

I must escape before I lose my strength and resolve, and before the storm makes my escape impossible. If I don't move soon, he realized, *I'll freeze to death.*

He shouted again to make certain that they hadn't posted a guard, and as expected, received no answer. Then he appealed for a blanket to keep warm. Again, no response.

He searched the inside pockets of his coat and found a small box of wood matches. Striking one, he made a quick inventory of his surroundings and didn't like what little he could see.

In spite of the gloom, it was clear that his little prison was a stout structure of post-and-beam construction. There was a pile of straw in one corner and a blanket laying on the floor. Evidently, that was the object they'd thrown after him.

Even if the rising blizzard hadn't made it pitch-dark outside, the only window was so filthy that he couldn't see through it, and was criss-crossed by several bars fashioned from angle iron. He was able to twist the latch and swing the window open, but when he tried to yank the bars loose, he found they were firmly attached with long bolts that went through the entire frame of the wall. The floor was simply frozen earth, so there was no hope of digging out. And there were no tools, not even a scrap of firewood that he might use to beat on the bars.

When he was satisfied that there was no hope of escape in that direction, he shut the window against the freezing wind.

He then put his shoulder to the door and heaved, but could do no more than rattle it slightly. Then he lay down on his back, with his feet toward the middle of one wall, and kicked as hard as he could between two of the studs. The impact made no impression on the boards. He realized that he wasn't going to make his escape that way either.

He struck a second match and noticed a trapdoor to a loft above. It was secured with a hasp and padlock. He pulled himself up onto a horizontal brace about three-and-a-half feet off the floor. To maintain his balance, he gripped a wooden peg that secured the end of one of the ceiling beams, then pushed up on the trap door with his other hand, using all his strength. The angle was wrong, so he couldn't bring much pressure to bear and he failed to even budge the trap door. He grabbed the lock, and tried to wrench the hasp free, but merely hurt his knuckles. *Not that it would matter,* he thought. *Once in the loft, I'd still have the problem of breaking through the roof.*

Nevertheless, he decided to try one more time before the muscles in his legs and shoulders began griping because of his odd position. He tried leaning out even further, again pushing up against the trap door, but this time he lost his grip. He fell hard, saved only by landing on the pile of straw, and a spasm gripped him where he had injured his chest months before.

He had done himself no good with his futile efforts, and now he was hurt. It was clear that his jailers had made a good choice for his makeshift prison and weren't so amateurish as he'd imagined. They'd probably used it on earlier occasions for others like himself. He wondered in passing whether anyone else had been left out here at risk of freezing to death.

Did they consider that the blizzard might kill me? he wondered. *Would they even care?*

The cold had long since penetrated his clothing. The exertion caused him to exhale great gouts of vapor, and he thought of the old New England fable about a person's breath turning to ice crystals and shattering when they fell to the ground.

Shivering now, he curled up on the pile of straw, wrapping himself from head to foot in the threadbare blanket.

"Please, Lord," he prayed, *"help me."*

His thoughts seemed to turn immediately from his prayer to what else he might be carrying in the deep inside pocket of his overcoat. He reached down, and felt a soft packet.

I could use some tissues, he thought, *but they won't make an earth-shaking change in my situation.*

He pulled the packet from his pocket, and opened it. It was a mylar sheet with a chrome coating. He fumbled with it for some time before his cold-stiffened fingers could unfold it. Then he spread it out over the hay, and lay the blanket his jailers had left behind over it. He lay down on one edge and pulled them over him. He immediately felt his diminishing body heat reflected back by the remarkable little plastic sheeting. His eyes filled with tears as he realized that he'd received an instant answer to prayer.

He was unable to sleep, but lay there in a semi-conscious state, drifting in and out, the cold eating into his reserves, draining his remaining strength and will. Finally he drifted off into a light sleep.

The Guest Bedroom

Butter Creek Tavern
December 24th, 9:30 p.m.

When the three men returned to the inn, cursing the cold, and kicking the snow from their boots, they discovered that the driver of the SUV had brought the woman and her two children inside, and was busy pointing out the place on the floor where they were to sleep near the hearth.

The children's mother overheard one of the men joke about the likelihood of their own prisoner freezing to death before they'd even get him to headquarters, and she cringed as the other two laughed. They did not notice as she turned an expressionless face toward them, then returned to her labors. The children had also overheard the comment and had tears in their eyes.

Their woman knelt down next to them, tucking the blankets the innkeeper had grudgingly surrendered to her, and smiled at them. "You don't think that the Lord is going to let your daddy die now, after bringing him all this way, do you?"

The little girl answered. "Really Mommy?"

"Really. Now we're going to pray for Daddy. Okay?"

"Yes, Mommy."

Then the little boy piped up. "God will take care of Daddy," he sniffed, and his big sister used the sleeve of her coat to wipe away her own tears. Then they closed their eyes while their mother whispered a prayer for the man who was their daddy and her husband.

While this was going on unnoticed in the dining room, the farmer made good on his earlier threat to the innkeeper, and offered the guards free drinks. When they happily accepted, he told the serving girl to bring them an entire bottle of bourbon, a very generous gift in a world where distilleries no longer operated, and after making eye contact with the farmer, the young woman filled a water glass for each of the four men.

As drunk as these esteemed officers of the Home Guard already are, she thought, *it won't be long before they are unconscious. I wonder if that's the farmers' plan.*

Burton wasn't paying much attention to his unwanted guests. In his mind, he had already counted the reward he would get for turning the guy in, and he was again focusing on the girl. He kept moving his weight from one foot to the other, staring at her and occasionally licking his lips.

When she was finished serving the drinks, he told her, "Get upstairs and make sure the guest room is all set up for business."

"Why?" she asked. "You put that woman and her two children on that cold floor, and we aren't expecting any other travelers tonight."

"Never mind," he snapped. "Just do as I say." Then he added, "I'll be up in a minute to check on you."

Hearing this, one of the farmers suggested that Burton join the others for a drink or two, and the man who'd taken charge of the prisoner grabbed him by the arm and drew him to the table..

"You might as well have a drink, Burton. We aren't going anywhere in this blizzard."

"Which means," one of the farmers added, "that you have no reason to force us out into the snow tonight after all?"

"Why would he do that?" the leader of the group asked incredulously, putting an end to Burton's plan to evict them.

"Well, we have one room for rent, and that bed is for me," Burton laughed, but he was staring after the departing girl when he said it.

While they were drinking their dinners, the serving girl reached the top of the stairs, and entered the room that the Burtons laughingly called their guest suite. She worked quickly. Aided by the light of an oil lamp, she stripped the bedding from the mattress and threw it into a corner, then slid the sagging mattress off the old springs so that it fell between the bed frame and the wall. Then she looked about for a weapon. Finding nothing in the bureau or the closet, she gave a cursory look at the lamp on the table. It was a frail thing, useless for her needs.

In frustration, she kicked the leg on the bed's footboard. Even with her hiking shoes on, she felt the shock in her toe, and was angry at herself for losing control. She grasped the bedpost with one hand while she bent down to massage her foot, and noticed that the post moved slightly. Using one hand, she continued wiggling it, then using both hands, she jerked hard on it.

It broke loose. It was a heavy piece of oak, a full two inches thick and nearly three feet in length. It sounded like a pistol shot in the confines of the room, and she listened carefully for any indication that they'd heard it downstairs. Hearing nothing, she raised the makeshift club to her shoulder and gave it a trial swing, as though it were a baseball bat.

A moment later she heard Burton's heavy tread as he slowly climbed the stairs, and she ran lightly across the room to extinguish the lantern. She moved back to the middle of the room and let her hand drop to her side, hiding her new-found club in the folds of her full skirt. Burton had climbed the stairs without a light, but she could tell when he padded into the room because she could smell his sour unwashed body.

As he closed the door behind him, he said, "You were to come back downstairs as soon as you finished here."

"I'm just finishing up."

"Well, no need to go down now."

"Why not?" she asked, trying to sound indifferent to the implied threat.

"The men from the Home Guard are drunk, and the two farmers are stretched out by the fireplace. So we have this room to ourselves now." Although it was pitch dark, he moved toward her unerringly, almost sensing her by the fear she believed she exuded in the darkness. Her heart was beating so hard that she was afraid he must hear it.

He was speaking in what he must have considered a kind and reasonable voice, and when he was just a few feet away she acted. The bat swept up behind her right shoulder, then she swung it around with all her strength, striking him on the neck.

The pain was so great that he only made a mewling sound, but he quickly recovered. Reaching for her, Burton intended to hit her with all his strength, but he found himself unable to lift his arm. He twisted around, raising his other arm, and she swung again, this time striking him just above the ear. He crashed senseless across the old bedsprings.

At the same moment, someone else pushed into the room. She swung at him, but missed, and he exclaimed, "Don't hit us. We just came up to help you."

"I don't believe you."

"Listen, the four guys down stairs are drunk. We've come to tell you that this is your chance to get out of here."

"I have nowhere to go?"

"Sure you do. Get that man out of the woodshed and go with him."

"That sounds like jumping out of the frying pan into the fire."

"No, he's a good man!"

"What about the poster."

The two men laughed. "If the Home Guard put a big reward on his head, it stands to reason that he's a very good man," the older farmer offered.

She had been coming to the same conclusion.

"I guess that makes sense."

"Right. So bundle up, and go help him."

"What about the men downstairs," she asked.

"We don't dare take an obvious part in this, but we can keep offering them drinks if they wake up. You, on the other hand, need to move fast."

"What about the woman and her kids?"

"We'd like to help them, but they're asleep, and there's no way those kids could walk far in this blizzard."

"One last question. What about Burton?"

"He followed you up here, and at least one of them saw that. It's obvious that you simply defended yourself from Burton. But you'd better understand this. To the Chinese, it won't make any difference. If they catch you, they will deal harshly with you, and your innocence won't protect you."

Her distrust had vanished. "So what do I do?"

"Fill a thermos with something hot to drink, take some of that fresh bread, dress in your warmest clothes, and get out there and free that guy. Then don't stop until you've found a good place to hide."

The Rescuer

Butter Creek Tavern
December 24th, 9:48 p.m.

It couldn't have been much later that CC heard a scratching sound at the door. He tried to pull himself to his feet, but was too stiff and cramped with the cold. Suddenly the door was dragged open a foot or so, its bottom scraping over the frozen earth. He sensed someone entering. A match flared, dazzling him with its glare. It was instantly snuffed out and dropped to the floor where it was ground underfoot. Someone moved across the shed and knelt beside him. The frozen air was clearing his senses, and the sweet odor of lilac came to him. It was the serving girl.

She knelt beside CC and helped prop him up in a sitting position. Unscrewing the lid from a thermos bottle, she poured a cup of hot soup. Holding it to his lips, she helped him drink. "Slowly," she warned. "You'll burn your mouth."

She was right, but he didn't mind. The warmth seemed to permeate his body, restoring not just his strength but his hope.

"I'd better save the rest for later," she muttered, and screwed the lid back on the thermos.

She began speaking with a sense of urgency. "We must leave here. I don't know who you are or what you've done, but they're all inside celebrating. They are so drunk that they're talking about your coming trial and execution."

CC handed back the empty cup. "Execution?" Then he realized there was no time to discuss it. He had to act quickly. "Why are you helping me?"

"Because, if they're against you, you must be a good person. And, if they want to kill you, you must be someone who poses a real threat to them."

He couldn't fault her logic, but it didn't make any sense to him. His problem was figuring out why anyone on earth would think him worthy of any attention at all. On the other hand, they seemed to know things about him that he didn't know about himself, things he wasn't sure he wanted to know. He now realized that he'd come to enjoy the solitude and security of Hidden Valley, the simplicity of his life, and the quality of the company he had with Jonathan and Sarah.

He strained to see the woman's face in the darkness. Maybe he was naturally suspicious, but he wondered how she could have gotten free to help him, or why she would want to. Maybe she was just there to get information.

"Even if you want to help me, what makes you think we can get out of here and survive this storm," he rasped.

Her answer was not reassuring.

"First, I've already decided that it's better for me to die out there in a snow drift than live under their control."

He couldn't fault her reasoning.

Then she said, "You had to come here from somewhere. Maybe I can go back there with you." It was a question.

That silenced him. Since the bad guys already had him, he couldn't figure what advantage they might exact by discovering the location of his hideaway. Then he realized, *Their skilled interrogators would get that out of me sooner or later.*

Then she said something that touched him with its pathos. "Those men have all been trying to get alone with me. They're inside, joking about ganging up on me. They think the Chinese will look the other way as a reward for their capturing you."

"Won't your employers protect you?"

"Burton is the worst, but he might be dead."

"Dead?"

"He had me alone in the upstairs bedroom. I hit him over the head with a bed leg. Twice."

"Really?"

She could hear the smile in his voice. He hadn't liked Mr. Burton either, and was interested in her opinion of him. "How bad is he?"

"I was able to get along for a while, but he's grown worse."

"Yes, I can't see how you could abide him. He literally stinks."

"I call him 'Rudolph'."

"Because of his nose?"

"Yes. It's swollen and veined and purple because he's a drunken sot. He's a filthy, evil man. The place is full of old pornographic magazines. His wife had gone home or she'd have put a stop to his plan. Not because she's a good person. She's just domineering and possessive, but she doesn't want anything to happen to me either."

"Why not," he asked, a hint of suspicion in the question.

She laughed. "It ought to be obvious. I do most of their work."

That put everything in perspective. With her arm around him, CC rose clumsily to his feet.

"Come on," she said. "Storm or no storm, we've got to hurry and get out of here."

There was a wicked laugh from the doorway. Then someone staggered in.

"Why," a slurred voice cut in, "you ain't going anywhere, Rachel. Jake and me, we were searching for our pretty little piece, and here you are, helping our prize prisoner to escape." He grabbed her arm and jerked her to his side, almost knocking the thermos from her hands.

"And your antics ain't gonna do you much good with our little yellow-skinned leaders either, honey. Now, why don't you come back to the inn with me and, if you treat me real nice, maybe I can get you a little special consideration."

CC reached out, put his hand on the drunk's chest, and thrust him away. The man reeled across the room, fell against the wall, and slid down in a sitting position, still laughing.

Then another figure moved into the room, but he wasn't staggering. He held a flashlight in one hand, and a gun in the other, and his movements seemed reasonably sure and steady. He spoke over his shoulder to the giggling drunk.

"Get up, Ronnie."

"Aw, Jake — gimme a break," he giggled, and began to croon it over and over. "Aw Jake... gimme a break." He laughed. Then, with a grunt, he slid sideways to the floor and passed out.

Jake uttered a sound of disgust, then pushed the gun into CC's sore ribs. "Out," he commanded.

The Escape

Butter Creek Tavern
December 24th, 10:40 p.m.

They started out the woodshed door, the serving girl leading the way. When CC stopped for an instant to get his bearings, his assailant rammed the gun painfully into his back. CC stumbled, then righted himself and resumed following the girl toward the back door of the inn. His joints were stiff from lying on the frozen ground, and the dim light that seeped through the inn's windows seemed to flicker in the heavily falling snow, making it barely possible to follow the vanishing path through the rising drifts. The wind-whipped snow was already nearly two feet deep.

CC heard a dull, meaty thud, after which the pressure of the weapon in the small of his back disappeared, and he turned his head just in time to see Jake collapse into a snow bank. Another figure stood over him, a hunk of firewood in his hands, and there was a hoarse whisper.

"CC, is that you?"

In amazement, CC asked, "Jonathan?"

"Yes. I'm sorry. When you didn't come home last night, Sarah started worrying. She begged me to find you. I peeked through windows in almost every house in town, but I didn't see you. If it hadn't been for the commotion out here, I think I'd have frozen to death before I located you."

His teeth were chattering, but CC's thoughts were on other matters. He didn't want to get caught again.

"Give me a hand," he ordered.

They dragged Jake back into the shed, laid him next to his unconscious partner, and closed the door. Rachel picked up a broken tree branch and jammed the end of it into the hasp.

Jonathan was holding a flashlight, and CC could see the woman's face. She looked at him, eyebrows raised, as if to ask, *What next?*

"All right, Jonathan," he said, "the three of us need to get to the mountain road."

"Follow me," Jonathan shouted above the rising gail. He led them back through a snow drift to an old stable further out in the yard. They stopped in the shelter of the building, and

Rachel divided the remainder of the soup between the three of them. Then Jonathan led them up a hill, across a small ravine, and up another slope. It was difficult making the climb, but CC realized that any pursuers were apt to assume they'd take an easier route. They soon found themselves north of the town, on the edge of the mountain road.

CC's chest hurt. The exertion made him gasp for breath, and the cold air increased the pain. He pulled his scarf up to cover his face. They walked through the deepening snow for twenty minutes before they got to the old feed and grain store.

In danger of freezing, they broke into the cellar, found some canned goods, started the gas range upstairs, and prepared a hot meal. They ate quickly, knowing that they dared not take time to sleep or linger.

Plunderer's Storehouse

Green Mountain Feed and Grain Store
December 24th, 11:25 p.m.

C C picked up the empty cans from which they'd eaten and dropped them in an empty cardboard carton. Then, gazing through the frosty window, he tried vainly to penetrate the darkness.

"We've been here too long," he warned, "and we have to get back while there's still enough snow falling to cover our tracks." He shook his head, as though struggling with a decision, then turned his gaze from one to the other. "We need to go, but I don't think that we can afford to walk away without looking through the stuff that the bad guys have hidden in the cellar."

None of them was in a hurry to leave the relative warmth of the unheated building, so they made their way downstairs and began rooting through various cartons. There were smiles when Jonathan tore open a box and they discovered that they were going to be able to replace their wet socks with brand-new dry ones.

Then the woman gave a cry of surprised delight, and CC turned to see her tearing open a carton.

Her face was a study in joy as she held up a filmy garment, then realizing she was being watched, she hastily stuffed it back into the box.

"What was that?" CC asked her.

She looked slightly embarrassed, and answered in a small voice.

"It's underwear."

CC displayed surprise at her evident excitement, and she rushed to explain. "They've emptied all the stores of women's lingerie. Rumor has it that it's saved for women who are willing to *co-operate* with the new order. Anyway, it won't be long before most women will have to revert to the expedient of tying old pieces of cloth around themselves to preserve any degree of modesty."

She lowered her eyes in embarrassment, and it occurred to CC that her modesty was like that of some of the Christians he'd known. *What Christians?* he wondered. Even as that question occurred to him, he found himself assaulted by a headache so severe that he had to close his eyes. He was instantly transported to a world of flames and smoke and death, where men in white suits pushed gurneys with body bags on them. The visions consumed his consciousness. He staggered, and Jonathan put out his hand to steady him, a look of deep concern on his face. The pain receded and CC shook his head as though to clear his mind.

Rachel remained oblivious to what was taking place behind her back, and continued to open cartons. She thought that the man was quite young to have a teenage son, but she inherently trusted both of them.

"This entire stack of boxes is full of incredibly expensive lingerie," she mused. Then, as though experiencing an epiphany, her conversation took a radical turn, and she spoke at just above a whisper. "It's very dangerous for us to be here."

CC was rubbing his temples, trying to get back from wherever he'd drifted, and fought gamely to get his mind back on the matters at hand. Forcing a grim smile, he tried to imagine what it would be like for a woman not to have proper underwear. For most men, it had been pretty much a choice of choosing small, medium, or large. Yet, realizing that it was important to her, he had decided that they could risk a few more minutes.

"Dangerous or not, you'd better take what you need, but, yes, please hurry." As an afterthought, he suggested, "Why don't you pack up a year's supply of a couple of sizes." He grinned at Jonathan and shrugged his shoulders. "The way we've been collecting strays, I can't imagine who else we might pick up along the way."

Rachel laughed. "A couple of sizes? It doesn't work that way." Then she laughed again.

"What?"

"Sizes. There is a lot of variety."

"Oh, yes, of course." He looked away in embarrassment, and she thought how refreshing it was to find a man in this day and age who seemed such an innocent.

"And your comment." She laughed. "I never thought of myself as a stray."

CC turned toward her in confusion, but she'd already resumed rooting through the cartons. While she was busy sorting clothes, Jonathan moved about, reading the labels on the boxes and searching through the cartons piled in the shadows.

He pulled something out of a large box, and turned to Rachel. "Catch," he said, and stretched out to hand her a bulky aluminum framework with nylon cloth and straps attached. She examined it and realized it was a backpack. Smiling her thanks, she began stuffing one pouch with the filmy garments. She wasn't frivolous. The first thing that went into that bag were four sets of flannel PJs and two ankle-length flannel nightgowns.

"If you see any pajamas that might fit a seven-year old girl, bring along a pair or two, will you?" CC asked.

"Sure," she answered, without comment.

Jonathan had continued to study the labels. When he reached the end of a row of cartons, he ducked under the stair-case. Suddenly he made a low whistle. "Hello. What do we have here?" He dragged a beautiful, aluminum-framed backpack from the corner where it lay hidden under a pile of flattened cartons. Opening it, he reached in and dragged out a one-pound can.

"Oh, just more coffee beans."

"Great. We'll put it with our stockpile when we get back."

CC made his way to the door to check the weather. There was a lapse in the storm's fury, and it was now snowing lightly. They prepared for the final push home while it was still dark.

CC had discovered a carton that contained handguns, and set aside three identical automatics, including a half-dozen magazines for each, plus several hundred rounds of ammunition. He showed the others how to load the weapons, how to set the safeties, and cautioned them to carry the weapons in their coat pockets.

Perhaps the most exciting find was a box containing night-vision goggles. Taking time to familiarize himself with the instructions, he pulled open the battery compartment and installed the required cells. He gave each of them a set of the goggles to pack away. In spite of their weight and discomfort, he wore his. Now he would literally be able to see in almost total darkness, giving him an enormous advantage over anyone who lacked such costly and sophisticated hi-tech equipment.

Rachel had stuffed her backpack to its limit, and was now struggling to get her hands through the straps. Jonathan stepped up behind her and helped lift it onto her shoulders while she slipped her arms through the straps.

This is the first time a man has stood behind me in nearly a year that I haven't been frightened, she realized.

CC and Jonathan had already slipped into the backpacks they'd filled with food, medical supplies, and ammunition. Jonathan had discovered a carton containing knit hats and wool-lined leather gloves, and had set aside a set for each of them. No one noticed that he packed two pair of children's gloves in one of the zipper pouches. Sarah was never far from his thoughts. When they were ready, the three of them buttoned up their coats, drew on their new gloves, scarves and hats, made their way outside, and headed up the slope in the blowing snow.

They were walking along the edge of the highway, just approaching the bottleneck, when the snow resumed falling with a vengeance. CC almost despaired of their making it. There was ice beneath the snow, and each of them had slipped and fallen several times because of the treacherous footing. Rachel noticed that it was easier to keep one's footing in the deeper snow on the side of the road, though it was much harder to push through it.

The blowing snow became so intense that they almost passed by the entrance to the valley. The storm had become a real Northeaster. Conditions improved considerably when they got among the trees in the bottleneck because there was little wind. CC took several candy bars from his pocket and passed them around. They had to gnaw hard to break off pieces of the frozen chocolate, then literally let it melt in their mouths.

They all wanted to stop to rest, but CC knew that they didn't dare remain in the gulch, exposed as they were to both the elements and to possible pursuit. He wanted to get far away from the highway, and hoped that the drifting snow would fill the deep footprints they were leaving behind them.

Rachel wanted to ask where they were going, but conversation was impossible. She hoped that they were headed for better shelter than a tent or a lean-to, and that they had some way to heat it.

It took them well over an hour to fight their way to the north end of the valley, and to find the entrance to the cavern. The night vision binoculars were almost useless in the intense darkness and blowing snow, but CC was finally able to pick out the top of the cave's portal above a deep drift.

When they finally pushed their way through the drift and stumbled into the cave, their flashlight batteries were almost depleted, providing only a feeble light. Their clothing and hair were matted with snow, and their faces were beginning to suffer the effects of frostbite. Hoping for some hot food and a warm bed, CC was totally unprepared for the scene that met his gaze.

The remains of a wood fire smoldered against his artificial wall. The choking odor of burned paint and charred fiberglass made a dramatic change from the pure winter air outside. Jonathan shined his penlight on the back wall. A hole had been melted through part of the fake partition. Worse, the camouflaged door was sprung open and hung by just one hinge.

The Interlopers

The Cave Entrance
December 25th, 1:25 a.m.

It was nothing less than a catastrophe. Someone had obviously stumbled onto the cave, then moved inside to escape the storm. In an effort to keep warm, they had built a fire against the fake wall, ultimately discovered the entry, and made their way inside.

Jonathan was choking on the fumes, and they moved back toward the cave's entrance to get some fresh air. Questions raced through CC's mind.

Who is inside? Have they come here looking specifically for me? Do they represent a physical danger? Most importantly, is Sarah safe? And, finally, how should we respond?

To make matters worse, the three of them were all now choking on the acrid smoke, and shaking so from the cold that they could barely communicate. CC realized that they didn't really have any choice. They had to take their chances and get inside as soon as possible.

They moved back up the tunnel, and he dragged the damaged door just far enough open to peer into the main cave. The front window of the motor home was dimly lit, but he could see no one moving about inside. He studied the scene for a several minutes, then looked toward the cottage.

There was no sign of activity there. Sometimes Sarah dragged a sleeping bag into one of the closets and slept on the floor. He could only hope that she was there, undiscovered, asleep, and oblivious to the existence of this unexpected and unwanted guest.

He wanted to kick himself. It had been stupid of him to go to town. Yet he could not discount the knowledge he'd gained, nor the importance of having been able to rescue Rachel. Or, more precisely, to have been rescued by her. For he had to admit to himself somewhat ruefully that Rachel rescued him, and that Jonathan had rescued Rachel.

And he rescued me, too, of course. So I can offer no rationale for my bad judgment. And because I wasn't here, we are now facing another crisis, although even if I had been here I don't know what I could have done to keep this person from happening along and breaking in.

There was no escaping the truth. He'd even compounded his foolishness further because he failed to take a weapon with him, a weapon that might have seen him escape the tavern. But again, that would have left Rachel a virtual captive there. It all seemed very confusing if God was left out of the equation.

For God had even compensated for CC's failure to carry a gun by motivating Jonathan to come after him, and enabled him to whack the bad guy with a hunk of firewood. And it was certainly providential that they discovered the handguns in the basement of the feed and grain store, or they'd have found themselves unarmed now.

He led them back down the tunnel where they could find cleaner air and talk without danger of being overheard. He had Jonathan hold a flashlight so that he could again demonstrate how to change the magazines in their handguns, and how to pull back and release the slide to load a round into the chamber. He made sure that they kept the muzzles pointed at the ground and watched carefully as each of them checked their handguns, and he again pointed out the little lever that put them on safety.

When CC was satisfied that they each had a round in the chamber, that the weapons were cocked, and the safeties were on, he led the way back through the cave. CC and Rachel slipped quietly through the broken fiberglass doorway, followed by Jonathan who tried to pull it back in place to reduce the amount of smoke entering the cavern. When they were all inside, CC whispered to Rachel to wait where she was. Pointing his fingers to indicate a pincer movement, he signaled Jonathan to approach the motor home's rear door while he moved toward the front.

When they'd reached their respective positions, Jonathan gripped his gun firmly in one hand and turned the door handle with the other, opening it very slowly. CC watched as Jonathan leaned forward to peer through the open door, and was suddenly concerned because the boy would be looking directly into the motor home bedroom.

That too was foolish of me. I should have gone to the rear door.

It was too late. The teen had already stepped up onto the threshold of the open door, and nodded to indicate that he was ready.

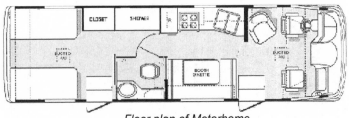

Floor plan of Motorhome

CC then slipped quietly into the living area at the front of the motor home. The night light over the little kitchen table provided sufficient illumination for him to work his way back toward the rear bedroom.

There was no one in sight, but the table was a mess of opened cans and unwashed dishes. As CC moved through the kitchen area, he counted two plates and two coffee mugs on the table. One of the mugs had lipstick on the rim. He wondered that a woman in these circumstances would possess any lipstick, much less wear it. As he tiptoed toward the back of the motor home, he heard a rasping snore. He looked down the hall through the bathroom and the open bedroom door. *No time for loitering about,* he thought. *Whoever these people are, there were obviously exhausted and hungry.*

CC's thoughts were black. Back in the village, they were probably already mounting a search for both he and the girl, though the storm might deter them for hours and even days. It didn't seem to matter. He tried to tell himself that he had done no serious harm, and the enemy might not feel compelled to search for him. Then he remembered the men left lying unconscious in the snow, and realized that they might even now be dead. Even that might not matter at all. The presence of these intruders indicated that the secret of his hideaway was already lost.

What would he do if the trespassers proved belligerent? He could only try to imprison them, which would be an impossible hardship on everyone concerned. Or he could kill them, but he blanched at the thought. It was a totally unacceptable alternative, an alternative for which he was neither emotionally nor spiritually equipped. Yet, if they weren't enthusiastically cooperative, he had a huge problem.

He rolled the sliding door open very slowly to reduce any rumble. He needn't have worried. He could see their unwelcome visitor sleeping soundly on his bed. He slipped through the bathroom door into the bedroom as Jonathan stepped through the rear door.

His thoughts flashed back to the night he found the motor home in the field next to the Green Mountain Feed and Grain

Store, and how he'd brought it back here to serve as his and Sarah's little underground home.

There was adequate light coming through the hall from the kitchen to keep he and Jonathan from stumbling around. There were two of them, one asleep on each of the twin beds. CC realized that it was to his advantage that the intruders had both pulled the covers over their heads to keep warm. The beds ran along the opposite sidewalls to the rear wall of the motor home, and Jonathan had already taken a position at the foot of the bed by the door.

CC had originally decided to use the same technique that Jonathan had once used on him. He would press the gun's muzzle against the guy's head. Then he was forced to acknowledge that he was no action-adventure hero.

Our lives are at stake here, and this is not make-believe. He might react by swinging at me, and my gun might go off.

He instead moved to the foot of the bed, just across from Jonathan. He wondered, *If this turns violent, do I have the nerve to pull the trigger?*

Jonathan stood still, his arms extended in what he must have imagined was the prescribed firing position, the rigid line of his lips revealing his stress. CC wondered if the teen had learned it while watching TV. One of the boy's legs was actually pressed against the bed, perhaps in an unconscious effort to brace himself. His handgun was pointed down toward the person beneath the covers, plainly a woman. He looked into CC's eyes and nodded to indicate his readiness. In response, CC wagged his finger back and forth in a "no-no" gesture, intending to forestall any rash action.

The boy had to remove one hand from his pistol in order to take the flashlight that CC held out to him. He turned it on, and pointed it toward the head of the bed. At the same time, CC gripped the blankets that lay over the man's feet, and jerked them toward him, pulling the covers down to the man's waist.

The man's reaction was so violent that CC almost pulled the trigger. In an instant, the guy was sitting up and sliding his hands around in the bedding searching for something. And that something, CC realized, was a gun. It lay just out his reach, slightly behind him, under the edge of his pillow.

"Don't move!" CC barked, realizing at once how trite the words sounded, yet unable to think of anything more appropriate. The man squinted into the light, and evidently saw the two of them with guns in hand. He immediately ceased his furious movements, but the way his eyes moved about, assessing the situation, made it clear to CC that he and Jonathan would have to be very careful.

"Hands behind your head!" CC ordered.

The man hesitated, then slowly complied.

"Now, move to the other bed and lie down next to your friend."

With all the racket, the woman had awakened and pulled the blanket down under her chin so that she could see what was happening.

"There's no way he's lying down with me." The sentence was spoken without inflection—flat, nerveless, definite.

CC didn't question her preference. He said to the man, "Okay, on the floor." Then, after a moment's thought, "On your stomach, and put your hands behind your head." As the man knelt to comply, CC saw his eyes flicker toward the gun he'd left laying by his pillow.

"Don't even think about it," he warned, and the man acquiesced.

While he was lowering himself to the floor, the woman raised herself abruptly into a sitting position. The blankets fell away from her shoulders, but she caught them before she was fully exposed. Her lips curled slightly as Jonathan began to look away in embarrassment, unaware that she was fully dressed. Then her little grin blossomed into a radiant smile. She had decided that she liked this innocent teenager.

Having assessed the teenager's personality, she now moved her attention from the boy to the man. She was not surprised that his eyes appeared to be riveted on her upper body. She'd met far too many men whose immediate response to her looks was a ravening lust, and she simply assumed from his stare that he was like all the others.

On earlier occasions, she might have turned red with anger, but her involuntary reaction now was to turn a pretty shade of rose. But she paled again as she realized that he wasn't examining her body. Surprising herself, she was at first disappointed, then frightened. *He's staring at the necklace,* she realized.

And he was thinking, *I can't believe the size of those gems!*

She realized that he was appraising the jewelry, and had just as obviously concluded, and quite correctly, that it was inappropriate for sleepwear. She was momentarily caught speechless.

CC was thinking along other lines.

If that necklace is genuine, it's highly unlikely that the woman would ever dare remove it. Keeping it next to her skin, well-hidden by her clothing, is probably the best place to safeguard such a magnificent treasure.

His thoughts raced. *Those jewels have got to be* artificial. *If they were real, they'd be priceless. On the other hand, she might be a looter who discovered them while rifling a jewelry box in the master bedroom of a vacant mansion.*

He had never been interested in jewelry, but this necklace was, in its own way, as beautiful as the woman. It looked worth a king's ransom. The chain appeared to be white gold, and was hung end-to-end with at least a dozen diamonds, each larger than any he had ever seen before. Hanging from its center was a huge, brooding, dark blue stone. It was fully an inch across and it seemed to become a sullen brooding eye when the beam of his flashlight touched it. The enormous stone was surrounded by smaller stones, but small only in their relationship to the larger one.

Even the smallest of them, he calculated, *must be at least several carats in size.*

The woman saw the incredulity on his face, and reached up to enclose the dark stone in the palm of her hand, an unconscious and futile attempt to conceal it from his stare, as though she were trying to guard her own innocence. It was so large that she was unable to enclose the entire setting in one hand. Realizing that an explanation was necessary, and with what seemed a forced ingenuousness, she almost stuttered.

"This is just an old piece of costume jewelry my father bought for me when I was a child. I wear it for sentimental reasons."

Though he considered her unsolicited explanation to be out of character with the combative personality she had displayed a moment before, CC said nothing. He decided that, for the moment, the source of the jewels and their genuineness were of secondary importance, and he resumed dividing his attention between the two intruders,

"Can I get up yet," the guy on the floor whined. "It's cold and dirty down here."

"In a minute," CC snarled. "Keep still!"

The woman spoke up. She was matter of fact, and introduced herself as though there was nothing strange about being found in someone else's bed in the middle of the night with a fortune in jewels hanging about her neck.

"My name is Elizabeth Ross." My companion, and she nodded her head toward the man lying prone on the floor, says that he is Jim McCord. We mean you no harm. At least I don't," which made them all wonder what sort of relationship she and McCord shared.

To CC, it sounded like some trite line from a movie about invaders from outer space. And just about as sincere. He could hear the dialogue.

"You are from Mars. I am from Venus. We mean you no harm. Zap!"

His expression did not change, however, so she barged ahead. "Several months ago, Mr. McCord rescued me from a gang that threatened to assault me."

Jonathan received an annoyed look when he commented, "Yeah, there's a lot of that going around."

"Then, yesterday, or rather the day before, we left the cave in which we were sheltering in order to try to locate some building materials. We were on our way back to the cave when we became lost in the snowstorm. We only stumbled on the entrance to this place by accident."

She chose to ignore the boy's perceptive question, when he asked, "Where are those building supplies now?"

She evidently assumed that her cryptic explanation was more than adequate, but CC wasn't at all satisfied.

What little she said, he thought, *sounds reasonable, but it seems too pat, as though it were rehearsed*

"If you don't mind," she continued, "I'd like to get up."

CC wasn't about to leave the room to let her put any clothes on. Besides, he reasoned, if she'd undressed in front of this man, he wasn't about to subject himself to potential harm by playing the gentleman. "Help yourself," he responded. "Just move very slowly, and keep your hands in view."

A peevish voice came from the floor. "Not very trusting, are you?"

"Not very. And if you are trusting of strangers, it's surprising that you're still alive."

His reply was a sarcastic, "No kidding."

Ross dropped her blankets as she pushed herself further back against the rear wall of the motor home. She was completely dressed.

Instructing Jonathan to keep his gun on them, and thinking how melodramatic the whole affair seemed, CC remained convinced that these two would prove very dangerous to his little community. He set one foot beside the man's prostrate form, and stretched across the bed to pick up his handgun. Then he stepped away quickly, backing down the hall toward the kitchen.

"Okay, we are at your mercy," the man acknowledged flatly, "but you can't blame us for taking advantage of your absence to warm up and get some food. We weren't hurting anybody."

"That remains to be seen," CC replied. "Jonathan, you keep your gun on the woman. You," he said, speaking to the man on the floor, "get up and sit on the bed."

After the man was seated, CC ordered the woman to move over to sit beside him.

"Now, Jonathan, pull the covers off her bed and see if she has a gun too?"

"I don't," she stated flatly.

The boy ignored her and dragged the blankets down toward the end of the bed. There was no sign of a weapon.

CC felt as though he'd seized the initiative and he planned to keep it. As he stepped backward, he waved his gun at them, indicating that he wanted them to stand and follow him toward the front of the motor home. "Suppose we all move into the kitchen and we'll make some coffee," he said. "Then we'll talk." It wasn't a suggestion.

When they reached the tiny kitchen, he made them slide around behind the pedestal table so that they were almost wedged together between its edge and the outside wall of the motor home.

He asked Jonathan to brew a pot of coffee, then took a moment to study the two intruders. The woman was as beautiful as the man appeared ascetic. Her eyes were ice-blue, and her was face framed with long auburn hair, but when she looked at him, she seemed to be focusing about three feet behind him, leaving him with the feeling that she was looking right though him, communicating a sense of cold indifference.

She left an impression of being an ice princess, both strong-minded and untouchable, but CC wasn't certain that his was an accurate appraisal. It seemed to him that this was a carefully constructed facade to protect her from a dangerous world. *Time will tell*, he reflected, *if I dare allow them any time.*

The man's character was even more difficult to appraise. His hair was pale brown. His nose was thin and aquiline, his mouth pinched, his gums edged with white where they met teeth yellowed by neglect, and his skin had an unhealthy pallor.

But it was his eyes that concerned CC. They appeared strangely flat and lifeless, until he was challenged or provoked. Then they seemed to ignite with a spark of fire that CC thought bordered on the insane. They reminded him of the eyes of those snakes he'd fallen in with a year before.

He felt he was being generous when he attempted to lay the blame for the man's appearance merely on stress or poor diet. *This man has been deeply troubled for a long time*, CC concluded. When he returned CC's stare, he did not give the impression that he was frightened or defensive, but arrogantly indifferent. And CC didn't know why, but he had a strange feeling that this guy knew who he was, and was hiding the fact.

The Examination

The Motor Home
December 25th, 1:55 a.m.

C C felt as though he was walking about in a daze. He had to concentrate before giving instructions to the boy. He knew that they were at a disadvantage because they were exhausted from fighting the cold and the snow, while their two unwelcome guests had enjoyed the advantage of a few hours' sleep.

"Jonathan, would you please get Rachel in here? And then check on you-know-who." Without a word, the boy stepped down from the motor home. When Rachel came through the door a moment later, CC suggested that she be seated in the swivel seat adjacent to the kitchen sink.

CC busied himself with setting out coffee mugs, sugar and fresh cream, but positioned himself so that he could keep an eye on his unwelcome visitors. It was necessary to set his handgun down on the counter top, but he knew he could grab it before either of them could climb over or around the table top. He was trusting his instincts, and had come to the conclusion that these two might just be okay. *Oh Lord, I hope so,* he prayed.

When Jonathan returned, he stepped over to CC and whispered, "She's asleep." CC raised his eyebrows in question. The boy added, "She's in the closet."

CC smiled and nodded his head.

The teenager took up CC's former position at the top of the entry stairs near the door. He was adjacent to the closed end of the dinette, and just a few feet from McCord, out of his direct line of sight, and separated from him by the waist-high end wall of the banquette. Jonathan had his gun out, and it was clear from the way that McCord's eyes flicked back and forth between CC and him that the teen's presence on his periphery made him uncomfortable.

Rachel offered to pour the coffee, and CC welcomed her help. He had forgotten how cold the three of them had been just minutes before, and how much they all would enjoy something hot. Could it be only a few hours since he had been held prisoner in that shed?

Rachel's voice brought a surprising reaction from Elizabeth Ross. The other woman's body stiffened and her head snapped around, her eyes studying Rachel as though she felt she ought to recognize her. It seemed obvious that she couldn't place her, and she finally looked down as though studying her hands. Elizabeth's interest in her hadn't escaped Rachel's attention, and she in turn glanced across the table to surreptitiously study the redhead.

When Rachel took CC's place at the kitchen counter, he used the tip of his shoe to hook a folding chair and drag it up to the table. Then, while the coffee was percolating, Rachel cleared the table of the empty tin cans and soiled plates, wiped it clean, and set down five empty mugs. Elizabeth looked startled when Rachel offered her a sympathetic smile, and turned away to study Rachel from beneath lowered brows.

Sensing her confusion, Rachel had to restrain a smile. Not many people would have recognized her as a girl who had attended college with the then-notorious Elizabeth Ross. After all, they'd only met that one time. She laughed aloud, drawing everyone's attention, but turned back to her work without explanation. *It was ironic*, she realized. She'd also been serving tables on the one other occasion when she'd met Elizabeth Ross, but she knew that the woman would be hard put to identify her as that same homely young woman. She had, in fact, made many changes to her appearance.

After graduation, and in confidence that she'd pass the bar exam, she began those changes. To improve her vision and do away with the need for her old eye glasses, she'd undergone corrective surgery. The simple act of discarding those dark-framed glasses had produced a remarkable change in her appearance. She'd borrowed money, and had her teeth straightened. And when she'd begun jogging, working out in the gym, and practicing martial arts, she'd shed twenty pounds. The exercise regimen not only slimmed her body, but trimmed the baby fat from her face. She's also had her hair cut shorter and carefully styled, and was much more delicate in her application of makeup. And she had found a sympathetic clerk at an upscale boutique who helped her assemble a professional wardrobe. As a result, the poised and confident women who stood in the kitchen of that motor home bore little resemblance to the girl whom Elizabeth Ross had attempted to bully several years earlier.

Elizabeth had changed as well, she observed, but the changes weren't external, except perhaps that she dressed more modestly. Rachel couldn't know it, but as the years passed Ross had begun to regret the way she'd treated others, and had started moving with a different class of people. She was now far more interested in a person's character than in their wealth, status, or physical appearance. And as a result of the troubles she'd experienced since college, and the abuse she'd suffered, she had more sympathy for the trials that other people faced. In consequence, she'd begun to regret the way she'd treated others.

Nor had Elizabeth forgotten the unpretentious girl who'd bravely stood her ground and given her back as good as she'd gotten, for that young woman's courage had left an indelible impression on her. Her lips curled slightly. Somewhere there was a photograph of herself wearing the tray full of food that she had schemed to have dumped on that young woman. Elizabeth was no longer bitter toward her for turning the tables. In fact, she had recently been praying that she might also have survived the holocaust. Regrettably, if she had learned her first name, she couldn't recall it. Many memories of the past had seemed to fade away in the horrors of the past year.

It certainly never occurred to her that they would ever meet again, much less that she could actually be studying her at that moment. But even in the midst of the present difficulties, it didn't seem strange to her that her thoughts would return to the girl. Elizabeth had come to admire that homely girl for the great character she'd displayed, and her thoughts had often returned to the scene that had proven a great embarrassment as well as a personal epiphany.

She realized that she'd been unconsciously remodeling her own character to conform with what she supposed was that of the younger woman who'd properly put her in her place.

Perhaps, she thought, *there is some intangible similarity between this woman and that young college student who brought her to my mind.*

A rumor had swept across campus suggesting that the same freshman student had somehow orchestrated the firing of a lecherous professor. She tried to recall the facts.

Rachel, too, was reminiscing about her college experiences, and it was not odd that the two of them had, for a moment, thought of that notorious event, one that would ultimately bring down the president of their little Ivy League school. Unlike Elizabeth, Rachel had perfect knowledge of the events. It seemed like only yesterday.

Rachel and her two roommates were serious students, each with ambitions that would require top grades. The highest grades, however, were often doled out to the highest bidders. That was because a number of the tenured professors were venial, and traded off their highest grades for things like a summer at a student's palatial summer residence, a trip to Europe, or even a sexual liaison.

As freshmen, Rachel and her two innocent young friends had arrived at school expecting to work hard, and assuming they would receive the grades they earned. As the weeks passed, they were to be sorely disillusioned.

Jaz, at 23, was a blonde-haired beauty with blue eyes. She already knew a lot about TV production because she'd helped out at the station her father had managed since she was sixteen, and except for two years at the local junior college, had spent nearly every waking moment at the station. She had returned to college after falling in love with motion pictures. She wanted to acquire the training she'd need to enter the industry.

Rachel's other roommate, Jeanette, was the daughter of a Scandinavian diplomat attached to the United Nations, and wanted to follow in her father's footsteps. She was majoring in world history and diplomacy. Many of the girls at the college didn't really care about getting high grades because they were there for what was laughingly called their "MRS" degrees, but students who wanted to make a mark in a particular career field competed for a limited number of higher marks. At the same time, their ambitions often left them at the mercy of those exigent teachers who shamelessly bartered their higher grades — A's and B's — for various favors.

One evening, when Jeanette failed to appear at her dinner table, Rachel noticed several of the women exchanging knowing smiles and making snide remarks about her. One woman, whose eyes maliciously followed Rachel as she moved about the table, made a supercilious comment that Jeanette was going to have to "put up or shut up." A number of similar remarks left Rachel confused and upset.

As soon as she punched off the clock, she rushed back to the dorm room that the three of them shared. She found Jeanette lying on her bed, tears streaming down her face, balled up tissues laying about her on the floor, with Jaz trying futilely to comfort her.

Rachel ignored the tears and got right to the point. "Okay. Let's have it! What's going on?"

Jeanette was now sobbing, so Rachel turned to Jaz.

"What's going on? What's this I hear about Jeanette having to put up or shut up?"

"You know Dr. Ranier?"

"The prof who teaches European political history?"

"That's him."

"What about him?"

"Don't say any more," Jeanette choked.

"Of course she's going to tell me," Rachel stated flatly, "unless you plan to."

Jeanette, though a kind and gentle soul, had real backbone. She sat up, wiped the tears from her eyes, and said, "All right. Everyone else seems to know."

Rachel flopped in their leather recliner and adopted a posture that suggested they should all relax because things were never as bad as they seem. She soon realized that she might be wrong.

Jeanette sat staring out the window. When Rachel cleared her throat, Jeanette finally spoke.

"When Dr. Ranier was assigning today's homework, he called my name and said that he wanted to see me in his office right after class. I heard a few laughs from girls around the room. Dr. Ranier ignored them, and I didn't understand why they were laughing."

Elizabeth, who was far less naive than Jeanette, thought she understood, but said nothing.

Jeanette began to cry again.

Rachel looked to Jaz, raising one eyebrow in question.

"Yes. Well, the dirty old man...."

"He's only in his thirties," Rachel interjected, and realized she was being flippant. "Let's call him a dirty middle-aged man, okay?"

That brought a tiny smile from Jeanette, and she resumed her story.

"When I got to his office, he was sitting on the love seat across from his desk, and he patted the cushion next to him, inviting me to sit beside him. I could tell he didn't like it that I sat in the chair across the room, but that didn't deter him. He immediately made his intentions clear."

"What intentions?"

"Wait until you hear what he said," Jaz interrupted.

Jeanette ignored her and resumed her account.

"'Jeanette,' he told me. 'I've had my eye on you....'"

"I just bet he had," Jaz interjected.

"Are you going to let Jeanette tell this?" Rachel asked.

"Sorry."

"He said, 'I've had my eye on you, and I think you could be one of my top students.' Then he went on, 'The reason I wanted to speak privately is because I don't want other students to think that I play favorites.' He seemed annoyed when I said that I didn't understand why other students would be upset because an outstanding student was rewarded."

"Then what happened?"

"He said, 'No, I can see that you don't understand, but I'll help you.' So I asked him, 'How?'"

"'Well, Jeanette,' he began, 'you aren't the only intelligent and gifted student in my class. But you are perhaps the most beautiful.' Something about the way he said that really bothered me."

"I guess," Jaz laughed.

Jeanette turned to her and snapped, "It's not funny."

"Again, sorry."

"Anyway, he said that if I wanted to be 'his outstanding student,' we were going to have to work very, very closely together, *intimately*, was the way he put it."

"And did he make any specific suggestions," Rachel asked, her voice very quiet and very cold.

"He said we could start by establishing that I was potentially as good a student as he thought, and suggested it would be beneficial if he and I were to complete a small project together."

"And that project would be?"

"He said we should discuss the political implications of Lucretia Borgia's sexual proclivities. We would meet in TV Lab A tomorrow night at 9 PM. He said he would videotape it so that he could play it back later to judge the quality of my participation."

Jaz slapped her knee and laughed aloud.

"And what did you tell him," Rachel asked, ignoring her.

"I told him that I'd like to bring a couple of friends along to watch."

Rachel smiled. "And his reply?"

"He said, and these were his exact words, 'Oh, I don't think so. We don't want the video to be ruined by someone making a false move or a silly comment.'"

"What did you tell him?"

"I said that I'd feel uncomfortable in that situation because in my country single women are not allowed to be alone with a man."

"And his response?"

"He said, 'Well, this is America, and you'll soon learn that we do things differently here.' Then he added, 'Besides, you're not at home, and no one there will ever know what you do here.'"

"What a jerk," Jaz commented.

Rachel ignored her. "What happened next?"

"He said that I could call him back any time this evening if I changed my mind; otherwise, he probably couldn't even assure me of being among even his top ten students." There were no longer any tears in her eyes. It was clear that the conversation had helped clarify her thoughts, and she was now very angry. She searched Rachel's face.

"Is there something I can do? Someone I can talk to?"

Rachel chewed her lip for a moment.

"I don't think so. It's your word against his, and he's obviously done this before. Worse, no one likes a whistle blower."

Jeanette was again on the verge of tears.

"Then what can I do?"

Rachel smiled, and looked over at Jaz. "Oh, I think we'll come up with something." She leaned forward, and in a near whisper, laid out her plan.

Jeanette asked, "Do you think it will work?"

Jaz tipped her head, a dazzling smile on her face, clearly ready to risk her college career if her participation in the plan might make a difference.

"Oh, yes!" she said, laughing along with Rachel. "Between the three of us, we have the expertise to pull it off, and I think it might very well work. Now you call the good doctor, and in your breathless little girl voice, you tell him you will meet him at 9 PM at the TV lab.

The university had both a sophisticated computer website and an integrated TV network. It provided information to the entire faculty and student body and enabled staff and students to post and check assignments, view lectures, study experimental data, examine grades, and much more. At any moment, as many as a thousand people were viewing one or another of the four TV channels.

This evening, however, proved to be something of a surprise. At exactly 9 PM, all of the channels began broadcasting the same picture. Dr. Thomas Ranier was suddenly centered on the screen, alone in one of the TV labs, adjusting a camcorder on a tripod and focusing it on a sofa in the middle of the well-lighted lab. Then he was seen to open a bottle of wine, pour some into one of the glasses, drink deeply and with satisfaction, and then top off his own glass and fill a second.

Curious as to what this was all about, many students continued to watch, while a few changed channels in the frustrated hope that they would be able to locate the information they'd been seeking. A few simply turned off the TV, but no one immediately called the communications office to complain. The majority kept one eye on the screen while attending to other matters, assuming that the mix-up would soon be straightened out.

Suddenly those viewing the scene heard a knocking and returned their attention to their monitors.

Dr. Ranier, dressed in khaki slacks and a polo shirt, a bright smile on his face, waved Jeanette into the lab, then locked the door behind her.

Around campus, people's eyes were suddenly riveted to the screen.

The video signal and sound were crisp.

"I'm glad you could make it," he said, and offered to help her with her coat.

What transpired over the next couple of minutes was a shock to some viewers, but only elicited knowing laughter from others. And it resulted in numerous students running up and down hallways shouting to friends and roommates to turn on any of the university's TV channels. Among the viewers were included a couple of administrators, the president of the college and an elderly and very wealthy member of the board of trustees.

What they saw was a young student calmly trying to explain to an angry professor why she felt it was wrong for him to try to make her trade sexual favors for a higher grade in his course. This was followed by a professor manifesting his frustration by ripping the front of the student's blouse away, exposing her underwear. She promptly screamed, then slapped him. He slapped her back hard, knocking her down on the sofa. He was leaning over her, ripping the remainder of the buttons from her blouse, when there came a loud knocking on the door, and a voice shouting, "This is campus security. Open this door immediately."

With a shocked look on his face, he backed away from the sofa, trying to figure what to do. "You've got to hide," he told her.

"Why should I do that?" she asked, rubbing her red and swollen cheek.

"So security won't find you here."

"I don't think so."

"Please," he begged. "I guarantee you'll get your "A.""

"She looked at him, her lips twisted in revulsion. She pulled the front of her blouse together even as she drew her shoulders back, stiffening her resolve as well as her body. Then, like a polished thespian, she uttered the words that Rachel and Jaz had coached her to say.

"Your conduct is immoral, illegal and unforgivable!"

As she was speaking, a uniformed campus policeman entered the room, passkey in hand. He took in the situation with one glance, remarked somewhat sarcastically to the doctor that it had been very informative watching this played out on the monitors in the laboratory hallway, then politely invited him to accompany him to his office downstairs. It wasn't a suggestion. As they left the TV lab, the campus nurse rushed in, and asked, "Are you okay, miss?"

"I'll live."

"Nevertheless, I think you should come with me for an examination."

"No thanks," she persisted. "I'm going back to my room."

As the nurse turned to go, two members of the campus security force entered the room. They didn't need to ask who she was, as they'd just watched the entire debacle on their monitors downstairs.

With all the arrogance of petty authority, one of them said, "Okay miss, you'll have to come with us for some questioning."

Jeanette looked as though she were about to cry, but then another voice intruded itself.

"On whose authority?"

Surprised, and angered, the two men turned to see that another woman had entered the room. They immediately dismissed her as just another student, hardly more than a girl. "I don't know who you are miss, but you'll have to leave. This is university business."

"Again, on whose authority are you acting?"

"The university president's."

The young woman failed to hide her smile. "I'm impressed. Do you mean to tell me that the president actually called you, and instructed you to try to cover this up?"

"Of course not," he replied, somewhat off-balance. "She called our boss, and he called us."

"Well, you've certainly made a rapid response. In fact, I can't imagine how the president could have responded so quickly to the events that just transpired." Then she smiled, "You're to be commended."

He looked at her suspiciously.

"I only wish you'd been as quick when that intruder entered our dorm last month and attacked another of our friends."

"That couldn't be helped."

He turned to Jeanette. "Okay, young lady, time to go."

The other woman stepped between. "She's not going anywhere with you."

"Says who?"

"Says me," she replied. "I'm representing this young woman."

"You're pretty young to be a lawyer."

"And you're pretty young to be going on trial with Dr. Ranier."

"We're not going on trial."

"This innocent young woman has already been assaulted once tonight. If you persist in trying to abduct her, you will be brought up on charges."

"On what charges?"

"Oh, where should I start? How about conspiracy, sexual harassment, exceeding your authority, perhaps even kidnapping?"

"We are policemen in the performance of our duties."

"You're rent-a-cops that are violating this woman's constitutional rights."

"Hey, you can't talk to us like that!"

"I just did." She held out her hand. "Let's see your warrant for this lady's arrest."

"Warrant?"

"By whose authority are you detaining this woman?"

"I just told you, the university's president. We don't need a warrant."

"Ah, and you represent the president of the university, do you?"

"Yes, we do," they answered together.

"Just as Dr. Ranier, who was about to rape this young woman a few minutes ago, also represents the university?"

"Of course not. But we plan to get to the bottom of this."

"I think that the hundreds of people who witnessed Dr. Ranier's actions via the university's TV networks have already gotten to the bottom of it, and they have correctly surmised what — or rather who — the professor was trying to get to the bottom of."

"Look, I have no intention of standing here arguing with a student. Stand back, or we'll take you in too."

"Really. What do you intend to do, kidnap us in front of your listening audience?" She swept her hand toward the wall of TV monitors that were behind them.

"Smile, you're on candid camera," she continued, pointing at the TV screens that covered much of the lab wall, all of them displaying a direct feed from the lab, all of them showing the two university cops accosting the two young women.

The two men paled, gave her a look of malice, spun on their heels, and left the room. A moment later, the screens returned to their regular programming.

Relief was evident in Jeanette's voice as she said, "Oh, Rachel, you were wonderful."

Rachel smiled to herself when she remembered that no one had ever discovered how the special programming came to be displayed over the entire university network. The administration had even hired a firm of detectives, and they in turn hired an outside computer security firm. Hiring them was one of the president's last actions before being asked by the board to resign.

These experts determined that someone had found a way into the university's computer servers, and had planted software that would override the systems on demand. Then, on the night of the debacle, someone signed in at an Internet cafe, sat down at a laptop, and took control of the university's TV network.

When the detectives hired by the college later questioned the owner of the Internet cafe, he reluctantly showed them his user log — including the data he recorded from what later turned out to be a fake ID. His closed-circuit system showed a tall woman, a little overweight, with long dark hair, operating a laptop. She'd worn a faded old raincoat, sunglasses, and bright red nail polish. On the basis of that information, the detectives were unable to associate her with any possible suspects.

When Rachel and Jeanette returned to their room that same evening, they walked in just in time to see Jaz stuffing some articles into a trash bag. Then kicked off a pair of elevator shoes and began massaging her feet.

Rachel took her by the wrist and turned her hand over. "Pretty garish fingernail polish," she commented.

"Yes," I guess I'd better remove it tonight."

They all laughed.

The video that the professor had begun to take of himself and the student might have proved to be damning evidence of his misconduct, but it had been confiscated by the college security people and subsequently turned over to the college president. Since the sexual harassment was a legal issue, the court later questioned how the recording came to be accidentally erased while in the president's custody.

Their clumsy attempts at a cover-up didn't matter because the live video feed was recorded on hundreds of DVRs all over the campus, and was uploaded to the Internet where it was seen by millions of people world-wide. Then it was broadcast on all the major TV networks, bringing considerable embarrassment to the school. After a thorough, but quiet internal investigation, the college administration cleaned house. For the next couple of years, there was no evidence of any similar misbehavior.

Not surprisingly, Jeanette graduated summa cum laude.

While Rachel was on the inside track, Elizabeth didn't know these details. Yes, she had among the multitude who had watched the drama unwind on the closed-circuit network, but she had no idea how the sting was made. She did know, however, that the college had a much more wholesome spirit for the remainder of her career, and that people thereafter tended to be rewarded on the basis of the quality of their work. It restored something of her faith in America's otherwise rapid moral decline.

The regret that she felt at her own earlier behavior constantly pressured her to change her own attitudes and lifestyle, and she had come to covet the character of the women who had brought these changes to bear. What's more, she realized that those qualities were sorely lacking in those she had formerly considered her friends, and that's why she had simply walked away from those old relationships.

As far as that other young woman was concerned, she'd often thought of trying to get in touch with her. A few years after graduation, she had even written the alumni association to see whether they might provide contact information, but since she didn't know her former adversary's name, it was hopeless. A little over a year before, it occurred to her that she should search through old yearbooks for the girl's photo, but that opportunity never materialized because of the war. And now, because of that same war, she never anticipated seeing her again. She certainly didn't recognize her.

Rachel, who might, if so disposed, have taken advantage of this situation, was never one to carry a grudge. And she'd been praying for Ross. In her view, Ross's presence in this motor home at this moment revealed once again that God not only answers prayer, but that he has a wonderful sense of humor. So she kept her secret to herself.

We will see what kind of person Elizabeth Ross has become, she decided. *Maybe we can start over from scratch.*

As Rachel began pouring the coffee, Jonathan removed a tin of home-made chocolate chip cookies from an overhead cabinet, popped it open, and set it on the table. Their guests exchanged wondering looks at this luxury, but made no comment.

A tea party was definitely not what CC had in mind, and his annoyance at Jonathan for serving them must have been obvious, but he overcame the temptation to snap at him. The three of them were shaking from hunger.

We are all exhausted, he thought, *but I have to deal with this situation tonight, and I have to make some serious decisions right now. There are three new people in the room. As far as I'm concerned, Rachel had proven herself by helping me escape from the tavern. I consider her a full-fledged member of our little group and will welcome her participation in any discussions. At the same time, I have little interest in treating these other two to tea and crumpets.*

As soon as they were all served their coffee, CC came right to the point. Slapping both hands lightly on the table top, and forcing a lightness into his voice that he didn't feel, he said, "I want to know who you are, where you came from, and why and how you got here."

The woman protested. "I've already told you that."

He shook his head. "Not good enough. I want to hear it all." Realizing he'd begun to sound confrontational, he added, "Take your time, so that you can make yourselves understood."

The woman remained silent, perhaps considering her options. CC continued to study her. At first, he thought her to be about nineteen, but he could see by the tightness around her mouth and the spray of wrinkles at the corners of her eyes that she was probably in her mid-to-late twenties. It was hard to judge, particularly with all of the cosmetic surgery and new makeup that women had enjoyed access to over the past few decades.

When she still declined to speak, he nodded at her and made a futile attempt to smile encouragingly. "Ladies first."

She revealed her displeasure by asking, "Must we go through this now?"

"Look," CC offered in an even voice, "assume for a moment that you had carved yourselves out a home here in the valley, but then two strangers showed up to threaten your security?"

The man gnawed his lower lip, and finally nodded. "Yes. I can identify with that. I found a cave too, and before you did. So I'd be very upset if anyone were to find that comfortable little hideaway."

His companion looked ready to erupt in laughter, perhaps because he'd possessively called it "my cave," or maybe because she wouldn't describe the cave as comfortable. Or even because he said, "before you did."

But then he became aggressive. "But so what? That's no reason for us to tell you anything."

CC's jaws ground. He didn't want to have to deal with this, and would like to throw them back out into the blizzard, but he realized he couldn't do that for several reasons.

First, he thought, *I won't be responsible for their deaths, and second, if they survived, they might very well divulge our location to others. Up until now,* he thought, *the soldiers who burned the Sennett house may have assumed that there is no one else in the valley. Apart from that, these two might wind up aggressively competing with us for the resources in this valley. Or, worse, even fighting us. Yet in spite of the fact that I'm trying to be amiable, and although it should appear that I hold all the cards, they both refuse to provide us with the barest facts. So I have to ask myself, "What have they got to hide?"*

He looked over at Rachel. How different she was, he thought. Forthright and helpful. Then he had another idea. Looking at McCord, he asked, "You claim to have a comfortable cave somewhere here in the valley?"

"Yes, and I was here before you." He spaced out his words, as though to hammer them into his hearer's minds, as though to legitimize some claim to the valley.

"Well, whether or not you arrived here first, and I doubt that because you never sought me out, I am here at the owner's express welcome. So I consider your claim to be specious."

McCord looked momentarily stunned, but immediately shot back, "I'd sure like to see evidence of your so-called claim."

"It's possible you might see it, but I doubt it."

"That's what I figured, so what's your point?"

"Since the two of you are so close-mouthed, and belligerent, I see no alternative but to set you loose to lean on your own resources."

"You can't turn us back out into that storm!"

"I had no intention of doing that, but your attitudes leave me with little alternative."

McCord looked like he was about to climb over the table to attack CC, but when he heard the sound of Jonathan chambering a round in his handgun, he instead slid deeper into the cushions. In a far less belligerent voice, he asked, "Can't you at least wait until the snow stops falling?"

I wonder if Jonathan noticed that McCord's eyes kind of shoot sparks just before he goes off, CC asked himself. He shook his head. "I'm counting on the snow to cover your tracks, so that others don't find them and follow them back here.

"And where are we supposed to go?"

"Why, back to that comfortable cave you boast of, of course!"

"I didn't boast of it," he replied a little defensively. The woman turned her eyes on him, a look of contempt on her face.

CC persisted. "I guess that's irrelevant. It's really your problem, isn't it?"

His eyes again flashing in that peculiar manner, McCord challenged, "So what's to keep us from going to war with you?"

What, is he reading my mind?

"Or telling the Home Guard where you are?" Before the threat was out of his mouth, it was clear to him that he'd made a serious error. For one thing, Jonathan's pistol was no longer pointing at the floor.

CC shook his head slowly back and forth, a wry, almost apologetic smile on his face. "Those were fateful words."

"Never mind my words," the man shot back. "Tell that kid to point that gun somewhere else."

"His name is Jonathan," CC corrected. "And don't worry. He only shoots when he has a reason. Oh, and I've never seen him miss."

Ross glared at McCord, and finally broke her silence. "My God, Jim! How could you say something so stupid?"

He looked at her indifferently, as though neither she nor her question had any meaning for him.

CC responded decisively to the threat just uttered. "You're quite correct, Mr. McCord. You two can go to war with our little group. You might actually murder one of us, or perhaps we would kill one or both of you. I venture to suggest that we are better equipped and prepared for such a foolish event, but under the circumstances I have difficulty grasping the idea that a sane man would even suggest such a possibility."

CC gave that a moment to sink in, then went on. "And I think that even an impulsive and pompous person, such as you've shown yourself to be, would soon realize that such an idea is counter-productive. What you really needed to do was to become part of a group of like-minded people with whom you might have labored for mutual survival and benefit. You obviously lack the wisdom, or is it the integrity, to understand that."

McCord stared woodenly at him, his eyes once again reminding CC of that flat reptilian gaze that had struck terror in his heart just before he'd fallen from the tree and subsequently discovered the caves. He shivered slightly, wondering if there was a relationship between this guy and the serpents that were now cosily nesting well below the frost line not too many yards away.

That's an unworthy comparison, he thought. *The snakes were trying to do what you'd expect snakes to do. You wouldn't expect a decent man to behave this way.*

As his mind continued to wander over his first morning in the valley, he suddenly had a clear memory of a flash of light catching his eye just after he'd awakened and climbed down from the truck cab. And he decided to take a chance and jab at McCord's composure.

"I'd venture to say I know where your cave is located," he mentioned offhandedly.

"Oh, really?" McCord responded in mocking disbelief. "What is this, some kind of a bluff?"

"No," CC answered, with all the panache of a magician about to whip the handkerchief off his top hat to reveal the rabbit within.

"Okay, where's my cave?" McCord challenged.

"Oh, maybe fifteen feet above the valley floor, in the face of the cliff in the southeast corner of the valley."

McCord couldn't completely hide his dismay, but CC wasn't finished.

"It's on the south side, west of the bottleneck about two hundred yards."

McCord looked stunned, but the woman looked thoroughly amused.

Bingo! CC thought, and he pressed on remorselessly.

"In order to find your way back to your palatial home, all you have to do is exit our cave, walk due south across the valley until you hear the roar of stream in front of you, turn left, and follow it down the canyon until you reach the bottleneck." Using a finger, CC was drawing a picture in the air. "Then go around the end of the lake, and back up the far side a hundred yards or so, until you reach your comfortable cave."

McCord didn't deny the location, but instead challenged CC again. "And what if we turn you into the Home Guard?" he blustered.

"If you do that, I think that the Home Guard will be glad to have you lead them to us, and then they will reward you by allowing you to share our cell." Then he added, "After, of course, they seize everything of value that both you and we own, and extract their pound of flesh."

He stared meaningly at the woman for a moment. "Oh, yes, and I suspect they will think of some meaningful work they can put your friend to. CC leaned his head back, and held the other man's eyes until McCord looked away. "There's another thing. No one trusts a whistle blower or a fair-weather friend."

McCord looked shocked, and CC wondered why.

Then CC had a bit of a brainstorm. It was obvious that McCord didn't like the way he pursed his lips and smiled, and he liked it less when he heard what CC had to say next.

"Now that you threaten us with the possibility of exposure, Mr. McCord, it occurs to me that the invaders are your kind of people. And that further suggests the possibility that you may have done something that offended them. Otherwise, it's reasonable to assume that you would be dwelling with them right now, not wandering around in the snow looking for something to eat."

Everyone could tell by the look on McCord's face that CC had struck a nerve. And it suddenly occurred to CC that the Home Guard might even be more interested in McCord than they were in him, and he said as much. But CC didn't hesitate to cap his accusation. "And if that's the case, you're dead if you go near them."

McCord did not respond.

The woman, the hint of a smile on her face, nodded her head in what might have been grudging admiration.

"Yes. That makes sense," she agreed. "Mr. McCord hasn't discussed his background with me, though I've asked him several times," and turning to CC, she added, "but you seem to have it worked out pretty well." She took a deep breath. "And without unnecessarily discussing our brief, and it would seem, terminal relationship, I for one am now only too happy to answer any questions you may have. I don't know that it will bring me any favor in your eyes, but it can't do any harm."

"And why should we care to learn that now? Earlier, I held out an olive branch. You had an opportunity to share your backgrounds, your needs and interests, but you not only insulted us, you threatened our lives.

"McCord did. I didn't."

"That's true, but you weren't forthcoming."

"No, I'm sorry to say I wasn't, but you have to admit that I didn't know you either, nor your motives or intentions."

CC nodded in grudging agreement.

She went on. "I've seen a lot of very bad people in the last few months, and most of them had come by their comfortable situations," and she waved at her surroundings, "by forcibly taking them from others." She hesitated. "Yet, after listening to your reasoned statements, and seeing the character of the people you are caring for, I'm convinced that you are decent people.
"

"Thanks a lot," Jonathan whispered, making no attempt to cover his sarcasm.

"And, above all," she went on, nonplussed, "I've concluded that you did not threaten us with bodily harm — until, that is, my associate vainly threatened you."

She turned to McCord. "How idiotic could you be, to start threatening people who clearly have our lives in their hands?" She didn't give him an opportunity to respond, and he didn't appear inclined to do so.

She took a deep breath, and CC asked, "So?"

"So," she answered, "I apologize for my behavior, and respectfully request that you permit me to provide the information you originally asked for. I assure you that I will provide full disclosure."

CC stared into her eyes to the count of ten, but she held his gaze.

"Okay," he said, "tell away."

Then, with an impish smile on her face, she said, "And I expect to learn who you are also."

CC weighed her words carefully.

She said, "I expect to learn," not "I demand to learn." What does that reveal about her relationship with McCord? Or about her own personality? This is a woman with a mind of her own.

Picking Up the Pieces

Butter Creek

December 25th, 1:05 a.m.

The Burton house was still and cold, blanketed as it was by the heavy snowfall. Mrs Burton drew the blankets closer around her, but it wasn't the cold that was keeping her awake.

She didn't trust her husband alone with that young serving girl back at the inn, but more importantly, she didn't want to lose her share of the reward for that fugitive. The amount promised on the poster was huge by any standard.

Giving up on the idea of sleep, she threw the covers back, slid her feet into her slippers, and stood beside the bed. She was a grotesque figure, almost pear-shaped, dressed in insulated long johns. Quickly putting on a man's slacks and shirt, she sat down and struggled to reach her feet in order to pull on heavy wool socks. Donning a pair of insulated hiking boots, she stomped down to the kitchen where a teapot of water was simmering on the back burner of her wood-burning range.

She lifted one of the stove lids, dropped in a couple of chunks of firewood, replaced the lid, and opened the damper. She could hear the wood begin to snap and burn as the draft up the chimney roared.

Then she ripped open a packet of instant coffee, poured it into a mug, and filled it with the hot water. Foregoing her usual packet of precious sugar, she sat down near the stove and sipped the bitter liquid. She was unable to shake her feeling of disquiet, and even though it was the middle of the night, she decided she had to return to the inn, and quickly dressed.

It was not necessary to go outside to reach their snowmobile, as it was parked in the woodshed that abutted the kitchen. She pulled on a knit cap and her parka, opened the outside door, and stepped down to stand between the cords of seasoned firewood.

She reached her leg over the snowmobile, straddled the saddle, made certain the transmission was in neutral, opened the choke, and hit the starter. The snowmobile was a new one, taken by force from an uncooperative member of the community — the owner of the Green Mountain Feed and Grain — and given to the Burtons by the Home Guard. When she turned the key, the machine started instantly. After she had it running smoothly, she opened the woodshed door and backed it out. With the headlight on, it took only a few exhilarating minutes to reach the front door of the inn.

She was used to a sense of relative silence after shutting down the snowmobile's engine, but the area around the inn seemed unusually so. She had to use the snow shovel hanging on the wall to clear enough of the snowdrift to drag the front door open, and she was angry that her husband hadn't made the serving girl keep the porch clear.

She stopped just inside the front door and looked about, trying to identify why things didn't seem right. She looked to her left, into the dining area, and saw a number of forms stretched out on the floor near the fireplace. Someone had kept the fire burning, but judging by the chill it had done little good.

The two children were still asleep by the hearth, but their mother was missing. Then she heard a noise in the kitchen, and moved around the end of the bar. At least she could vent her spleen against the serving girl. But when she reached the kitchen, it wasn't her servant who was moving about, but the children's mother.

"What are you doing in my kitchen?" she demanded, her voice almost a hiss.

The woman scarcely turned her head, answering indifferently, "Making my children oatmeal."

"You'll answer for this."

The younger woman turned toward her, her eyes filled with
contempt, slowly examining the innkeeper's wife. She shook her
head and laughed.

"What are you going to do, have me arrested?"

"I'll kick you out of my kitchen."

"The woman laughed, and took a step toward her."

"You and what army? Those drunks asleep out there?"

The older woman licked her lips nervously, and backed toward the dining room. When she reached the door, she turned.
"I'll deal with you later."

"I'll be around," the younger woman promised.

When Burton's wife entered the dining room, no one was
awake. She recognized the two farmers who were lying furthest
from the fireplace and ignored them. She didn't realize that they
were awake, and had been following her every movement. Then
she leaned over the two men who had arrested the suspect a few
hours earlier. They were snoring loudly, and when she shook
them, it became obvious that they weren't going to wake up any
time soon. There was still no sign of her husband and the serving girl, so she started up the stairs toward the guest room, her
anger building.

The moment she was out of sight, the two farmers stood to
their feet. The pastor moved to the kitchen to fetch the mother
of the children, while the other went outside and around back
to the shed where Mrs. Burton had just parked her snowmobile.

When the pastor reached the kitchen, he held a brief but intense conversation with the children's mother. She never spoke,
but simply nodded her head in agreement, then followed him
back to the dining room. When she woke the children, they
looked at the pastor with fear in their eyes, but she put her finger to her lips and they kept their silence. The other farmer returned, brushing snow from his coat, and they helped the

woman bundle her kids into their snow suits, then saw them out the door to the waiting snowmobile. It was Mrs. Burton's.

Pastor Kenzy held another brief conversation with the woman, this time about where she should take her children. He opened a map and marked a rough course for her to follow, then pointed out across the fields.

Although she looked confused and frightened, she also seemed resigned to the fact that she had to attempt their escape.

The pastor made sure the gas tank was full, then he and his friend pushed the machine about a hundred feet down the drive so that it was less apt to be heard from the inn when the woman started it. He showed her how to start the engine and adjust the choke, and the two men watched as she moved slowly forward, experimenting with the controls, and getting a feel for the machine.. Then they returned to the inn, found places on the floor near the hearth, and lay down to again feign sleep.

In the meantime, Mrs. Benton discovered her husband unconscious on the floor of the guest room. She looked about, and it was fairly obvious what had transpired. He'd cornered the girl, and she'd fought back, successfully. She wondered for a moment where she might be hiding, then decided to handle one matter at a time.

She looked down at her husband with contempt. She had an urge to kick his blood-encrusted head, but instead knelt down to check his pulse. Since it seemed reasonably strong, she began to shake him. He groaned and when he tried to open his eyes, he cried out with pain, but she was totally indifferent. Cursing him, she got him to his feet and quickly enough ascertained that his injuries weren't life-threatening.

She helped him down the narrow stairway, and just as she reached the bar, she heard what sounded like a snowmobile engine. Letting go of her husband, he slid to the floor, while she moved as quickly as she could toward the front door. The black SUV was buried in a snowdrift where they'd parked it the night before, but her snowmobile was gone.

She waddled back to the dining room shouting, "Did you hear that?" There was no reply. Everyone was asleep where she'd left them. Everyone except the children. She moved surprisingly quickly toward the kitchen, thinking they'd be eating their oatmeal, but they were gone. She correctly assumed that the woman with the two brats had taken her snowmobile, and wondered how she'd explain leaving her key in the ignition.

She began taking a mental inventory, and concluded that the male suspect must still be locked in the shed out back, probably frozen to death. That was okay. She'd still get her reward. But the SUV was still outside, so where were the other two men who were to guard the prisoner?

She was in such a panic that she left the front door open as she began pushing her way through the deep snow toward the shed out back. When she reached it, she found the door wide open, with the snow drifting inside, partially covering a body.

I was right, she thought. *He's dead.* She leaned down to examine his face, and realized with shock that it wasn't the suspect, but one of the men who was supposed to have guarded him. She cursed vehemently, and spinning on her heel, almost fell on the frozen dirt floor.

Trudging back up the path, she tripped on something buried beneath the snow.

My stupid husband left a chunk of firewood in the middle of the path, she thought, and bent down to brush away the snow so that she wouldn't trip on it on her return. It wasn't a log. She had to scrape the snow away from the face to identify the body. Now she was frightened. Not only would she not receive a reward, but she'd have to try to explain the deaths of the two guards as well as the escapes of the prisoner and the serving girl who had been put in her trust. Worse, the woman and her two kids were gone too.

Elizabeth Cool

The Motor Home
December 25th, 2:15 a.m.

Throughout the discussion, Rachel had been surreptitiously studying Elizabeth. She thought it ironic that she had been accepted into this community after only a few hours, while Elizabeth was, quite literally, fighting for her life.

Rachel had recognized Elizabeth Ross, not from the cover of a magazine she'd glanced at while awaiting her turn at the checkout counter, but from that encounter at college. And it wasn't a matter of personal appearance about which they'd been competing. The fact that Rachel wasn't in the same league for beauty was of no consequence to her.

She had long since come to terms with what she considered her average appearance, and after a lot of painful deliberation, had determined that it really was character, not looks, that mattered, both in herself and in those she befriended. It was not a matter of sour grapes, for as she had matured, she had come to realize that she could take little credit, or blame, for her appearance, while she had a great deal of responsibility for her own character.

Outward beauty, she concluded, *is a gift from God, while character must be attained, often at great personal cost. I think that this woman — in spite of her beauty — has reached the same conclusion, and more power to her.*

Rachel had come to believe that most people who glory in things like their appearance, intelligence, or success, take unjustified pride in their gifts.

Most people credit their own wisdom and knowledge for their success. Others consider it a matter of being in the right place at the right time. Many think that it's just a matter of being lucky, while still others believe it's not what you know, but who you know. Few people, she knew, *ever acknowledge divine help, or express gratitude for what they've been given.*

It was after she'd finished college that a Christian friend helped Rachel to understand that, although beauty is only skin deep, that a little judicious attention to her appearance could pay amazing dividends. As one politically incorrect college professor once commented, "God invented makeup in order to level the playing field for homely women."

Rachel had dealt with the issue of her outward appearance long before this second unexpected meeting with Elizabeth Ross, and had begun to focus on far more important things. And now she planned to remain mute until she'd had an opportunity to determine whether Elizabeth had made any similar discoveries. She was looking for anything new that the woman might reveal about herself. It was only the men's obvious effort to appear indifferent to Elizabeth's beauty that caused it to register at all, and brought a hint of a deprecatory smile to Rachel's lips. Unlike many people born with extraordinary beauty, Elizabeth seemed comfortable in her own skin.

Observing Elizabeth several years after their college confrontation, Rachel believed that the woman had truly changed. She'd already seen indications of that from reports in the media. Early on, Elizabeth had become a darling of the public because she was that rare rich girl who spurned her family's wealth and strove to earn success on her own.

For a short time, she had been the subject of endless discussion on TV talk and gossip shows. She'd been featured on the covers of the sensationalist tabloids and celebrity magazines, but the publicity was clearly not a matter of her choice, and she had ultimately begun to avoid such exposure. And then came the difficult times.

For the past several years, Elizabeth had sought privacy, a very different goal than that of her college years. She was considered intelligent and beautiful and, because she had no brothers or sisters, was destined to inherit her parents' enormous wealth. So the harder she fought to avoid the limelight, the more the paparazzi pursued her. The media made it impossible for her to separate herself from her family's shadow, and the people with whom she was forced to deal invariably tried to pave her way in the belief that they would win her family's patronage.

Those who considered themselves privileged enough to meet her took particular pleasure in dropping her name. As a result, it became an unending struggle for Elizabeth to identify the rare individual who would value her for herself, as opposed to the multitude who wanted to exploit her.

Rachel didn't hold Elizabeth's past behavior against her. In spite of the highly biased sociology and psychology classes Rachel had taken, she was able to compensate for their often erroneous conclusions by referencing the wisdom of the Bible. And she understood that the simplistic conclusions that the social scientists and the media had drawn about Ross — with their need to conveniently pigeonhole every individual — were frequently based on flawed studies, anecdotal evidence, and a rejection of God's eternal principles. Rachel's view of life in general, and her evaluation of Elizabeth in particular, was substantially different from the world's view.

Rachel understood that an individual's heart, mind, and soul are too complex for anyone but God to truly comprehend, let alone to blithely and indifferently catalog. More importantly, she was convinced that God can change circumstances for anyone at any given moment. Having just escaped a world gone mad — a world in which almost everyone was doing what was right in their own eyes — Rachel was doubly grateful that the Lord had rescued her.

And yet Rachel also recognized that she frequently made snap judgments about the character of others based on their behavior and body language, and found herself interpreting those characteristics on the basis of some combination of her own education, experience, and intuition. To that, she added her understanding from the Word of God. She considered any success in this process of evaluation to be the result of meditation and prayer, and a matter of spiritual maturity.

When all was said and done, she found it necessary to pray for an individual's best interests, particularly those who seemed to oppose her. Sometimes her conclusions were painfully wrong, but this time she was betting on Ross.

Others might marvel at her for being so in favor of a woman who had attempted to embarrass and injure her in the past. Yet, during the past few minutes, Rachel had somehow come to the conclusion that Elizabeth might conceivably have made peace with God through Christ. There was no immediate evidence of this, nor anything in what Elizabeth had said, but Rachel detected a change in attitude that she believed could only be the result of God's grace.

And the longer Rachel scrutinized the woman, the more certain she was of her conclusion. She studied Elizabeth's appearance. In spite of the fact that she'd lived for months in the wilderness, that she had just been awakened from a deep sleep, was dressed in ragged clothes, and that her hair was a greasy tangled mess — she had made no excuses or apologies. Nor did she have to. Everything about her, from the smudges under her eyes, to an errant leaf stuck in her hair, seemed to amplify her beauty like a rustic frame would enhance a great landscape.

And Rachel didn't resent this. To her, everything balanced out. She understood too well that intellect, beauty, and wealth are burdens as well as blessings. That's why most people who are born with good looks or great intelligence often seem to fail in life. People who are richly endowed often have compensating problems. As far as Rachel was concerned, it's how each of us handles such seeming assets and liabilities that demonstrates our true character. *To whom much is given, of them much is required*, she remembered, and it was enough that she had to bear her own burdens.

While pretending to occupy herself otherwise, Rachel found herself taking delight in the other woman's poise and self-control. Elizabeth didn't so much as push a hair back from her forehead, much less look for a mirror in which to primp herself. And now, clearly exhausted from months of struggling for her very survival, she was still able to maintain her dignity.

Rachel further surprised herself by concluding that Elizabeth's initial self-righteous belligerence spoke better for her than would have a simpering and coquettish effort to woo the men. Elizabeth obviously wasn't expecting something for nothing, and she wasn't giving anything away either. There was no hint of any sort of concession or condescension in her behavior.

When Elizabeth began speaking, it was in a somber but melodic voice. She stared off into infinity, unconsciously providing them with an opportunity to search her face, to look beyond her beauty. And that beauty was a classic thing, enhanced, not diminished, by the marks of her exposure to the real world. Her face was an oval, with a wide expressive mouth, teeth as regular as pearls, a few nearly invisible freckles across her slightly upturned nose, and eyes that were wide apart and of a striking turquoise. She was of medium height, and her hair glowed like coils of copper bathed in sunlight. Her complexion was a pale peach, and if she'd had a few more inches in height, and were a bit less voluptuous, she would easily have qualified as a top model in their former world.

When she began speaking, the others were quickly captivated by her intelligence and sincerity. Her words revealed that her worldly afflictions had sharpened her mind, but her eyes, poorly defined in the semi-dark room, prevented anyone from attempting to peer into her soul.

CC also attempted to study Elizabeth's appearance for a clue to her integrity, but quickly realized that a knowledge of her history, and the consistency in how she related it, was far more important to his understanding. He needed to grasp the things that motivated her, the moral values she held, and whatever usefulness she might have to the group. This wasn't crass. This was practical reality. And he dared make no mistakes.

He was surprised to find himself fascinated with her story. Ross had just begun her survival account when she suddenly stopped in mid-sentence. With her lips turned up in a slight smile, she nodded to either side of CC. He turned to look at whatever had captured her attention and gave an involuntary laugh. Both Jonathan and McCord had slid down in their seats and were nodding with fatigue.

"Yeah," he said, "I guess we're all pretty tired."

Jonathan opened his eyes. "I'm not asleep; I was listening."

Ross laughed, a low rumbling sound.

CC was all business. "It's too late tonight to carry on with this discussion. You can both stay here for the night, and we'll talk tomorrow morning. If you are liars, it will give you a few more hours to work out your stories." *Now why did I say that last?* he wondered. *Am I that tired?*

In spite of the implied insult, Elizabeth looked relieved. McCord, on the other hand, looked as though he'd received a stay of execution, or even some sort of opportunity.

"Where will everyone sleep?" Jonathan asked.

"Elizabeth will bunk with Rachel, and with the oldest, or more correctly, the youngest lady in our group." The women looked confused. They had seen no other women since their arrival. Even as they were pondering that fact, however, Rachel had not failed to note that CC had called Ross by her first name. So while mulling over the revelation that there was a third woman here, she also felt an odd twinge of jealousy over her possible relationship with CC.

CC was totally focused on practical issues, and looked appraisingly at McCord.

"Mr. McCord," he continued, nodding toward the back bedroom of the motor home, "will return to the bed he was sleeping on when we discovered him. First, however, we'll have his slacks and his shoes."

McCord started to object, but CC had already turned to speak to Jonathan. "Would you do something for me before you turn in?"

"Sure!"

"Show the women to Sarah's room, and get them settled. Then get the cordless drill and a couple of sheet metal screws and fasten the back door of the motor home closed. Mr. Mc-Cord might be prone to walk in his sleep, and we wouldn't want him falling out the door onto the floor of the cave."

Jonathan smiled. "I'll take care of it right away."

"Thanks."

McCord gave CC a sour look, but made no comment. Rachel and Elizabeth followed Jonathan outside, and he led them to the cottage.

After the women had departed, McCord went into the back bedroom of the motor home, stripped off his outer clothes and shoes, and threw them down the hall to CC who was converting the fold-down dinette set into a bed.

As McCord was climbing into bed, CC told him that he too would be remaining in the motor home for the time being. He didn't add that he was determined to keep McCord separated from the rest of them until he'd formulated some sort of plan. If McCord tried to run, CC might not be able to stop him, but by taking his clothing and shoes, he had severely limited his mobility. If, on the other hand, he did escape, there were simply too many places in the valley to hide.

The plain fact was that they were all physically and mentally exhausted, and there were too few of them to mount a guard over both Ross and McCord. McCord, however, was also exhausted, so hopefully he'd cause no problems, at least for the remainder of this night.

After CC had finished making up his own bed, he closed the sliding door that separated the back bedroom from the tiny bath and kitchen, and set the little brass latch. Hopefully he'd be awakened in time if McCord tried to slide the door. He heard the sound of the battery-powered drill as Jonathan secured the back door. Other jobs, like cleaning up and re-camouflaging the cave entrance would have to wait until CC had gotten things sorted out and under control. He lay down on the dinette cushions fully clothed, gun close at hand, and was soon asleep.

Christmas Breakfast

The Motor Home
December 25th, 10:30 a.m.

Troubled as he was with the challenges of his exploding community, CC awoke early after a fitful sleep. There'd been no noise or movement from the back bedroom, so he slid the door slightly to make certain that his unwelcome guest was still in his bed. McCord was snoring softly, so CC slipped into the bathroom for a shave and a quick shower. Quietly gathering some fresh clothes from the closet, he returned to the kitchen to change while McCord slept on.

After grinding a quantity of beans, CC brewed a large pot of coffee. Then he set out a jug of apple cider, and whipped up a batch of pancake batter from their stores. Slicing off strips of bacon, he dropped them into a pan. The smell of the sizzling bacon reminded him of how little he'd eaten in the past twenty-four hours, and he found himself almost shaking with hunger. Was it possible that it'd only been a matter of hours since they'd escaped from the tavern?

He was putting together what had become a typical breakfast for his troglodyte family, but would comprise an unimaginable feast for most people in the world. He could hear muted rustlings and whispers from the cottage across the cavern, and patted his holster to reassure himself that he was as ready as could be for whatever might be coming.

Then Ross stuck her head in the outside door, her nose wrinkled, her face a beatific mask of joy.

"I thought I smelled bacon," she said incredulously. "And are you making pancakes?" She looked truly impressed. "It can't be. First this wonderful underground home. Then this meal. You're incredible!"

Her words reminded him that he was going to have to master the unpleasant skill of hog butchering in the very near future. Then he had the equally unpleasant thought that she was merely trying to ingratiate herself with her flattering words. He thought it ironic that she had complimented him on his ability to provide shelter and to produce a pre-war quality breakfast, when, just a few hours before, she'd insulted CC while being protective of McCord.

If the two of them hadn't accidentally discovered this cave, he thought, *they'd have almost certainly died in the blizzard,* then chastised himself for such an uncharitable thought. He restrained the impulse to say something critical, and instead attempted to return her pleasantries.

"Pancakes and bacon," he replied in answer to her comment. "And we even have real creamery butter and pure maple syrup for the pancakes."

"Wow, sounds like an ad for a country inn. What do we use for a credit card?"

"Your smile is more than adequate." And he realized that he meant it. "Just sit yourself down right there," and he pointed in the general direction of the banquette. She noted that he hadn't insisted she sit on the back side against the wall.

"Thank you, kind sir, but I'd rather help. I'm a pretty good flapjack flipper myself."

"Okay. You asked for it! Have at it," and he handed her the spatula.

He heard rustling in the back bedroom, then some gurgling and splashing from the lavatory. Finally McCord slid the door open far enough to expose his head.

"Hey, may I have my clothes back?"

Elizabeth turned toward him and said, "Please?"

"Yeah, yeah. *Please* may I have my clothes back?" he echoed, but there was nothing pleasant in the look he gave her or in the sound of his voice.

When McCord stepped through the door a couple of minutes later, CC wasn't about to comment on his appearance. He remembered how he had looked with several days' growth of beard and a lot of grime on his face. McCord had clearly not taken advantage of a soap and razor in many days.

A moment later, Sarah came stamping in, leading Rachel by the hand. She'd obviously accepted her as a member of the household, but she let go of her hand when she spotted CC, and immediately ran over to demand a kiss.

Then, hands on hips, she leaned back to look up at the stranger who was staring at them through the bathroom doorway, but instead of asking who he was, she simply said, "Oh, yuck. You need a bath!"

Rachel's rebuke was spontaneous. "SARah!"

"Oh, I'm sorry."

McCord surprised everyone when, instead of taking offense, he looked at the girl through sleep-dulled eyes and said, "Yeah, sweetheart, right after breakfast, I hope."

Maybe a night to meditate has convinced him to lighten up a little, CC thought.

Jonathan joined them just after Sarah finished offering McCord her unsolicited comment.

"Mmm, that sure smells good," he said. "I'm starved."

To which the irrepressible Sarah responded, "Oh, Jonathan, you've got a hollow leg!"

That brought stifled laughter from the women, but no rebuke.

CC set two platters heaped with pancakes and bacon on the table, and was startled to see that Elizabeth had bowed her head, evidently in prayer. *What is this*, he wondered, s*ome kind of act?*

As she looked up, she saw the surprise registered on his face.

Her explanation was simple enough.

"If there weren't a God, I wouldn't be here today."

"I'm sure we've all had to adjust our premises to adapt to reality," CC replied evenly.

"Yes," she agreed, "but those same events, when put in perspective, make me realize that someone's been watching over me. For example, there is no comparison between what I had to eat a few days ago and this marvelous breakfast."

"Amen," Rachel whispered.

McCord said nothing, but gave them both a sour look.

CC thought, *Maybe I need to reexamine some of my premises as well. I suspect I've judged Elizabeth too harshly. And she really didn't know whether we would be favorable to, or offended by, her praying.*

CC had also noticed the angry look that McCord gave Elizabeth. *Was it because she prayed, or because of her comparison with his meals? Or both?*

Then Elizabeth surprised CC again by turning to McCord without a hint of malice. "You've always been offended by my praying, Jim. I guess that I've returned to the God of my fathers." She seemed to think that over. "Or rather, I've returned to the God of my grandfathers." Then she added in a soft voice, "They were deists, too. I don't think that my father believed in God, and I have no idea whether he's gone to a godless eternity."

McCord gave her a stony look, then continued wolfing down his breakfast.

As they were eating, Jonathan and Sarah went back out the door together. A few minutes later, while the adults were still stuffing themselves, Jonathan pulled the door open, and he and Sarah marched back in. He was carrying a small evergreen tree that was decorated with strings of popcorn and cranberries and sprinkled with bright-colored ornaments cut from foil. He'd nailed a little wooden stand to the base of the trunk, and they set it up in the corner of the motor home next to the driver's seat. Everyone applauded but Jim He offered a sardonic smile.

While they continued eating, the kids again left the motor home, returning almost immediately, singing, "O, Come All Ye Faithful," and carrying crudely wrapped packages. The surprise was complete. This was one occasion when the thought really did mean more than the gift.

Jonathan had secretly brought candy from the Green Mountain Feed and Grain, and it proved to be a rare and welcome treat. Apart from that, the two children had raided the storage area, and had wrapped up an article of clothing for each person. The surprise turned their first breakfast together into a Christmas celebration.

How the kids had achieved the surprise baffled CC, but he was very pleased with their thoughtfulness and imagination. They had turned an almost-forgotten holiday into a significant sacred event. It became especially poignant when Jonathan stood and interrupted their conversation to read the Christmas story from Luke, chapter two.

After Jonathan closed his Bible, McCord cleared his throat, his disdain clear to all, but Rachel forestalled any comment when, speaking to no one in particular, she remarked, "I've always wondered about the wise men. Who were they? Where in the east did they come from? How did they know that a Savior was to be born at that time? And how did they find their way to the holy land?"

McCord gave an airy wave of the hand as he dismissed the questions. "I'd say we'll never know because this is just another Bible myth used to present some sort of outdated moral principle."

No one seemed surprised that Jim brushed aside the story, or that he disdained moral principles, but they were surprised when CC spoke up in defense of the biblical account. It wasn't so much that he spoke up to defend the Christmas tradition, but that his arguments seemed to flow so smoothly and logically out of an unexpectedly deep well of knowledge.

When he first began speaking, Jim laughed aloud, then announced that CC would no doubt use the Bible to prove the Bible. "It's just circular reasoning," he sneered. "Everyone knows that the Bible has little in the way of historical or archaeological support."

At which CC in turn laughed.

"Nonsense!" he countered. "Here's just one example. For many years, critics of the Bible challenged its veracity because it spoke of the kingdom of the ancient Hittites. 'What Hittites?' the critics demanded. 'There were never any Hittites. Show us proof that any such people ever existed.' And then the archaeologists discovered clay tablets as well as several historical sites that proved the existence of that once-powerful nation." He slapped his hand lightly on the table. "The Bible is better supported by archaeology and by contemporary historical accounts than any other ancient history. And it's certainly more reliable than any contemporary book about Julius Caesar or Vladimir Putin."

McCord pulled himself more erect in his chair, obviously excited at the possibility of a debate, but CC raised his hand to forestall comment. He wasn't about to provide an opportunity for interruption.

"The truth is that there is an enormous amount of archaeological evidence as well as historical documentation to support the Bible. Unfortunately, after World War II most high school students were introduced to the Bible as a third-rate piece of literature that contains only a few worthwhile portions, and they were taught that it didn't justify the time or trouble to read it. Instead, educators pointed students to contemporary social propaganda like, *A Catcher in the Rye* and Chairman Mao's *Little Red Book.*

"Students were left in ignorance of profound and sacred literature, while every reference to God was systematically removed from schools and public places. Even the Ten Commandments, which are honored by Christians, Jews and Muslims alike, were proscribed. The words, *In God We Trust,* were removed from our money, along with prayer from the classroom and all public events, and even religious jewelry and clothing was forbidden in schools and places of employment. Simultaneously, secular values and rules were imposed on Christian organizations, while other religions like Islam were actually promoted by government. How could our children conclude other than that Christianity is wrong?"

"And quite right they were," Jim intoned piously.

And quite wrong they were, thought CC, but rather than argue, he simply forged ahead.

"Consider that passage about the wise men who visited the baby Jesus. It's covered in the first thirteen verses of Matthew, chapter two." He looked over at McCord. "You obviously prize yourself as a scholar, Jim. How many wise men were there?"

"Everyone knows that," he replied with thinly veiled contempt, almost disdaining to reply. "Three!"

"No, that's a tradition. Anyone who had taken the trouble to read this important account of the birth of the world's Savior would notice that it does not provide the number. The first verse simply says, '...there came wise men from the east.' That's men, plural!"

McCord shrugged his shoulders in feigned indifference, but as a pedant who obviously took pride in using precise information to stifle his opponents, he instead found himself embarrassed. Although he clearly didn't believe the story of a Savior born in a manger, it was obvious that he was embarrassed because he didn't know what the story purportedly said. But that didn't stop him.

"That book was written over a thousand years ago and has absolutely no bearing on our situation today."

CC was tempted to mention that McCord's ignorance was typical of those responsible for taking God and morality out of the classroom, and essentially destroying the nation, but instead said, "Since this is Christmas, it's the perfect day to discuss Christ's story. Unfortunately, we have other more pressing business that cannot be ignored."

While the adults were nursing their refilled coffee cups, and Jonathan and Rachel were cleaning up, CC told Jim that they were ready to hear his survival story. CC could only hope that, following a good night's sleep and a better breakfast, McCord had considered his tenuous situation and was prepared to tell them the truth, the whole truth, and nothing but the truth.

It was a forlorn hope. McCord stared with ill temper at the children until they took note of him and stopped fidgeting. When he finally had everyone's undivided attention, and with a pomposity unusual in a man of his age, he began his account. It soon became obvious to CC that McCord was more interested in polishing his own image than in relating any facts. Indeed, he seemed to have a unique ability to reveal very little of importance, while somehow making his listeners feel as though he'd introduced them to a number of precious and profound truths.

McCord did a lot of name-dropping, and spent a great deal of time needlessly embellishing meaningless details. CC found it difficult to believe that a man of such incredible vanity could have held all of the positions of influence in government that he claimed for himself. Then, remembering some of the men in government he had known, he wasn't in the least surprised.

What am I thinking? What men in government have I known, influential or otherwise?

CC tried to drag his mind back to the present, hoping to get some answers to his questions from what McCord was saying.

McCord Unmasked

The Motor Home
December 25th, 11 a.m.

C C realized that he had underestimated McCord. The man was both entertaining and glib.

He's obviously playing to his audience, CC thought, *but, why? To displace me? Just like that?* He frowned. *On the other hand, why not? Instead of my exiling him into the wilderness, perhaps he thinks he can generate enough leverage to get rid of me. After all, before last night I had just Jonathan and Sarah with me. He might beguile the two women. I really need to be careful here.*

CC looked from face to face, trying to assess their feelings. With the exception of Elizabeth, they all seemed rapt. *I'm not counting votes yet, but I definitely need Jonathan and Rachel, or, at least control of all the firearms. Lord,* he thought in frustration, *this seemed such a peaceful place until yesterday.*

CC's suspicion that McCord would use obfuscation to confuse and mislead his listeners was being corroborated. He had asked for a brief account of McCord's life, along with details of what McCord had experienced over the past few months, but every time he asked a direct question, McCord found a way to avoid a straight answer, and had become increasingly evasive. When the question was raised of how McCord happened to survive the war, he evaded a direct answer, instead responding with a lengthy and profane invective against society in general, and against the government in particular. Instead of talking about himself, he pontificated about anything that came to mind.

But the only thing that CC did was remind McCord that, even if there weren't children present, he wouldn't tolerate the sort of language he was using.

McCord didn't deign to respond, but instead startled all of them by standing to his feet as though addressing an auditorium full of people. "Society," he asserted, "became nothing more than a flock of willfully ignorant sheep, milling about the truth, yet never capable of recognizing it, or acting decisively. And our government," he loftily opined, "was composed of people more interested in the perquisites of power and personal advantages than in leading the people to meet the necessary realities of life."

High-sounding phrases, CC thought, *but this isn't anything that any other demagogue might not say to win the backing of voters. I still can't figure out whether this guy has any real substance.*

At first McCord said he had been a government trade negotiator for several years, and had good friends around the world. When pinned down, he remarked that one of them was a retired colonel who'd worked in Air Force counter-intelligence. "So," he went on, "when I anticipated the opening of hostilities, I contacted the colonel and got myself invited to join him and his family on his private plane, flying from Baltimore to a small airfield in the Adirondacks. We landed at his private airfield and made it into his underground bunker just minutes before Chinese, Russian, North Korean, and Iranian missiles began falling across North America."

McCord's ability to tell his story in a very precise and careful manner seemed to lend it authenticity. Even when he contradicted himself, he somehow sounded credible. He started his account by describing an alleged visit to Moscow about a week before the war started. Then he commented on how different the political situation appeared after he'd returned home to the USA, and began comparing what his Russian counterparts had told him with information he later discovered on various intelligence websites.

"I was profoundly shaken," he related in his pedantic manner, speaking through and down his nose as at lesser beings and carefully pronouncing each word. In very precise language, he began to recount his adventure.

"I sat staring at my computer display. I had downloaded two top-secret files from NASA and the CIA." Then, perhaps a bit too smugly, he proclaimed, "I was using a program that I developed myself. I called it 'Cryptic One.'"

CC stifled a cynical laugh, and received an annoyed look from Elizabeth. *I wonder,* he asked himself, *whether before the war McCord might also have openly competed with the one or two others who had the temerity to claim that they had invented the Internet,* but he kept the thought to himself.

Jonathan stared wide-eyed at McCord. Then, with his elbows resting on the table, he raised one hand head high. "Excuse me?"

McCord's only acknowledgement was to glance at the boy for the briefest instant, then continue his lecture without losing a beat. "My program has a sub-routine called 'Ought Control,' which is an advanced artificial intelligence feature similar to those used on high-performance mainframes, mostly by social websites dredging data for advertising purposes, but also employed by the NSA to keep tabs on possible terrorists and the potential enemies of the administration. It does what it ought to do, what I want it to do."

"Excuse me," Jonathan repeated. This time he spoke louder, waggling his hand above his head.

And this time McCord's cold reptilian eyes rested on him for an instant longer before he again resumed speaking.

"Some would call it a sort of 'fuzzy logic.' In this case, it guides itself through incredible number-crunching processes that can penetrate just about any computer system, no matter how sophisticated or well-protected. I tested it with the toughest codes ever devised, and it decrypted them all in mere seconds."

"May I ask a question, please?" the boy politely persisted.

Clenching his teeth, McCord glared at him. "What could you possibly ask that would contribute to this discussion?"

"Well, I've done a little programming...."

"Yeah, yeah. Every twelve-year-old is a programming genius."

Rachel sighed audibly, and McCord's eyes turned to her. Indeed, everyone around the table had heard her, and CC wondered whether McCord might have injured his own case a little.

If I'm right, McCord will be supersensitive to the reactions of his audience. So I don't understand why he responded to Jonathan in that manner. I don't think Jonathan is trying to curry favor, and he didn't seem to be challenging him. It seems to me that he was intrigued with what McCord was saying. If anything, he seemed almost ready to worship at McCord's altar. And though the boy doesn't look offended, I'll bet he's wondering with the rest of us why he is being treated in such a cavalier fashion.

Unperturbed by McCord's icy response, the teen revealed surprising maturity.

"I'm sorry to interrupt," disappointment in his voice. I just wanted to ask a question."

"And, again," McCord replied, "I'm wondering what value your question might have, what it might contribute."

This megalomaniac is rude, officious, and supercilious, CC thought. *If I try to intercede on Jonathan's behalf, McCord may well turn it against me and make me the bad guy. If I don't, he might hurt Jonathan's feelings. Then, again, he might not.*

CC studied the boy, and realized that Jonathan might have a better intuitive grasp of who they were dealing with than he appreciated. CC's lips shaped themselves into the briefest of smiles. *Let's see how it plays out,* he thought.

To his immense relief, Elizabeth snapped, "Oh for pity's sake, Jimmy! Let the boy ask his question."

"Who's telling this story?" McCord demanded. If I allow questions now, we'll never finish."

"Only because you're an old windbag," Sarah whispered behind her hand, and Rachel almost choked trying to suppress her laughter.

McCord doesn't know Jonathan, CC thought. *I think this boy is one of those rare computer prodigies. On the other hand, maybe McCord's evading the question because he's afraid of it. Maybe I should get involved.*

With a tone that declared, I'm still in charge, CC stated flatly, "Jonathan is a vital member of this community, and if he has questions, we'll take time for them." Then, in a conciliatory tone, more for his audience than McCord, he asked, "We won't know what value Jonathan's question might have until we hear it, will we? We are all trying to learn, and we certainly don't mind taking a couple of extra minutes for Mr. McCord to answer his questions."

CC looked around the table, as though seeking consensus. "Isn't that right ladies?" While they were nodding in agreement,

CC added, "That is, if you aren't afraid of a simple question from a "twelve-year-old computer genius."

McCord flushed at the implication, but he clearly understood that he needed to moderate his tone if he didn't want to alienate his small audience. He screwed his mouth into an almost grotesque smile and spoke between clenched teeth, "Okay, kid, ask away."

"I was just wondering what program language you worked in?"

"What programming language I worked in for what? I just told you. I created the program."

"Yes. I heard you," barely hiding his own impatience. "You created a program. What I want to know is, what language you used to develop your app — I think you call it *Cryptic One.* I mean, did you use C++, or JavaScript, or Python?"

"No. None of those."

"Well, what did you use?"

"I don't like to share my secrets."

"What secrets?" the teen asked, still sounding conciliatory. "You can share the name of the language you used to develop the application without revealing anything about the app itself."

McCord looked from face to face, assessing how much currency he might have, and was obviously not reassured by the looks he was receiving. And it was clear that he wasn't about to be rescued. When no help was forthcoming, he said, "I suppose there's no danger in telling you now."

It was clear to CC that Jonathan had gone from being curious to very suspicious, but instead of exposing his misgivings, he appeared to feign excitement and admiration. "Well, okay," he said. "Did you use one of the more powerful languages used by the professionals?"

"Of course."

"I bet it was either Serpent, Incubus, or Spirochete," Jonathan offered, in a voice that dripped with respect.

"You're pretty smart, kid."

"Which one?"

"I used both Spirochete and Incubus."

"Wow, that's incredible! Thank you for sharing that."

Rachel thought the teen's effusive response was less than sincere, perhaps even bordering on sarcasm, and found herself leaning forward to hear what might come next.

McCord looked at Ross, and when it was clear that he had her attention, he commented smugly, "See, the interruption wasn't important."

She looked toward Jonathan, and suddenly realized that McCord's smug remark might not have been prudent. The teen wasn't about to crawl into the woodwork, and he was again raising his hand.

"What now?" McCord demanded impatiently, frustrated that he hadn't yet rid himself of this adolescent annoyance.

"Maybe, as you just said, my question wasn't important, but your answer was certainly informative."

McCord sighed, obviously impatient to move on, but striving to look unruffled. After a moment, he asked, "How so?"

"It was informative," he replied, "because there are no computer languages, advanced or otherwise, named Spirochete or Incubus. I just made those names up on the spur of the moment."

McCord's face reddened and it took him a moment to frame a reply. "That's what you think, kid. They are languages, top-secret languages developed by the military."

"No, they are not!" Jonathan stated flatly.

The angry red had faded from McCord's face, but he recovered quickly. Again affixing that almost cadaverous grin of his, he looked from face to face. Shaking his head, he stared at Jonathan as though pitying him. "Like I said, every kid thinks he's a computer guru."

CC on the other hand had no doubt that Jonathan really knew what he was talking about, and the women clearly recognized it too. CC had been watching their faces when Jonathan dropped his bombshell, and it was as though he could see blinds close over both women's eyes when McCord tried to squirm his way out of it.

Perhaps in an attempt to make everyone forget Jonathan's challenge, McCord went blithely on. "I could break codes that were keyed to obscure novels and textbooks," he pronounced. "I even had my program run through series of probabilities to check the contents of millions of volumes in an a matter of minutes." He paused, staring pointedly at Jonathan.

"Are you listening to me?" He went on without waiting for a reply, speaking more rapidly. "I was able to mine social websites for related data on questionable individuals, then correlate that information to discover anything significant, such as current activities, personal associations, items purchased, criminal and financial records, personal interests, even sexual proclivities."

But Jonathan even popped that bubble when he remarked that, "Anyone could have gone to any number of websites where, for a few dollars, he could download all that private information on almost anyone in America." The boy didn't stop there.

"Where did you get that kind of computing power?" he pursued, obviously not expecting a response. "Did you rent virtual computers from one of the major web retailers?"

He was surprised when McCord bit. "Look kid, your name is Jonathan, right?"

When the teen nodded, he went on. "Look, Jonathan. You're a bit confused. Those people sell stuff, you know — books, cameras, software — they don't rent computers."

"Actually," the boy replied, "the major on-line retailer expanded into leasing computer resources to developers and businesses years ago. They allowed the developers to get access to raw computing power without having to shell out big bucks to buy expensive gear. And even some of the biggest companies in the world used their services when it was to their advantage."

McCord's face appeared impassive, but his eyes sparked with fury. Still, he managed to remain expressionless, simply shaking his head as though in disappointment at the boy's ignorance, holding his palms up in a gesture that suggested, "What can you expect from a kid?" Again ignoring Jonathan's statement, he pressed on.

But before he'd completed a phrase, Rachel asked, "Why did you want all this very personal information claim that you gathered? You weren't one of those people who stole identities, were you?"

"McCord's expression again changed. CC thought the transformations his face was undergoing were wondrous, and when he caught Elizabeth cupping her mouth to cover up a cynical grin, he almost laughed aloud. He'd been growing increasingly skeptical of what he considered McCord's snow job, but Jonathan's exposure of his ignorance and dishonesty, plus the fact that Rachel seemed to accidentally strike a nerve, convinced him that McCord was a nasty character who would like others to imagine that he played with the big boys, while he was in fact merely a shell of a man. Still, he couldn't help but conclude that, even if his story were only partly true, McCord must have had some direct means of securing national security information.

CC realized that everyone else in the room had been starry-eyed with McCord's initial self-effacing remarks, but that had subtly changed. Their trust had melted away. And then he thought, *It doesn't really matter. It's important to have people in agreement with me, but the truth is that others in this room aren't going to have much input in the outcome of this conversation, nor of my final decision concerning the disposition of Mr. McCord. Right now I'm marking him down as extremely devious, and probably dangerous.*

McCord did not correctly interpret CC's look, and instead went blithely on.

"My computer program worked great, but the data correlations sobered me."

What a pompous fool, Rachel was thinking. *He's remorseless, like those flawed documentaries that college students used to be forced to listen to.*

"It seemed clear to me that war was imminent. Oddly it was a Russian who put me on to the danger, and I have to confess that I didn't at first believe him. He gave me a briefcase full of documents to bring back to the United States. And I really did try to intervene. I took the information to the appropriate people, but my efforts were futile. My contacts were willfully blind, or worse, they were serving as conscientious agents of one conspiracy or another."

Tell us something we don't know, Elizabeth thought.

"Our government had become riddled with hypocrisy. Corruption was rampant, and many had sold out to one or another foreign nations. A number of people were even taking money from competing powers. So it was a waste of time. I was too late with too little. Worse, I got my name on a couple of lists I would like to have avoided."

He took a breath, and went remorselessly on. "I'd already been accused of crying 'wolf' about our treatment by other nations. My superiors regularly criticized me and threatened my career. They destroyed my credibility. I can't help but believe that their effort was orchestrated by unnamed individuals to neutralize me."

McCord hesitated for a moment, staring meaningly at CC. "I think they found ways to silence a lot of other voices so that they could pull this thing off. Obviously, some whistleblowers in the U.S. intelligence apparatus had more than an inkling of what was going on. They began sending warnings on unsecured channels, and in the clear. Then, very suddenly, there was silence, and their IP addresses disappeared. They'd been neutralized."

For the first time, Jonathan nodded in agreement. He too had seen such warnings. McCord might just be restoring some credibility in the eyes of his listeners.

"I lost security clearance and legal access to many important networks when I was mysteriously fired from my key position, but I could still find ways to get into the computer nets. I wanted people to understand that we should always negotiate, even if it meant giving up our wealth and power. After all," he added, "America stole everything it had from others."

CC couldn't let that go by. "We Americans built the greatest nation on earth because we provided people with the freedom to pursue life, liberty, and happiness, and until we lost those freedoms by turning from God, we held up the light of liberty, and the fruit of faith, to the entire world."

McCord started to scoff, but CC went on. "Our faith in Jesus Christ is the only distinctive underlying our republican form of government that could possibly explain our unique and extraordinary success." He hesitated, as though searching his memory for something. Then he went on.

"There's something in the Bible. Ah, yes. *Righteousness exalts a nation, but sin is a reproach to any people!*"

"On the other hand," he went on, "it doesn't take a great student of world history to realize that the last and lowest form of diplomacy results from a corrupt leader wanting something that belongs to some other nation, and his last resort is always war.

Most people will resort to violence rather than surrender any significant economic advantage. That's why we have jails and policemen. That's why I encouraged negotiations through strength, and peace through preparedness. I am sometimes cynical, but I am also a realist. To my thinking, the human race hasn't improved a bit in terms of moral character. The problem is that predators have become far more effective. They have found more powerful means of exerting their will over an ever-increasing number of people in a shorter time."

As the words poured from him, he looked up to find that everyone was staring at him open mouthed. It was a moment before he realized that he'd just divulged something about himself that he wasn't consciously aware of. He squinted as his head began to ache again. Was it his imagination, or was McCord the only one not surprised at his unexpected outburst.

The Mockingbirds Sing

Ross and McCord
Motor Home
December 25th, Noon

It was obvious that McCord and CC were not far from exchanging blows.

In an attempt to defuse the situation, Rachel asked McCord and Ross how they'd met. CC considered her interruption timely, as he didn't feel that it was time to confront McCord. McCord must have had similar feelings because he almost smiled at her.

"I'd just escaped a roadblock set up by pillagers, and drove my motorcycle off the highway to evade capture. With bullets zipping around me, I rode up a hill into some woods, hoping to get out of sight. Instead, I drove right into their campsite, at the same moment that Elizabeth was scrambling out of a tent."

She picked up the account. "I saw him coming, but I figured he was one of my captors until I saw a couple of the men from the roadblock running up the hill shooting at him."

"She came staggering out of that tent," Jim continued, "and I didn't know which of us was more afraid of the other. So I gunned my bike, getting ready to head deeper into the woods."

"That's true," she interrupted. "He didn't know that I'd been a prisoner, and he wasn't the one who freed me. Just before he arrived, I thought I'd been left alone in camp, with all the nasties down at the roadblock. Then I heard someone sawing through the tent canvas, and looked up to see a big hunting knife just above my head. The next thing I know, some guy was leaning down through the opening. I thought he was going to stab me, but instead he started cutting the ropes on my wrists and ankles.

"I couldn't see him well, but he reassured me that he wasn't going to hurt me. *Oh, sure, I trust you!* I thought, and as soon as he helped me out through the hole in the tent, I tried to get away, but when I stumbled out of the tent, I was disoriented.

That's when I heard Jim's motorcycle approaching, and I saw the two guys shooting at him from down the hill, so I figured he had to be one of the good guys. but all of a sudden the big guy comes running out from behind the tent shouting, "There you are, you son of a...."

McCord interrupted with that icy smile of his. "She picked up a chunk of firewood and hit him on the side of his head, dropping him like a rock."

They're like two people singing in rounds, CC thought.

"I felt really bad," Elizabeth added. "He was the guy who'd cut me loose, and I couldn't imagine why he was calling me names, unless...," and stopped in mid-sentence to stare at Jim, and her voice trailed off, "...unless he was yelling at somebody else."

McCord seized that moment to divert their attention. "The other guys were now only about a couple of hundred yards away," he interjected, "and one of them had stopped and was aiming his rifle at us. I wasn't about to hang around waiting for her to make up her mind, so I gunned my bike again, and started away. Then I heard her scream." In a falsetto voice, he mimicked her cry: "Please don't leave me here alone!' So I spun the bike around and pulled up next to her. 'Why shouldn't I leave you?' I asked her. 'I have no reason to take you along.'" He paused. "For all I knew, they might have had a good reason for tying her up. She might have been one of them, and after I saw her KO that guy, I wasn't sure I wanted her sitting behind me on my motorcycle." Ross broke in on him, and McCord gave her a look of annoyance.

"I understood his fears. I don't think he realized how important we might be to one another, two heads are better than one, and all that kind of thing. Anyway, I begged him to take me at least a mile or two so that I'd have a head start on the guys who were chasing him up the hill."

CC watched carefully to see whether they were exchanging signals or fabricating the story, but it appeared they were sincere.

McCord picked up the account. "I told her to climb on behind me, still a little worried that she might attack me too. I'd already heard some real horror stories about what people were doing to one another in the name of survival, but I decided to take the chance." He went on with his precisely worded account.

"I almost popped a wheelie getting out of there, then started swerving back and forth among the trees, bullets whizzing around us, and doing everything I could to get out of range.

"When we'd gone about a mile, I slowed down, and she started shouting in my ear, telling me we had to stop. I asked her if she was crazy, and she said, 'No,' that she'd hidden something important among some rocks just before they caught her. I told her that I wouldn't turn around, and she told me that I wouldn't have to. She pointed off to our left, and I drove through the trees for about a quarter-mile until she spotted the place she was looking for."

She again picked up the tale. "He kept asking me whether I knew the name of the guy I'd knocked unconscious, and I kept telling him, 'No!' And when I got off his bike, he told me that he was going to leave me there. I begged him to reconsider. He asked me again whether I knew the guy I'd knocked down, and I guess he believed me that time. When I asked him why he wanted to know, Jim said that the guy mistakenly believed that he had something belonging to him."

"I asked whether he knew the man's name, and he told me 'Joseph.'"

Jim picked up the account. "She argued that we'd be better off together, keeping an eye out for bad guys, sharing chores, and keeping watch, so I said, 'Maybe.' She went off into the rocks to pick up whatever she'd left there, and kept turning to see whether I was waiting for her. When she came back, she had some sort of a strange backpack. She climbed on behind me, and I took off. Remembering that some of those guys had

4-wheel drive trucks, I decided to continue riding cross country, hoping they wouldn't be able to follow us through the woods."

Again Ross interrupted. "That night we camped by a stream in an apple orchard. About then, I think we both realized how frightened we were of others, and while we might decide to split up at any time, we both realized we were, for the moment, safer together than traveling alone."

"At least one of us could be on watch while the other slept," he added.

"And although we later had some pretty bad arguments, I don't believe that I ever had anything to fear from Jim."

"And she pretty much carried her own weight," he added somewhat grudgingly. "In fact, she's the reason we found this valley. We'd stopped on the highway uphill from the entrance. The sun was going down, and we had to get under cover because there was a low-flying plane coming up the valley, obviously hunting for people. And while I was pulling the bike under the trees beneath the cliff, I told her to keep an eye on the plane."

She again picked up the account. "That's when I noticed the back end of a tractor-trailer pulling under the trees a couple of hundred yards downhill from us," she exclaimed.

"So," McCord added, "Elizabeth saved our necks by finding the way in."

"Yes, I followed the wheel tracks of the truck into the woods, until I found where it had almost slid into a pond. I didn't want to run into whoever was driving that truck, so I went back and got Jim. He was pretty angry with me for disappearing."

"Yeah, I'd been trying to figure out whether to continue down the mountain road, hoping to find a place to camp, when I realized that I hadn't seen Elizabeth for several minutes. First I was afraid she'd stumbled onto someone, and might lead them back to me. Then I wondered whether she'd gotten lost in the darkness. It would be just like a woman."

Rachel's lips tightened at that comment, but she said nothing. Oblivious of her feelings, he pressed on.

"I was afraid to move far from my bike, but I spotted her about a hundred yards away down the side of the road. It was almost dark by the time we'd pushed the motorcycle back along that wood road and reached the big pond. She pointed out the truck up on the right side, so we decided to follow the opposite shore."

Elizabeth picked up the account, and there was now no question in CC's mind that they were telling the truth about their discovery of the valley. Or of who had arrived here first.

"Jim was very interested in the pond because of our need for water, as well as the possibility of providing fresh fish for our meals. We spent the night beside the pond. My later discovery of a cave settled the matter. In spite of the truck parked across the valley, we decided to stop there for at least a day or two.

"We figured that if we could shelter in that cave, we'd be able to reduce the amount of radiation we might be receiving, and it would probably be warmer and safer from predators. There were some large boulders beneath the cave, and evergreens grew between them. Those trees made a great place to hide the motorcycle."

"After all that," Jim added, "I was a little hesitant to explore that cave."

"That's for sure!" Elizabeth laughed. "He stopped just inside the entrance, and I thought he was about to jump out of his skin when we heard an animal make a screaming sound. Jim drew his gun and moved into the cave carrying a torch, but he came running out a moment later, after which a family of raccoons came ambling out."

"I noticed that you waited outside while I did the exploring."

She laughed. "You bet! Tangling with wild animals is not my thing."

Jim told them how he'd fashioned a torch from a dead branch that he'd snapped out of the base of a pine tree. He glanced at Elizabeth, indignation in his voice. "I was blinded by the flame in the darkness of the cave, and when the coons rushed out, they were under my feet, and I almost stumbled over them." He was clearly angry when he added, "I suppose that Elizabeth, standing in safety at the mouth of the cave must have thought I was frightened."

"Right," she agreed wryly. "That and the fact that you screamed."

"I didn't scream," he retorted angrily. "I just shouted a warning to you."

"Yeah, right. Okay."

Rachel could see that things were again getting out of hand, and tried to pour oil on the troubled waters. "Did you find anything interesting in the cave?"

"Actually, yes," Elizabeth replied before Jim could open his mouth to speak. "Jim stumbled over an ancient fire ring, and tripped over the remains of several clay pots, one still intact. "The were obviously hand-made," Elizabeth said, then added, "I estimate they are of Native American manufacture, probably a couple of centuries old."

"We carried our gear and what little food we had up the steep incline to the cave, and set up our camp near the back. From there, we felt secure from prying eyes. From the mouth of the cave we had a great view of most of the valley, though much of it was hidden by trees. After running for our lives for so long," she added, "it was great to feel a little secure."

Jim's face looked less grim after her next remark.

"I built a fireplace about ten feet back inside the cave, placing a couple of large slabs of rock on end so that they'd hide the flames from anyone out in the valley. It seemed important because we thought we had caught sight of a campfire through the trees at the far end of the valley, and we didn't want to duplicate their carelessness."

CC grimaced, but said nothing.

Jim finally broke his silence. "After supper, we agreed not to have any more open fires or to use any lights during the hours of darkness."

"So, how have you survived?" CC asked.

McCord hesitated, then looked at Elizabeth. They both shrugged their shoulders, obviously agreeing that it wouldn't hurt to share some secrets.

"We knew we couldn't last long once the weather grew cold," Elizabeth told them, and we had to get more food. So we went exploring. We found an abandoned feed and grain store a few miles north on Route 19. It was full of things we needed, like clothing, sleeping bags, food, even building supplies and tools. There was a little two-wheel garden trailer there, designed to tow behind a lawn tractor. Jim jury-rigged a hitch on the back of his motorcycle, and we made several trips after dark. We were even able to bring back some light framing lumber and tarpaper, so that we could close off the outer end of the cave to keep it warm."

Then McCord admitted, "We had trouble with smoke from the fire, so we brought back a little cast iron stove and smoke-stack piping, and set it up near the tarpaper wall. It allowed us to warm the cave without smoking ourselves out. With a kerosene lantern and a couple of gallons of fuel from the feed and grain store, we were able to light the cave and read the books we brought along."

"Things were fairly cozy for a few days," Elizabeth added, "but since Jim strained his back, and since I could only carry a limited amount, things soon got a lot tougher. I made several trips to bring food back, but I was frightened away one night when I discovered someone else in the building. In order to get a head start, I locked them in and took off on the bike."

CC didn't bother mentioning that he was probably the "someone" she'd locked in.

Rachel was staring at the two of them, and CC wondered whether she was thinking what he was thinking. *Exactly how cozy were the two of them?* Then CC looked at the way in which McCord occasionally stared at Jonathan and concluded that McCord and Ross enjoyed at best a platonic relationship.

His thoughts were interrupted by McCord. "Elizabeth picked up all the dry fallen wood within about a hundred yards of our cave, and carried it up the rough path. Then I stacked it the best I could."

"You mean you tossed it in a heap just inside the mouth of the cave," she countered.

There was a little bitterness in that comment, CC thought.

"We were running out of food again," she continued, "so we set out to look around the valley. That's when this blizzard came up. You know the rest."

CC sat staring at the two of them, weighing their stories. Everything they'd said sounded reasonable, and their stories seemed to dovetail. It seemed likely that she was the ones he'd heard the night he was at the feed and grain store, but he hesitated to ask whether she'd been the one who'd tried to lock him in the cellar. Nonetheless, he wished he had questioned them separately. Elizabeth came across as a woman that CC might befriend, and he believed her story. On the other hand, McCord had been caught in several lies. There was something inconsistent and terribly phony about him.

The Price of Failure
Green Mountain Feed and Grain
December 25th, 2:35 p.m.

A long semi-trailer was parked by the gas pumps in front of the feed and grain store, and a crew of shabbily uniformed men were loading it with cartons they were bringing up from the cellar beneath the store. Another trailer was backed up to the loading dock, and a man on a forklift was moving heavily loaded pallets out of the warehouse and stacking them inside the trailer.

An old man dressed in flannel shirt and overalls stood alone on the porch, watching the activity. His face paled when a black SUV broke through the line of men and stopped a few yards away.

The driver's door opened, and the driver leapt out to open the rear door. An elderly oriental in a very crisp military uniform stepped out, placed a brimmed hat on his head, squared it carefully, then in an unmilitary gesture, put his knuckles in the small of his back and stretched. After a moment, he turned slowly to appraise the work going on. He was well over sixty years old, and wore three stars on his collar points as well as above the brim of his hat. His eyes became frosty when they settled on the man who waited on the porch. Unlike the others at the feed and grain store, the subject of his attention was not in uniform.

The officer didn't bother climbing the stairs to the porch, and was obviously resentful that he had to look up to see his inferior. He nevertheless lacquered his words with a false politeness.

"Mr. Copeland, it is good to find you still here."

"I did not realize that I had a choice in the matter, but since your words seem to indicate that I do, I think I will be on my way."

The general was momentarily taken aback by his glibness, but when he spoke, his voice lost its false geniality, and his deeply etched face turned to stone.

"Perhaps we both need to rethink our previous statements." He didn't attempt to hide a sly smile. "Please plan to remain here indefinitely."

The man did not respond, and the general's patience wore thin. In clipped tones he said, "I don't have much time."

The old man, realizing that the general wasn't going to climb to the porch, shuffled slowly down the stairway to the parking area, and without bowing or demonstrating any other form of respect, simply said, "What is it you want now?"

"I want to know why you've been far too busy to notice that a substantial quantity of precious materiel has disappeared from my storage facility."

The man, now with his emotions under tight check, swept his arm behind him, indicating the warehouse and store. "You are referring, I assume, to my property?"

"The concept of private property no longer exists."

"Well," the man smiled, there seems to be some confusion. You just referred to it as your property. Are you suggesting that some pigs are more equal than other pigs?"

"An unfortunate mischaracterization," the general snapped, embarrassed to have this brought to the attention of his men. "I repeat, private property no longer exists."

The old man's lips curled slightly as he remarked, "This too shall pass."

"I think that is hardly likely," the general responded coldly, "but your opinions are hardly relevant. The question is, what happened to the items we stored here, and how do you plan to get them back?"

Copeland knew the general didn't expect him to have any answers, and simply wanted to toy with him — a mouse between the paws of a ferrel cat. Unlike a mouse, however, he was indifferent to his fate, and was anything but paralyzed with fear. His lifetime friend, Joseph Sennett, had taught him how to find the peace of God that passes understanding.

His wasn't reckless courage, but it wasn't cowardice either. He'd done what he could to help the fledgling resistance movement, and he had hoped to be able to do more, but he was now resigned to whatever the Lord had in mind.

What these people simply don't understand, is that we Christians are confident of our ultimate destiny. We count on the Lord making a way of escape that we may be able to bear whatever we face. Those three that Daniel wrote about, the three in the fiery furnace, demonstrated their faith when they told King Nebuchadnezzar, "...our God whom we serve is able to deliver us from the burning fiery furnace, and he will deliver us out of thine hand, O king."

All he replied, however, were a few words. "Alive here, or alive in heaven, General Eng, you do not control my destiny! I will ultimately be delivered."

"Then, Mr. Copeland, I will take great pleasure in helping to speed your deliverance. The general scowled, angry that he was not eliciting the sort of response that he'd been able to get from most of these American cowards. He nevertheless persisted.

"Save me your religious drivel, Mr. Copeland. Do you have any idea who took these items, or where they were taken?"

"Why do you expect me to know?"

"I placed this facility under your authority. You were responsible for its contents."

"This facility, being my property, has always been under my authority, but since you stole everything in this building from me, I am no longer responsible for it."

"You are treading on very thin ice," the general warned. "Let me remind you that your success in caring for this facility and its contents would have been to your benefit."

"My benefit? You invaded my country, caused the death of my wife, murdered many of my friends, and destroyed my business. And you have the gall to suggest that you can benefit me?"

"So you admit that you stole from this facility?"

"I make no such admission. I have taken nothing for myself. I have eaten only the poor fare that your men have given me. I have not taken anything away, though it is mine."

"It is not yours!" raged the general."

Copeland simply smiled, which made the general furious, and his fury reminded him of the description of Nebuchadnezzar when the three Hebrew men defied him. He could even quote it. "Then was Nebuchadnezzar full of fury, and the form of his visage was changed."

The general, however, had played this game before and willed himself to be calm. "I wonder how is it that someone was able to just walk in here and get away with over half the food and virtually all of the firearms and ammunition. And yet you say that you weren't in any way involved with their removal?"

"I was not, but..."

"But what, Mr. Copeland?"

"I would have freely given to help others survive, and if they were committed to defeating you, I would have happily contributed everything I own."

The general stared at him a moment, one side of his tightly closed lips turned up in a smile. "But you don't own anything, do you? So you really had nothing to give."

"Apart from your accusation that I somehow failed you, I would remind the general that I've been a captive, completely under the control of your subordinates. At the same time, you yourself made it impossible for your henchmen to effectively guard this place because you ordered them not to make their presence obvious."

"You dare not remind me of anything?" he roared. "How is it that you didn't post a guard inconspicuously? I gave you that responsibility!"

"You cannot demand responsibility where you do not give commensurate authority." The old man's voice was quiet and authoritative. "It wasn't my responsibility. If it were offered, I wouldn't accept it. If it were ordered, I would refuse." He hesitated for a moment, putting his words in order. "Your real problem, Eng, is that your own misfit subordinates failed you."

His voice didn't falter, even when he saw the general's change of expression. He didn't know what else to say, so he pushed boldly onward, no longer caring about the outcome.

"You told them not to post a guard, as it would draw attention to this facility. You told them that the rundown condition of the property would..."

"Don't you dare tell me what you think I said," the general screamed, a string of spittle flying from his lips. "The fact is that you failed to protect vital military materiel that was placed under your control."

"The fact is that your subordinates failed to protect the materiel. For all I know, they may have sold some items on the black market. And therein lies your problem, general. Therein lies the cause for your ultimate defeat."

"We will be victorious!"

"Really? Just look at the faces of these men. Ex-convicts, derelicts, men who've never earned an honest dollar in their lives. Hungry, bitter, greedy and rapacious. This is your ragtag army. A thousand of them couldn't stand against one godly American citizen. Your defeat can be seen in the character of the despicable people who flock to your banner for the loot you offer. And...."

The general's hand swept up, striking him across the face, knocking him down. A growl rose from several of the men who had been loading the trucks, and only subsided when the armed guards nearby raised their weapons and shouted warnings.

One of the workers ignored the guard's threats and bent to help the old man to his feet. When Copeland was able to stand unaided, he took a handkerchief from his pocket, and wiped the blood from his lip. He brushed dirt from his sleeves before turning to again face the general and completed his fatal comment. "... and it may well be one of your own men who ends your life."

Old man Copeland had been a popular member of the community. He had always been fair and open-handed with everyone. During economic downturns he had supplied food, seed, and equipment to responsible farmers who lacked money and credit. Some of the people who had been brought to the feed and grain were farmers forced to load the trucks at gunpoint. During this verbal exchange, they had stopped working and were listening keenly to the discussion.

His own hand swept around in an arc, not to strike the general, but to take in all those who were listening. He seemed to grow in stature even as his quavering voice steadied and took on a tone of deep conviction.

"These men you are treating as slave laborers may soon take up arms against you, using the teachings of your late Chairman Mao to defeat you."

The general was angered that the man might be planting ideas in the heads of these foolish westerners. He realized that when he'd knocked the old man down, some of them had been held in check only by the sound of his troops cocking their weapons.

No one had noticed as two of the men who'd been working nearby had quietly set down their burden and sunk to their knees unnoticed behind several cords of firewood. They had no trouble hearing the general's next words.

He had turned his back on Copeland to whisper to the sergeant.

"Do you have any idea where these stolen items were taken?"

"No, sir."

"Well, we can do without the food, but I want the weapons recovered. And we must deal severely with the people who took them. This sort of thing cannot be tolerated. Such success will embolden our enemies."

"I don't believe the people who have these things came from very far away, General."

"Oh?"

"Some time back, one of our pilots reported seeing a couple of people on the mountain road. I thought I'd take a squad and check out that area."

"Excellent. But how is it that you didn't check out the area before this?" Before he could respond that he had been refused permission, the general abruptly changed direction. "Never mind. I know I can count on you. Just keep me informed."

"Yes sir."

"When you have removed everything of value, burn the buildings."

The man's response was one of shock. "Burn the buildings?"

"Do you have a problem with that order?"

"No, sir!"

"Oh, and leave Mr. Copeland behind to guard what's left of his property." His smile was not pleasant. "I suggest that you drag him down those stairs and tie him to a post in the cellar where he can keep a closer eye on his property than he did for me."

The sergeant's face was impassive, but his affirmative reply sounded choked.

The men kneeling behind the wood pile turned to one another, nodded in agreement, and began crawled undetected beneath the length of the porch until they reached the far side of the building. Coming out behind some shrubs, they rose to their feet and walked quickly toward the woods just beyond the rear of the store. A number of their well-armed friends were waiting there with Pastor Kenzy. At one time or another, they had all experienced the kindness of the Copelands.

After they told the others what they had heard, the young farmer who'd been at the Butter Creek Inn the night the bar maid escaped turned to Pastor Kenzy.

"Well, Jack, you still want us sheep to try to lie down with those lions?"

The preacher shook his head. "I'm afraid the time for talking peace is over, Ted. Right now it's time to turn our plowshares into swords, and do something to save brother Copeland." His words were met with a chorus of amens.

Who's in Charge Here?

CC's Motor Home
December 25th, 1:45 p.m.

CC stared at McCord until the other man fidgeted and looked away. "Tell us," he demanded, "how you came here."

"I've already told you that."

"Not really."

"Well, let me think about it for a moment."

"What do you mean, 'think about it for a moment'? Don't you know how you got here?"

"Yes," Elizabeth asked, "or will it take you a minute or two to contrive a story that sounds plausible?"

"I just meant that I wanted to get my thoughts in order, that's all!"

"Why not simply tell us, moment by moment, what happened to you, and what you did, from the time you decided that this war was inevitable. Where were you at the time?"

McCord glared at him for a moment. He seemed a little uncertain, even belligerent, obviously hesitant to answer and very careful about choosing his next words.

CC turned to the boy. "Jonathan, please go in the bedroom, find Mr. McCord's wallet, go through it, and bring me anything that might identify this guy. In fact, bring the wallet and you can go through it right here."

"Hey, wait a minute," McCord blustered, "you have no right to do that."

"I don't want another word out of you until you're ready to provide three concise pieces of information. First, where were you when the bombs went off? Second, how did you survive? And, third, how and why did you come here?" CC held his eyes until McCord finally turned away. Then he went on.

"Do you understand those three questions?"

In a voice quaking, but filled with bluster, McCord finally replied. "I think I've given you about all the information I intend to."

"You've given us nothing except obfuscation. Do you know what obfuscation is," Mr. McCord?

"Of course."

"Well, just to make certain that we are on the same page, and that you're not obfuscating about the word, obfuscation, I'll give you my definition. Obfuscation is pulling the wool over people's eyes, it's blowing smoke, it's adulterating silver coins with copper, it's distorting the truth by mixing in the false, it's diluting a drink with water, it's a politician's stock in trade. In short, Mr. McCord, obfuscation is confusing the facts on purpose. To put a point to it, it's lying. My dad used to say that he hated liars worse than thieves. He said that you could tell when someone stole your possessions, but it's far more difficult to know when someone has stolen the truth."

CC stared at McCord until the other man looked away.

"What I'm wondering, Mr. McCord, is why you find it necessary to lie to us. You do understand, don't you, that we can't afford to have any liars here."

When McCord didn't respond, CC said, "Let me rephrase. Tell us, please, Mr. McCord," and he ground out the mister, "how you induced your associate, the retired air force colonel, to allow you, of all people, to fly with his family to their bomb shelter in that Adirondack park. Then tell us exactly when, day and hour, that you arrived there, where you stayed, how long you stayed, when and why you left, and how you happened to travel all the way to this particular valley." It was a command, not a request, and CC did not attempt to hide his anger.

McCord tried to hold his gaze, but again dropped his eyes. "All right," he finally replied. "As I've already told you, I sat out the war in a shelter in the Adirondack Forest. The colonel agreed to take me along because I'm his only nephew." He exhaled loudly.

"Let me digress. My uncle's father served at Pittsburgh with the Strategic Air Command back in the 60s, while he was a teen. As an officer, his father frequently visited the twelve Atlas missile sites that had been completed within a fifty-mile radius of Plattsburgh. They were, incidentally, the only ICBM sites ever constructed east of the Mississippi River. Each missile silo was built inside a gigantic hole they dug into solid rock. They were nearly two hundred feet deep and over fifty feet wide, and they used about 8,000 yards of concrete and tons of steel to make each one into a blast-proof, underground silo.

There he goes again, CC thought, *pontificating. But if I interrupt him, I'll never get him back on track.* McCord droned on.

"Each silo was protected by massive overhead doors to protect the missile. All but the two sites in Vermont were located in New York State. The entire base was officially closed down about 1965. Many New Yorkers didn't like having them anywhere in the state because they were either anti-war activists or they considered the silos to be too close to home, prime targets for enemy missiles."

"Okay, thanks for the history lesson," CC interrupted, but it was clear that he was anything but grateful. "What's your point?"

McCord put on the face of a kicked puppy, designed, CC believed, to win the sympathy of his audience, but McCord's eyes held that deadly opaque threat of a rattlesnake. He waited a moment before continuing.

"What most people didn't know was that some of those silos, less their missiles of course, have since been offered for sale to civilians. One of those silos was located in the wilds of New York's Adirondack State Park. It was on nearly thirty acres of land, had originally been offered for several million, but my uncle bought it from an investor who had already converted what had been the control center and crew quarters into a beautiful underground home. He bought it for less than a million, with a small down payment, and with the balance carried by the seller. The Air Force had also built a 2,000 foot runway nearby to service the original missile silo, and that's where my uncle landed our plane. So we weren't really flying to Plattsburgh, but to the middle of a vast forest where we weren't apt to be bothered by anyone."

"You said the Adirondack Forest?" CC asked.

McCord puffed himself up a little as he described the place.

"We felt safe from marauders there because the site is in a remote part of the forest, and there is only a population of 120,000 in the entire park of over six million acres. The park is roughly the size of Vermont, and greater than the total area of Yellowstone, Yosemite, Grand Canyon, Glacier, and the Great Smoky Mountain Parks combined." He grinned. "It's really huge!"

"Yes," CC commented. "I bet the people of New York State loved having six million acres set aside as forever wild wilderness, while they were stuck elbow to elbow in dirty cities and crowded suburbs."

"Well, what very few were aware of was that a lot of powerful individuals with the right political connections had luxury getaways hidden away in that forest, with access only by helicopter. But that's another story. For my part, I felt pretty secure. We were in a luxury home built within the silo, with massive steel doors to protect us from any eventuality. It was the perfect getaway home and was almost capable of withstanding a direct nuclear hit. Of course," he added, "since there was no missile there, it had no strategic value as a target."

"And since it was in the middle of nowhere," CC added, "it was unlikely to attract any attention."

"Exactly," McCord replied.

"This is all news to me," Elizabeth said.

"I know of no reason why I needed to share this information with you."

"No, nor can I think of any reason why you wouldn't have," she countered. "We were, after all, stuck with one another for months, totally bored to death." Then she asked a question that clearly caught McCord by surprise.

"So why aren't you still there?"

It was obvious that he didn't want to answer that, and might not have if CC hadn't pushed him.

"Yes, answer that. Why aren't you still there?" he pursued.

Again McCord hesitated, but finally answered in a voice so low that they had to strain to hear him.

"Well, things went pretty well for a few days, but then the isolation and the tension seemed to get to my uncle's family."

"And?" Rachel asked.

His response was little more than a grunt.

"What? I didn't hear you."

"He told me I had to leave."

"Huh. Your uncle's family was living in isolation, and they threw out the only other human being around?"

"Oh, I wasn't the only one there."

"No. Pray tell, who else was there?"

"His wife, his adult daughter and her family, and his teenage son."

"And your aunt and cousins didn't object to the colonel putting you out on your own in the midst of a war," Rachel asked.

McCord shrugged. "People are funny, especially when under stress. They were pretty irrational."

No one seemed to question that generalization, but Elizabeth didn't hesitate to pursue the subject.

"It seems to me that you must have done something highly offensive to get yourself thrown out by a relative who went to the trouble of saving your life by flying you a thousand miles in his private plane, and allowed you to survive the holocaust in a shelter with his family."

The arrow struck home, and it was clear that McCord had no satisfactory answer. His embarrassment was almost palpable. His face became suffused with blood, and his teeth audibly ground together. But still he did not reply.

"So what happened next," Jonathan asked, providing McCord a way of escape, and earning a smile bordering on the lascivious.

Still he hesitated, clearly formulating a reply.

"The underground silo was huge, and though they wouldn't let me stay in their home, they did give me food and blankets, and let me move into the area that had served as the missile control room. When two weeks had passed, I was asked politely to leave."

"And you didn't argue that decision," CC asked.

"Not while he had a shotgun in his hands, no," McCord replied.

"I wonder what offense he committed that drove them to that extreme," Rachel mused.

McCord said nothing, and there was silence while the others considered the possibility.

Then Elizabeth, dripping sarcasm, asked another question.

"So your uncle sent you out into the cold, cruel world with just the clothes on your back?"

"Not exactly," McCord answered.

"What, then?"

"He let me have a motorcycle."

"That's it?"

"No, of course not." He appeared to be taking a mental inventory. "He gave me some camping gear and as much food as I could carry."

"So that explains the bike," Elizabeth mused.

"I got on Route 73, drove east to 9N, and south to Chimney Point where I crossed Lake Champlain into Vermont." He chewed his upper lip for a moment. "From there, I followed 17 east, zigzagging across Vermont, following various roads, and suffering a few misadventures, until I chanced upon Ross." He looked at CC, and there was belligerence in his voice when he said, "And that's the truth."

Right, CC thought, *the truth, but not the whole truth*, though he nodded his head as though to affirm McCord's claim. *You'll let more of the truth slip out as time goes by*. And then he realized he'd actually decided to give McCord a little time. *Enough time to prove himself? Or maybe enough time to hang himself. Or maybe kill me?* But he wasn't ready to let McCord know that yet. He had to make at least one more test.

Elizabeth broke in.

"You were with your uncle for two weeks. What were you doing during the three weeks from the time you left the silo until the evening you rescued me?"

He was clearly angry that she raised this question, and answered with just one word.

"Surviving."

"That's it? Surviving?"

"That's it!"

McCord had a number of techniques for confusing listeners, but when unable to attack his opponent, or to offer a plausible lie, he simply talked around an irrelevant subject to get people's minds off the real issues. He had a tendency to mix in observations about the war with accounts of his own experience. No one seemed to mind because they were all hungry for information. Everyone, that is, except little Sarah. They'd all been sitting around the breakfast table for nearly two hours, and she'd fallen asleep leaning against Rachel, whereupon she'd laid the little girl beside her on the bench, with her head in her lap.

The entire group looked as though they were about to doze off, but they came sharply awake when CC slapped his hand on the table and said, "All right, let's stop this nonsense!"

The women seemed surprised by his words, but he forestalled any comments by raising his hand peremptorily.

CC began critiquing McCord's story, bringing to everyone's attention a number of the statements that had bothered them earlier, statements they had forgotten in the course of his often suffocating dialogue. He again braced McCord.

"In the past two hours you implied that you have worked for, or been involved with, a least three world powers and one or two multinational corporations. At one moment, you were a political activist, then an analyst. At another, you've were the world's greatest computer scientist. You imply that you were a spy, a diplomat, a businessman, and an expert on world affairs. Yet none of us has ever heard your name before."

CC shook his head in amused tolerance.

"And in spite of all your grand titles and important friends, you were unable to have any impact on circumstances. Then you told us that you somehow induced a relative to let you fly with his family to the wilds of New York where you survived the war, were then kicked out of their shelter for an undisclosed offense, somehow eluded your enemies, made your way to this valley, and accidentally happened upon this cave. Next you'll be telling us that your real name is James Bond!"

To which McCord responded cooly, "Shaken, not stirred."

"Well, if you're all that dangerous, we'll have to load our guns, hide our alcohol, lock up our women, and take steps to deal with you."

Both little jokes fell flat, but the confusion in the women's faces began clearing as CC continued pointing out the general contradictions and inconsistencies in McCord's account.

CC turned to Rachel. "Would you please bundle Sarah up and take her out for a little walk? It should be a nice day, though pretty cold. I don't think she needs to hear this conversation."

"Actually that sounds like a very good idea."

Elizabeth stood up and stretched. "I think I'll join them, if that's all right with you. I'm getting a little uncomfortable sitting here."

They were all surprised when CC said, "That's fine."

As Rachel handed the sleeping child through the door to Elizabeth, CC returned his attention to McCord.

McCord gave CC a baleful look.

"So what's next?" McCord asked.

"Temporarily, we will take a chance on you."

"Oh, wow! Aren't you just the generous soul?"

"You just don't quit, do you?"

"And don't you ever forget it."

"And don't you make me regret my decision."

"So what's next?" McCord repeated.

"You will remain in this area of the caverns only. You will be given lightweight clothing to wear, including shoes. You will not be permitted access to firearms."

"How will you enforce that?"

CC shook his head in frustration. "You really do push, don't you?" Then he went on. "Except for the firearms that Jonathan, Rachel, and I carry, the remainder will be locked up."

"Humph!"

"I want to make one important point here."

"Yeah, what's that?" McCord replied.

"If we see you attempting to secure a firearm, if we at any time see you with a firearm, we will assume you are a belligerent, and we will shoot you."

"Maybe. Maybe I'll shoot first. Time will tell."

"Perhaps it already has. I'm about three seconds from terminating your part in this conversation permanently."

McCord instantly sobered. "Okay," he answered, none too sincerely, "I'll play your silly game."

Camp Craft

The Meadow fronting the Cave
December 26th, 9:15 a.m.

E lizabeth had risen late, only to discover that everyone else had already eaten and gone about their business without waking her. She grabbed a cup of coffee, buttered a piece of the crusty homemade French bread, and followed the sound of voices through the tunnel that fronted on the meadow.

CC was kneeling in the entrance, the meadow behind him obscured by low-lying fog, the trees beyond almost lost in the murk. Rachel, Jonathan, and Sarah all knelt on a ground cloth facing him, paying rapt attention to whatever it was he was saying. His voice traveled clearly up the tunnel to where Elizabeth was standing unnoticed in the shadows, and since their activity seemed innocent enough, she decided to remain where she was until there was a break in the conversation.

"You'll each go and gather a couple of rocks to build a fireplace," CC instructed them, "and bring them back here." He rose to his feet, took a stick, and drew a circle in the dirt. "You'll need to dig down here to make certain that there are no leaves or roots that might catch on fire. When you are satisfied with that, you'll build a low wall, maybe two feet in diameter, to contain the fire. Do you understand?"

He received one 'uh huh,' one smile, and one head shake.

"Before you start that little project," he went on, "I want to talk to you for a few minutes about the importance of what we're really doing here."

Rachel and Sarah looked at him with raised eyebrows, while Jonathan blurted, "You're teaching us to build a fire, right?"

"Hopefully," CC smiled. Then his face took on a serious mien. "There is much more than a simple lesson here. It may not have occurred to you, but thousands, even millions of survivors may die this year simply because they do not know how to accomplish this one simple task. They are worn down, malnourished, unable to beat back the cold. And many are very discouraged."

"The two youngsters became more serious, and Rachel's eyes took on a pensive look. Elizabeth thought she understood CC's point. *Had it not been for my ability to build campfires, as well as my skill in finding suitable shelters, I would probably be lying out there somewhere, either seriously ill or dead.* CC's campfire training had suddenly taken on a new importance to all of them, and Elizabeth wondered, *How many other skills must I learn to assure my survival? Dumb question. I can't assure my survival. Only God can.*

CC had continued speaking to his little class, and the avid attention they were paying made it obvious that they respected and trusted him. He spoke to them of the benefits and dangers of fire, and of how the human race had used fire both to build and destroy.

Then he took them through the steps of building a proper campfire, explaining the importance of protecting the environment, and of being able to survive in the worst weather. Finally, he told them that he expected them to be able to teach others in order to help them survive. "This," he emphasized, "is the most important thing — to prepare yourself to help others." Then he sent them off to begin gathering rocks for their fireplace, and for the other materials with which they'd build their fire.

When they'd finally gathered and assembled the kindling and heavier materials, and were ready to light them, CC thrilled little Sarah by handing her a match. After she had lit the kindling, and the fire began blazing merrily, he glanced out across the clearing, then seemed to freeze in place.

Rachel followed his fixed gaze, and noted that the rising sun had driven away the fog and was throwing long shadows across the snow. She became concerned when she saw CC stumble forward a couple of steps, his face going from ruddy to white. He seemed unable to accept what he was seeing.

To CC, a world which a moment before had been full of promise, had become an impossibly dangerous place. All thoughts of fire-building had dissipated with the fog.

Elizabeth lifted her eyes to see whatever it was that had upset him. It took her a moment to identify what they were looking at. Out beneath the trees she saw dark stains in the snow. As she studied them, she realized that they were actually melting footprints that trailed out across the meadow and into the trees. She lowered her eyes to examine where the footprints had their origin, then followed the trail back almost to the cave entrance where the four fire builders were standing. Kept to the windswept mulch at the base of the cliff, and then walked boldly out across the snow into the valley.

CC was stunned. To a pilot flying over the valley, those tracks in the snow would be like an arrow pointing directly back toward their hideaway. And since planes occasionally flew over the valley, he had little doubt that there were searchers out looking for them. The only hope his little community had at this moment would be that either the snow would melt quickly, obliterating the tracks, or that more snow would fall immediately and cover the footprints. Both possibilities seemed remote.

CC stood pondering the tracks in the snow for almost a minute, his jaws working. Then he seemed to come to himself, and ordered the others to help him smother their fire with snow. He told his disappointed students that they'd have to finish their lesson another day. Then they followed him inside.

When they returned to the motor home, they found Elizabeth, an innocent expression on her face, drinking coffee in the kitchen. A quick search revealed that McCord was nowhere to be found.

Absent Without Leave (AWOL)

The Motor Home
Hidden Valley Cavern
December 26th, 9:45 a.m.

J ust two days after he and Ross had stumbled upon CC's cavern, McCord was missing.

At first, no one would admit to having seen him leave. Elizabeth finally suggested that he might have been planning to return to their cave in order to retrieve something. When she implied that she was confident that he would return, and that he wouldn't turn them in to the enemy, CC asked for a justification for what he considered her misplaced confidence. When she sought to avoid answering, he became angry.

CC was furious with himself for letting down his guard, and realized that he'd have to calm down and begin to think rationally if he were to have any chance of controlling the outcome. Once again, with everyone but McCord sitting around the table in the motor home, he was trying to figure out just what was going on, and then appraise their chances.

"McCord seems like an opportunist to me," CC observed quietly. "Since he left here without so much as a 'by-your-leave,' I wouldn't trust him any further than I could throw him."

He gnawed his lip, gazing off into space, then turned to stare fixedly at Ross. "So," he asked, "what do you know that we don't know that would cause you to reach such a conclusion? In other words, why do you think he will return, and why do you think he won't turn us in?"

"I don't know," she answered, shrugging her shoulders, her nervousness apparent. "I've only known him a short time, but I just don't think that in these circumstance he'd do that. At least I hope not."

"Indeed? And if our enemies haven't made him a good enough offer, perhaps Mr. McCord had something else in mind?"

Elizabeth was clasping and unclasping her hands, and made no attempt to reply.

Then CC snapped his fingers, his lips turning up in a cynical smile, as he again turned to her. When she sensed his eyes on her, she turned to look stonily back at him.

"What?" she asked defiantly.

"What's in your cave that's more valuable to McCord than the reward he'd receive for turning us in to the Chinese?"

"I don't know." Her answer came a bit too quickly to be convincing.

Even to the ears of the others, it came out more like, *If I knew, I wouldn't tell you.*

CC spoke very slowly, pronouncing ever word carefully. "Elizabeth, we can't afford any useless mouths here." After a moment, he added, "Or anyone who's working at cross purposes with us."

Her lower lip quivered slightly, and it took her a moment to respond, because suddenly she realized how important it had become to her to remain here. "What do you mean?"

"I mean that we can't afford the manpower and precious resources necessary to feed someone who we have to lock up in order to keep them from endangering us."

"Well, if you don't want me here, I guess I'll have to be on my way," she blustered.

"Hardly." He clipped his words. "You must realize that we can't risk having people running around the countryside sho know about this place and who do not share our values and concerns. To put a point to it, individuals like you who might pose a threat to our survival."

She looked up, trying to hide the shock in her eyes. "You are not savages. You can't mean what you're implying. I don't believe you!"

"These are not normal times."

"You wouldn't dare. I don't believe you," she repeated. Then a perceptive comment.

"You couldn't. "You're not that kind of man."

CC knew she was right, but covered his bluff well. He turned to his right and lifted little Sarah onto his lap. Then he gestured to Jonathan and Rachel, who were hanging on every word, neither of them quite certain whether he meant what they thought he had implied.

"You just don't understand, do you?" he challenged. "This is one time when I'd invoke the ungodly philosophy that the individual should be sacrificed for the good of the community."

Elizabeth's face paled as she muttered, "Oh, my God!"

The others looked down, but no one spoke.

After finding every face turned away, Elizabeth realized that they believed that CC might very well carry through on his threat. Her thoughts raced.

McCord is the wild card in the deck. He's gone, and I really don't know what he might do, or whether he'll keep his promise to me to come back. And he doesn't need me to carry out his plans. In fact, he will undoubtedly examine the things I wanted him to bring me, and might decide to keep them for himself. Worse, he might irreparably damage them. And if he doesn't return soon, there is no telling what will happen to me. Yet, how much more do I dare to divulge to this man? He's already indicated that he seems willing to kill me.

She bit her lip, shaking her head slightly as though trying to negate this possibility, trying to come up with some reply, while CC remained mute. Then she decided, *When in doubt, tell the truth. It doesn't look like it will cost me anything to keep some of my secrets, and it might cost a great deal if I divulge them, so I'll tell the truth, but only some of the truth.*

"Okay," she said, "I'll tell you what I know."

"Well, let me suggest," CC warned, biting off his words, "that it's pretty late in the game for you to do any more dissembling."

What is he doing, reading my mind?

"I understand." She began worrying her lower lip, on the verge of tears, but trying to concentrate on framing her next words.

"All right," she surrendered. She looked down for a moment. Then, chin firmly set, she looked up into his eyes with her characteristic boldness. "I think McCord went back to his cave to get something he considers valuable. I don't think he trusts those other people, the Chinese or the Islamic terrorists, any more than we do. That's why I'm hopeful that he'll bring it back here."

CC had tried to imagine any thing that was more valuable in these times than isolation, food and shelter. He stared at her, his anger palpable.

"How stupid!" he fumed. "Nothing that he or you might have left in that cave could be worth compromising the location of our hideaway." *Not jewels or even gold,* he thought. *And, unless he's an addict, not drugs or alcohol. It just doesn't make sense.* He decided to push her.

"And just what might that valuable something be," he pursued, bitterness in his voice."

Elizabeth was slow in replying.

"I don't want to have to pull these answers out of you a question at a time." CC had been trying to ignore the fact that McCord might, at that very moment, be divulging their whereabouts to the bad guys, so he would have very little time to get his little family safely away with enough food and equipment to give them even the slimmest chance of survival. And, he admitted to himself, the odds against them surviving were enormous. Even while he was filtering those thoughts, his attention was focused on Elizabeth's reply.

"I don't know what that valuable thing might be," she told him. She reasoned to herself that she wasn't really lying. Mc-

Cord might actually have something of his own that he considered valuable that she didn't know about. So it was sort of a half-truth.

What she did realize was that she'd been a fool to trust him. She should have returned to the cave with him instead of letting him talk her into trying to cover for him during his absence. Better yet, she should have left the objects where they were.

Picking up on her hesitation, CC suspected the truth, but decided not to challenge her.

"What surprises me is that you would trust him enough to let him return alone to get it."

He is reading my mind!

"Whatever the case," he went on, "I intend to have you locked away by the time McCord returns, and unless he is able to hide the item or items before that time, I plan to examine whatever he brings back very carefully. I will not allow our home to be further endangered by permitting anything our enemies might consider valuable to be kept anywhere in the valley.

Elizabeth's eyes followed CC's hand as he unconsciously touched the handgun holstered on his belt. It was obvious that he no longer trusted her any more than he trusted McCord. She opened her mouth to say something, swallowed hard, then turned away.

"What," CC demanded.

"There is something." She bit her lip and avoided his eyes.

"I thought so, but so what?" There was the glint of suspicion in his eyes, but it seemed clear that he'd already made some sort of decision. "Even if there is anything of value, why would you go after it now?"

She gulped. *He obviously considers me in partnership with McCord. And in a sense he's right.*

"Whatever it is, it was probably safer where you'd hidden it than it will be here. Valuable or not, all you've done is provide a clear path for any potential thief to follow."

Elizabeth's lips curved down in defeat, and she nodded her head in grudging agreement.

"It was stupid," she acknowledged. "I realize that now."

CC shrugged her words away. He was surprised that she'd make such a confession, and concluded charitably that she probably didn't have any more control over McCord's actions than he did.

In an attempt to deflect his anger from herself, she said, "I only know that he thinks the items I brought along might be valuable, and he told me that we need to guard everything from somebody named Joseph Sennett."

"Joseph Sennett?" CC's mind raced. *What does McCord know about Joseph Sennett?*

"Look," he replied. "It's true that a Joseph Sennett once lived in this valley, but he's dead."

"Joseph Sennett lived here? And he's dead?" It was Rachel, and there was no questioning the shock and sorrow in her voice.

"Well, a man named Joseph Sennett lived here. I don't know whether he is the one you are referring to, but no matter what McCord returned to your cave to pick up, it isn't worth giving our location away."

"Some things are worth any risk," Elizabeth countered.

"Some things, perhaps, but not what you or he are likely to value."

"It's not a question of what we value. It's a question of its value to others...to America. And to what lengths to which I...correction, to which we are justified in going to keep it safe from our enemies."

"Well, that's certainly a bold claim."

"Yes, I suppose it sounds far-fetched. But consider this. Jim claims he has a list of the leaders of various forces who, independent of one another, are trying to take over our country, including Muslims, Chinese, and Soviets — and he assured me that his information he went to retrieve is vital." She really doubted that McCord had anything of importance, but she knew that she did.

"Then all he has is something useless to us, but so important to our enemies that they'd stop at nothing to get their hands on it, is that it?" His eyes opened wide, as though he'd just realized something. "Wait a moment! Are you suggesting that you both have something that is of interest to the bad guys, and that neither of you knows what the other has?"

When she didn't respond, CC pressed on. "Okay, you say that he assured you he has a list of names?" CC looked at her, his anger and unbelief getting the better of him. Something had finally clicked.

"So you knew he was going, and you didn't warn me?" His mind was racing. "And if McCord has such a list, why didn't he leave it with some trustworthy official somewhere along his route, say in Washington, Baltimore, or even Plattsburgh? Or, for that matter, why'd he come this way at all? And why in the world would that old man, Joseph Sennett, have been interested in such a list?"

"I don't know anything about any old man," Elizabeth whispered, tears appearing at the corners of her eyes. "The Joseph Sennett that cut me loose was a young man.

Rachel interrupted, a forced smile on her face. "CC, it isn't going to do any good to badger her. Can't you see that she's confused and sorry?"

CC almost snapped at her, but reigned himself in, realizing that she might be right. He moderated his tone. "That may well be, but our lives are now at stake."

Rachel nodded silent assent. Sarah started to cry, and Rachel hugged her, giving CC a poisonous look. He lifted his hands, palm up, then shook his head in frustration. *I've frightened Sarah, and now I'm the bad guy.*

Nonetheless, he heeded Rachel's censure and ceased his questioning for the moment.

"Well," he thought aloud, "we can't follow McCord, or we'll just leave more tracks. We'll have to hope that it snows." The tone of his voice made it clear that he didn't expect snow any time soon.

His frustration was obvious. "If I'd known McCord felt that he had to leave, I could at least have shown him a much safer way to go."

In a soft voice, Rachel asked, "Would you have let him go?"

CC sighed. "No, probably not."

"Isn't there anything that we can do?" she asked.

He had been groping for a solution. "My boots are about the same size as that pair that Jim stole from storage. I'll walk up to the farm."

Her surprise was evident in her expression.

"There's a farm in the southwest corner of the canyon," he explained.. The Chinese know it's there. They've already burned the house." He couldn't hide his anger over that terrible waste. "It was Sarah's home."

"I'm thinking of walking out across the valley stepping in McCord's footsteps. When I come to the place where he passed under a tree, I'll change direction and walk up to the farm. I'll try to make it look like he made a round trip from the lower end of the valley, out to the farm, over here to the caves, and back down the valley. I can only hope it fools anyone flying over." He could see from their expressions that they weren't following him.

"Since McCord's footprints will go 'round trip down the valley, and mine will go round trip to the farm, a casual tracker may not realize the tracks really started or ended here. He hesitated, trying to reason it out. "It's a risk, but it's the best I can do."

He turned to Jonathan. "Get a broom, and drift the dust around in the tunnel. Make sure there are no foot prints on the floor of the entry cave. Do what you can to hide the damaged doorway in the fake wall. Oh, and move the ashes left from the fire that Ross and McCord started in the cave. Throw them into the little fire ring that the three of you just built. If anyone follows Jim's tracks, maybe they'll think he just stopped here to get warm."

"Right away, CC."

"Then all of you get back into the cavern and keep the noise down."

CC knew that it was already probably too late.

McCord has left a tell-tale path across the valley, and the pilot of any small plane or any remote-controlled drone might already have spotted his trail. If I add new tracks, it will simply indicate a high level of activity in the valley. Much too high!

Then he thought, *Not good! I need to rethink my idea about making more tracks. It's probably a waste of time, and might only make things worse, especially if I'm spotted.*

"Time's too short," he muttered. "I'm not going out there. McCord could be in the act of betraying us right now."

"Rachel, he asked, once again decisive, "would you please take Sarah, and gather up freeze-dried foods, sleeping bags, first-aid supplies, and some cooking gear, along with rifles, ammunition, and anything else you think we might need if we have to run? Sarah will help you find them."

He looked at Jonathan and smiled. "As soon as you're done disguising the cave, you know the place to take them. Help them carry everything deep into the caverns where it will be handy if we have to get out of here. Okay?"

Jonathan nodded his head, "Sure." He pointed at Elizabeth. "What about her?"

"She's going to wait right here, tied to this swivel chair. Get some of those long plastic wire ties, and we'll bind her ankles and wrists."

The boy opened a kitchen drawer and removed a half dozen of the ties. After he handed them to CC, he headed for the tunnel entrance to clean up the mess.

Elizabeth was both furious and frightened, but she realized that it was pointless to resist the inevitable. "Okay," she said, "I'll stay here and promise to be quiet, and maybe that will prove to you whose side I'm on."

CC stared at her for a moment. "It might help," he agreed grudgingly. Then he relented. "If you'll promise me not to leave the motor home, and not to warn McCord, I'll leave you untied."

"I promise," she told him, and then she thought with a sense of enormous relief, *This is the man who threatened to kill me. Ha!*

A few minutes later, armed with a rifle, CC exited the tunnel into the valley. *Talk about a double-minded man being unstable in all his ways,* he thought. *Here I am wandering around the valley, when at any moment McCord might come back with a gang of his friends.*

The snow formed a pristine blanket of white against the backdrop of cliffs and trees. Pristine, that is, except for that set of footprints that formed deep blue shadows in the bright sunlight that marched out across the valley.

Broom in hand, Jonathan had followed him out into the tunnel. "I thought you decided not to walk around the valley after all."

As CC moved off across the small meadow, he shouted, "I'm just going to the edge of these woods to see if anyone is out there. I'll stay under cover."

"Ah, good idea."

"Do your best to clean up that false wall."

As Jonathan turned back into the cave, CC disappeared among the trees.

When Jonathan returned to the motor home twenty minutes later, he found Elizabeth untied. He forced her at gunpoint to sit back on the chair while he bound her wrists to the chair's arms. Her protests that CC had left her untied did nothing to sway the teen.

The Mysterious Portfolio

Motor Home
December 28th, 1 p.m.

W hen CC returned from surveying the valley, he was in an even worse mood, but felt better when he found that Elizabeth had evidently kept her promise and remained in the motor home.

He stood unnoticed on the cave floor, peering through the screen door, trying to understand what was going on. Then he noticed McCord sitting in the shadows on the swivel chair, his gaze intent on Elizabeth.

She was unbuckling the straps on a backpack that CC hadn't seen before. It was a high-priced rig, and she was unfastening a portfolio that was strapped to the back of it. The portfolio was large, over two feet high and nearly three feet long, and nearly three inches thick.

He knew that the two of them didn't have that portfolio with them when they'd arrived two days earlier, so it must have been among the items that McCord had carried back from their cave.

I wonder why he'd bothered bringing that back for Ross. And I wonder what he brought back of his own. CC's eyes widened when it came to him that she might have stolen a painting from her museum.

She finished unbuckling the various straps that secured the portfolio to the backpack, then, with a grunt, handed the backpack to McCord who immediately opened one of the zippered pouches on the side in order to check the contents.

Evidently the backpack belongs to McCord, CC concluded. *I wonder what he's got in there. It doesn't look like Ross knows. Maybe she does, and considers it none of her business.*

As she straightened up in her chair, the portfolio balanced across her knees, she noticed CC's reflection in a wall mirror. She turned so quickly that the portfolio slipped to the floor. She bent quickly to recover it, snugging it to her breasts.

CC opened the screen door and stepped up into the motor home. At the same time, McCord leaned forward from where he was seated, and gave CC an arrogant smile. Then he leaned back against the cushions, a smug expression on his face, as though dismissing CC's presence as unimportant.

Jonathan stepped up into the motor home and stood behind CC.

"What's in the packs?" CC asked quietly.

"None of your business," Ross snapped. Her response was out of character for someone who, just a half-hour before, had supposedly been concerned about her relationship with the group.

There was a metallic whirring noise from the chair, and CC turned to see McCord spinning the cylinder on a revolver.

"She wouldn't tell me either," he said, "but I have little doubt that she's walked off with some priceless painting from her art museum."

His tone was condescending, the voice of an opportunist who'd willingly turn against one acquaintance to gain advantage with another who might possibly have more to offer.

As he leveled this accusation, he also leveled his revolver at CC and said, "Bang, bang. You're dead." At the same time he used his heel to push his own knapsack into the shadows between the swivel chair and the motor home wall.

"Where did you get the gun?" CC asked in a cold voice. *Stupid question,* he thought. *It's obvious that he picked it up at his cave, and now he intends to intimidate me with it. Or worse.*

His thoughts were interrupted by the sound of a cartridge being slammed into the chamber of a shotgun, and he couldn't help smiling as McCord swiveled his head toward Jonathan. The teen had been standing behind CC, but had moved off to his side, and was pointing a 12-gauge at McCord's midriff.

"Hey, kid," McCord warned, "you'd better watch it. This isn't a toy I'm holding."

"Someone once told me that you shouldn't point a gun unless you plan to shoot it," the boy retorted. Unless you plan to shoot that pistol, you'd better not still be holding it by the time I count to three," the teen warned. "Set it down on the floor, now," he commanded, "or I'm going to pull the trigger."

"McCord aimed the pistol at the boy," and CC took a step to his left, drawing his own automatic from the small of his back and leveling it at McCord.

Jonathan laughed, and McCord looked surprised.

"That looks like a 32-caliber revolver you're holding," Jonathan replied. "And this is a 12-gauge automatic shotgun, loaded with six rounds, each round containing eight pellets of double-ought buckshot."

"So?"

The teenager shook his head. "Each of the eight pellets is the same caliber as the one round in your chamber. That's eight pellets! Each of these pellets is about the same size as one of your bullets. You might hit me," he calmly told McCord, "but these will spread enough so that there's no way I'll miss you."

"Maybe I'm willing to take the chance."

"And since this is a semi-automatic," the boy went on as though not hearing him, "I just pull the trigger as fast as I can."

"And if Jonathan should by some stretch of the imagination miss you, I definitely won't," CC added. He didn't think McCord would take the risk, but he added, "Maybe you'd better do what Jonathan told you, and slowly and carefully set that revolver on the floor."

When McCord finally complied, CC stepped forward, hooked the gun with the toe of his shoe, and slid it across the floor out of his reach.

"I cannot believe you would do something as stupid as draw a weapon against us."

"I assure you," McCord said, "that you were not in danger."

"Really? What was that you said, 'Bang, bang; you're dead?'"

McCord shrugged his shoulders. "It was a joke."

"Sure it was," Elizabeth interjected, her sarcasm heavy, expressing the feelings of everyone else in the room.

"I'm sure you remember," CC went on, "that I forbade you to touch any weapon."

McCord didn't acknowledge his statement, but in an attempt to deflect their anger, McCord pointed at Ross. "She has more explaining to do than I have."

Elizabeth was glaring at McCord, bitter denial in her glance. "I didn't threaten anyone's life," she said. And then with what sounded like great sincerity, she added, "My fondest wish is to become part of this little group."

"Maybe they don't want someone who is a liar and a thief."

"I'm not a thief!"

"How do you explain the paintings in that portfolio?"

I didn't steal any paintings," she said evenly, "but I admit that I am sorry that someone couldn't have rescued all those magnificent works of art. They're probably all ruined by now."

"Ruined?" Rachel had just entered the motor home, slipping around CC to find a place out of the way at the table.

"Yes. Without electricity, the pumps that kept that underground vault dry will have stopped operating, and I have no doubt that everything down there is now immersed in ten or fifteen feet of muddy water, probably forever."

She turned to CC. "I didn't steal any paintings, so you can just forget that." Turning back to McCord, she almost hissed, "Some friend you turned out to be!"

McCord looked back at her, his mouth drawn in contempt. "There's never been anything between us except the need to cooperate for mutual survival."

"Yes, and I did all the co-operating," she snapped.

CC wrapped his fingers around McCord's upper arm. Pointing at her portfolio, he asked, "Wasn't it you that brought that here?"

Jim yanked his arm free, his eyes fixed on Elizabeth.

"Yes, but now I regret it."

"Why?" CC asked. "Do you know what's in it?"

"No," he replied, even more caustically.

"Why not?"

"She asked me to bring it back to keep it from being damaged by the cold. I just figured it must be valuable or she wouldn't have been dragging it around with her."

"You didn't answer my question. Why don't you know what's in it?"

"I didn't look."

"That doesn't make sense," CC countered. "You told us that you were a spy, and that you examined everything that interested you on the Internet. And now you expect us to believe you lacked the curiosity to look inside that portfolio?" CC laughed. "As a supposed spy, and as an unscrupulous opportunist, your curiosity would have compelled you to look inside the case."

"All right! So I looked, but whatever is in there is heat-sealed in a plastic wrap, and I could see foil and some kind of foam board under that, and I figured if she packed it that way, it might damage whatever it is if I broke the seal."

"Thank God!" Elizabeth whispered.

"Besides, it has no value to me. There's not much of a market for works of art right now, in case you haven't noticed. Besides, I didn't think there was any need. If she stole a painting, it is undoubtedly one of the finest. And if a market for rare paintings should develop, well, time will tell what happens to any artwork that she may have stolen."

Elizabeth's eyes widened. "Those words suggest that you mean to wind up with whatever's in here."

"I didn't say that," but a sly smile made his intentions clear.

Jonathan turned to CC. "Did you cut Elizabeth loose?"

"No, I left her untied."

"Oops." The teen was chagrined. "I didn't believe her when she told me you'd left her loose."

"So you tied her?"

"Yes."

"Then who untied her?" He looked at McCord. "You?"

"Yeah, what of it?"

"You seem to have an unusual relationship, sort of 'love-hate'."

"Again, what of it?"

"You don't understand, do you?" CC asked incredulously.

"Understand what?"

"This little community has to be based on trust. And when, for example, you do such things as take off without permission, endangering us all, or set your co-conspirator free, then point a revolver at me, I can no longer trust you.

"So?"

"So! So, it indicates that we dare not allow you to stay with us." Before he could elaborate, another scene began to be played out across the room.

Jonathan leaned over and started to unzip the portfolio that Elizabeth held in her arms.

"Don't open that!" she shouted. Without rising from the chair, McCord leaned forward, grasped a handful of her hair, and jerked her head back, providing Jonathan the opportunity to snatch the portfolio from her hands and move it to the table.

"Please," she pleaded, almost in tears. "Please, you'll damage them." She turned to slap McCord in the face, causing him to release her hair, and was across the small room in two steps, struggling to wrest the portfolio from Jonathan's grasp.

She looked at CC, tears in her eyes. "Don't let them open it," she begged.

He turned to McCord, his hand raised, ready to backhand him. "Don't touch her again. Don't ever touch anyone here!"

McCord sneered at him, but leaned back out of his reach.

Almost in the same breath, CC ordered Jonathan, "Leave it alone."

The teen immediately set the portfolio down on the table top, raising his hands palm outward to indicate his acquiescence.

McCord immediately rose, stepped between them, snatched it off the table, backed up to the chair, sat down, searched for the zipper, and began to open it. The familiar zipping sound was drowned out by the metallic sound of a handgun being cocked, and McCord's hands immediately ceased their movement. He looked up to discover CC holding the muzzle of the weapon just inches from his ear.

CC stepped in front of him with his left hand extended, and McCord very carefully hooked the handle of the portfolio over his fingers. Then he put his hands in his lap, commenting, "Once again, I prove that 'might makes right.'"

CC ignored him, and held the portfolio out to Elizabeth. With a smile of gratitude, she took it from him, and leaned it against her knees on the floor. He stared at her for a full minute, the pulse in his temple visible, revealing that his patience was razor-thin.

"All right," he asked, "what's in the case and why can't we open it?"

She hesitated a long moment before framing her reply.

"Okay, first the reason for not opening it." Her fingers drummed on the portfolio until she noticed that everyone was looking at her, and she forced herself to sit still. "I had to wrap the contents so that they wouldn't be destroyed by exposure to air."

"Why in the world for," CC asked.

"I don't understand either," Rachel said. "Why all that special packaging?"

"They are very delicate," she explained.

"I bet I know," Jonathan interjected, but CC's frown silenced him.

Elizabeth's answer was succinct. "If they are exposed to air, they will probably crumble."

"Never mind that. I want to know what you've got there."

"I know, I know!" Jonathan shouted, unable to contain himself, and holding up his hand for permission to speak.

Annoyed more with Elizabeth than with Jonathan, CC nodded tolerantly at the boy.

"I saw an article in a newspaper about a year ago, and asked my father if we could go to Boston to see them."

"See what?" CC demanded, still irritated, but now curious in spite of himself.

Elizabeth, realizing that Jonathan did in fact probably know what was in her portfolio, and that there was no advantage in refusing to answer, opened her mouth to speak, but not before the boy blurted out his incredible revelation. "She has the *Declaration of Independence!*"

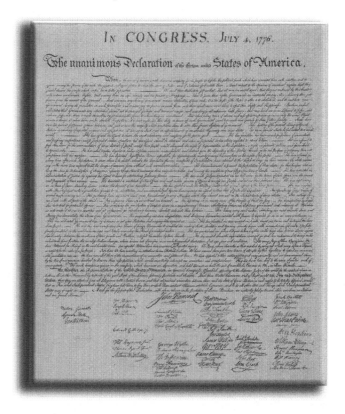

Not knowing how to react to Jonathan's words, Rachel's mouth dropped open in unbelief, and Jim, for some unknown reason, laughed aloud.

CC was staring down at Elizabeth. "That's not possible. The original *Declaration* is in the National Archives in Washington. I've seen it. At least, it seems to me that I remember seeing it there."

But searching Elizabeth's face, CC realized that as incredible as it sounded, she might actually have the document in her possession. In a tone of unbelief, he asked, "You actually have the original signed copy of the *Declaration of Independence* in that case?"

"More than that," she replied. "I not only have the original autograph of the *Declaration of Independence*, but I also have all four pages of the *Constitution*."

"But, why, how?" he stammered.

"The documents were in the basement where I was working, scheduled to be displayed at the museum the day following the attack." She looked around. "For me as an individual, they had no special monetary value, but," and she leaned down to wrap her arms around the case, "for me as an American, they are now more valuable than all the masterpieces in the world."

"So," McCord challenged, "you stole them."

"Don't be absurd," she countered. "With the electricity off, they'd have been destroyed within a few days." She shook her head in anger at his willful stupidity. "I didn't steal them, idiot. I saved them!"

For a moment, everyone was too stunned to speak, but CC's exhalation turned into a low whistle.

Jim muttered something under his breath.

CC turned to him. "What did you say?"

"I just realized that everybody playing tug of war over the future of the United States would love to get their hands on those."

"Who do you mean," Rachel asked. "Why?"

"The Chinese and Russian communists, as well as the radical Muslims, would all love to get hold of those documents."

Jonathan showed his surprise. "What would they want with our Constitution?"

"It's in their interests to destroy anything and everything related to our political and historic traditions," McCord pointed out. "Although I'm an atheist, I'm realistic enough to recognize that Christian traditions and the rule of law were vital to our survival, and our own leaders have pretty much gotten rid of those. Apart from their efforts to crush Christianity, which they understand breeds a hunger for freedom in people's hearts, those documents would certainly top the list of things to destroy. It's more than lip service to say that those documents undergirded our way of life."

"I studied political science, but I guess I still don't understand," Rachel persisted.

"Consider the wording," and McCord began reciting aloud.

"When in the Course of human events it becomes necessary for one people to dissolve the political bands which have connected them with another and to assume among the powers of the earth, the separate and equal station to which the Laws of Nature and of Nature's God entitle them...."

"Did you hear me? They wrote 'Nature's God.' So, no, I've never been more serious."

"I see," enjoined CC. "In the eyes of a depraved world, that document melds God, country and freedom."

McCord seemed to have forgotten his anger and was getting into the moment. "One doesn't have to agree with the sentiments expressed in those documents to appreciate the power that those ideas might have over little minds."

CC looked at him. "Little minds? Those documents were the product of some of the greatest minds in history!"

McCord went blithely on. "The Chinese are subtle," he observed. "As a people that prides itself on thousands of years of their own traditions, they recognize the importance of history and tradition in the life of any nation. As you know, over the past few decades, the debate over the constitutionality of every law we pass has become more and more heated, and it was even suggested by one president that we scrap the Constitution itself."

"Yes, and he did everything he could to circumvent it," CC conceded softly.

"Those documents, if indeed they are genuine," McCord suggested, as he pointed at the portfolio now wrapped protectively in Elizabeth 's arms, "have greater intrinsic value now than at any time in our history. They could become a rallying point for any counter-insurgency. More than that, they symbolize American history and serve as the foundation for its future."

McCord was waxing eloquent, but CC couldn't help but notice that he was separating himself not just from God and from this document, but from the United States. Yet no one in the room could disagree with McCord's suppositions.

"Without those documents," McCord concluded, "Americans cannot prove to future generations that they ever even existed."

Jonathan asked, "What about all the books?"

"What books?"

"You know, history books and school books. They all talk about the Constitution. Some even have pictures of the documents, and there are countless facsimiles."

McCord's shook his head. "So what?" Extending his hands, palms upward, he declared, "People burn books! It's no secret that the Muslims burned the ancient library at Alexandria during the first millennium after Christ. The Nazis burned books. The Chinese and Muslims destroy every copy of the Christian Bible and the Hebrew Torah they can get their hands on. People in America burned their own flag. What's to stop America's enemies from burning what's left of the libraries, or at least the books they find offensive to their views?"

"The question of who burned the greatest library of antiquity is disputed," CC remarked.

McCord shook his head. "These invaders include the Taliban who not too long ago blew up the gigantic 2,000-year-old Buddhas in Afghanistan and leveled entire historic sites. They will stop at nothing to obliterate every religion but their own. It ought to be obvious that whoever has sufficient power can rewrite history with impunity."

"Think back," he challenged. "Remember those so-called "freedom fighters" that a past president helped to overthrow their governments. They went on to create radical Islamic regimes throughout the middle east, establishing Shariah Law, pursuing ethnic cleansing, and ridding those lands of any religious and political views not in keeping with their Islamic doctrines. Whether or not you agree with me about the intentions of the Russians, Chinese, or Muslims, you'd better understand this."

McCord walked over to where Elizabeth was sitting, and dramatically pointed his index finger at the portfolio. "You cannot overestimate the importance of these documents, nor the danger that their presence represents."

McCord looked at Elizabeth, a frown on his face. "In a way, it would have been better if you had stolen priceless works of art. Instead, you risked your life to preserve something which, because it is of inestimable political value both to America and its enemies, places us all in grave danger."

He turned his attention to CC. "You must find a way to get these to one of the invaders so that they won't be pursuing us."

The idea was repugnant. Even if the likelihood of their shaking off pursuit by numerous enemies seemed absurd, they must try to do so. CC didn't bother dignifying McCord's absurd suggestion with a response.

Instead, he smiled at the group. "It does put us in a fine fettle, doesn't it?"

"Yes, it does," McCord responded, leaving everyone else wondering at the turn of events. But McCord persisted, not realizing that CC had no intention of passing those documents to an enemy.

"They were already searching for you. And now, anyone that suspects those documents exist, and that they are in this part of Vermont, will put their priority on locating them, which means finding the rest of us."

Already focused on the documents, CC evidently missed the significance of McCord's remark about his own danger.

"I'm not sure we should be so concerned," CC said. "These documents will be extremely difficult for anyone to trace. Many of those people who would remember that the documents were in Boston would have died as a result of the attacks. Others might not remember or care. Those who might know are un-likely to speak with anyone interested in finding them. And if any of the museum's employees survived, it's unlikely that they'll return there. And if anyone does return to the museum, they will probably be more interested in the paintings than the docu-ment."

He sat down at the table. "One more thought," he added. "Who would know that Elizabeth worked there, or indeed that she survived, let alone that she took the documents? In fact, I doubt that anyone is apt to get down below the street level and find that room. It might, as she said, be flooded, and if so, it will be assumed that these documents are submerged and unsal-vageable."

He paused, pondering the possibilities. "I simply can't imagine that anyone has survived that would know of Eliza-beth's access to them."

McCord shook his head. "I suppose it's the greatest piece of luck for you when you consider it."

"How so?" CC asked.

"It's fortunate that she has withdrawn them from the imme-diate access of the Chinese and the Islamic terrorists, but it's also helpful that they are in the hands of someone who knows their value and is qualified by education and training to preserve them."

"And the Russians?" CC reminded him.

"Huh? Oh sure, right, and the Russians."

McCords failure to mention the Russians somehow acted on CC's mind as though someone had waved a red flag before a bull. Or a red star before a liberty-loving American.

"The Chinese and Russians have been cooperating on a limited scale for quite some time," CC reflected, "though they've been on-again, off-again enemies for centuries."

"Nonsense," McCord retorted.

"Nonsense? Even you must be aware that not too many years ago the Chinese and Russian navies partnered for the largest joint naval drill in history."

"It's true," Rachel agreed. And moving from that macrocosm to this microcosm, these documents become more vital. They could be the rallying point for a nation that feels itself defeated."

Jim nodded his head in grudging agreement. "My point exactly, but we're all apt to wind up dead in a failed attempt to save them."

Elizabeth made a sort of choking sound.

"What?" CC asked, in a far more solicitous tone than before.

"I'm afraid that your confidence in my anonymity may be a bit overblown."

CC smiled. "How so? As a matter of fact, I've been breathing a lot easier since these thoughts occurred to me."

"Well..." Ross began, but didn't complete the thought.

"What?" CC persisted, with a touch of uneasiness in his voice. He grew impatient as he waited for her to respond.

"Well," Elizabeth finally replied in a voice that was flat and lifeless, "I spray-painted a message on the wall of the museum lobby before I left."

"You what?"

Her head was down now, and they had to strain to hear her words.

"I was removing the state papers, and I wanted to make certain that any authorities searching for them would know that they were in competent hands."

Everyone simply stared at her, waiting for the other shoe to drop.

"In big letters, I painted, *Curator Elizabeth Ross has removed the state papers for safekeeping, and will return them to the appropriate authorities ASAP.*"

No one spoke. There was obviously no point. Rachel realized that, under the circumstances, Elizabeth's actions would seem appropriate.

CC chose to change the subject. Keeping his voice conversational, he asked, "How have you protected them? They'll be damaged by air, won't they?"

"They're not exposed to air. I placed each document between layers of a soft padding, and sandwiched them between hard sheets of non-flammable art board. Then I shrink-wrapped them in a special plastic, evacuated the air, and replaced it with argon gas. After that I wrapped all the individually packaged documents into one bundle using bubble wrap, and put them in the portfolio. That's probably why Jim thought I had paintings, because the entire package is so thick." She frowned. "And that's all you would see if you opened the portfolio."

Holding it across her knees, she tapped on it with her fingers. "The packaging is effective, but laughingly fragile. That's why it's vital that no one touches them. They must be stored at room temperature in normal humidity and air pressure in order to keep the plastic seals from leaking the argon. And as soon as possible they must be put back in special gas-filled cabinets, with the correct atmosphere and preferably little or no lighting. Until then, they should remain untouched."

"Where'd you find the stuff to package them like that?" Jonathan asked.

"We have all that sort of thing in the vault at the museum." She looked down, sorrow clouding her face. "At least we did have those things. And the curators from Washington who accompanied the documents had special materials on hand in case of an emergency." Her thoughts seemed to be drifting. "I used those materials to pack them."

Jonathan touched the small leather satchel that was strapped to the larger portfolio, and she snatched it away.

"Don't touch that."

"I just wondered if it contained the stuff you need to care for the documents."

She hesitated a moment before responding. "Yes, of course. That's precisely what it contains," and some of it is quite fragile, so I don't want anyone touching it." She lowered her voice to speak in a conciliatory tone. "Is that all right, Jonathan?"

"Oh, yeah, sure," he answered, "but it was obvious that even he believed that she was lying about the contents of the package.

Elizabeth turned to CC "I need to find a dark, fairly dry corner, to store them."

He stared at her a moment. Then he sighed, nodding in agreement. "I know just the place. There's another cave that's essentially salt, and it's very dry."

"Salt?"

"Sodium chloride. Table salt. I think the native Americans must have discovered it centuries ago."

"That would be perfect."

McCord spoke up. "I may have been wrong about the paintings, but I still believe you took something valuable from the museum." As he stepped down from the motor home, he shot back, "You're not to be trusted."

"Presumably, neither of us is," Elizabeth muttered under her breath.

Another Unwelcome Visitor

The Outer Cave
December 29th, 5 p.m.

At twilight, a big man made his way up the valley. He was on cross-country skis, carried a light pack on his back and had a massive fifty-caliber bolt-action rifle with a scope slung over his shoulder. He moved easily, propelling himself forward with his two ski poles, obviously following the tracks Jim had left in the snow.

He didn't hesitate, but turned directly toward the caverns where CC was standing watch. He first saw the man as he came out of the woods on the far side of the meadow, and quickly ducked back through the now-repaired secret door, carefully closing and latching it behind him.

The man was wearing a white camouflage smock, and as CC watched him through the small peep hole in the artificial wall, he gave the impression that he knew just what he was about. His eyes kept moving around, searching the terrain and the cliff face, as though he were trying to penetrate the depths of the mountain. He kicked the skis off at the entrance to the tunnel, unslung his oversized sniper rifle, and moved into the cave. As he walked slowly back toward the false wall, he inexplicably smiled. He looked as though he were enjoying some sort of private joke.

CC couldn't understand his strange behavior. He knew that his own camouflage work was excellent, and with the repairs they had made, and even with a good flashlight, the interloper would have difficulty determining that he was looking at a fake wall. Yet he felt as though the man was focusing his eyes through the partition, and staring right at him. CC's fingers clenched the stock of his own rifle, for he realized that this man was familiar with this cave.

The man raised the muzzle of his rifle to waist level, pointed toward the wall behind which CC was standing, then smiled, and said, "Bang, bang!"

CC had the uncanny feeling that the man somehow knew he was there. All he'd have to do would be to kick the wall, and it would be obvious that it wasn't rock.

But instead the man lowered his weapon, and laughed aloud, the sound carrying easily through the thin fiberglass shell. Whistling under his breath, he turned, moved back to the entrance, slung his rifle, bent to pull on his skis, and started through the woods in the direction of the farm.

CC breathed a sigh of relief, but remained where he was until darkness covered the valley. In spite of his relief at the man's departure, he was certain that he'd somehow known that someone was there.

The Crow's Nest
One-year anniversary of war
The Meadow
January 24th, 9 a.m.

I t was an indescribable day, that twenty-fourth of January. The temperature had reached the mid-forties, the sky was the fairest blue, and the evergreens created a glorious splash of blue and green against the pristine snow.

Light breezes occasionally wafted across the remaining drifts, bringing a reminder of the cold that had already invaded the valley, and presaging worse weather yet to come. The air was so crisp and clear, the sun so bright, and the pines so gloriously green that it made CC feel almost happy in spite of his concerns.

He was reveling in the bracing air, seizing this morning to escape the growing oppression of the caverns, and enjoying a brief respite from what promised to be a brutal winter. He was out early, dressed in a heavy wool shirt, flannel-lined canvas work pants, and insulated leather boots. He set a steaming cup of coffee on his chopping block and bit into a fresh croissant.

Who would have imagined, that these two women would exhibit such incredible culinary skills? I've never eaten so well! Life is full of surprises, he thought, *and it is certainly a surprise to walk into the kitchen and find Rachel and Elizabeth up to their elbows in flour, with the smell of baking bread in the air.*

It was a blessing to realize that Elizabeth, who at first had stood apart with seeming contempt for Rachel, was now working side by side, sharing responsibilities.

CC thought that the turning point in their relationship came when the two of them began discussing books, really great books, and Rachel demonstrated in her uniquely modest way that she knew as much about great literature as Elizabeth. What really surprised Elizabeth was that Rachel also knew a good deal about art. From that point on, CC realized, their relationship had blossomed into a warm and growing friendship.

And here he was eating an honest-to-goodness croissant and drinking excellent coffee.

As he stood in the little meadow that lay between the cave and the forest, he realized that he was enjoying one of those rare moments of peace and pleasure that one rarely experiences in the course of an entire lifetime. *And this,* he thought, *in a world turned upside down.* He realized that he was pessimistic about their outlook for the future, and he knew that letting down his guard could prove catastrophic. Yet he also understood that he must not allow himself to labor under that burden, and must make every effort to provide a sense of normalcy for their little community.

Deep in reverie, it took a moment before he realized that someone had spoken to him. When he looked for the speaker, however, there was no one in sight. *Must have been imagining it,* he thought. He picked up the ax to make certain it was sharp, and heard the voice again, this time more distinctly. "Good morning!" It sounded like Jonathan, though there was a hollow sound to the voice.

CC leaned the ax against the chopping block, and with a broad smile on his face began searching the area, this time examining the cave mouth where he assumed the teenager was hiding.

"Where are you?"

"Up here," Jonathan laughed.

CC did an about-face and found himself staring at the base of the giant oak that stood at the edge of the wood. The boy's voice had traveled down the inside of the hollow tree as though through a pipe. CC leaned back and looked up into the branches. Jonathan was waving to him through a hole in the tree's trunk that was about fifty feet above the ground.

"You're up early," CC observed. "Way up!"

"You, too," Jonathan laughed. I wanted to get up early," he punned in turn, "to check the valley."

"See anything?"

Instead of answering, the boy disappeared from the window for a moment. CC knew that he'd moved to the other side of the tree, and was looking down the valley through another opening. From his perch high up in that ancient oak, he could see out over the other trees in the nearby woods. He couldn't see the Sennett farm because it was hidden by the tall pines that surrounded it, but he could see the chimneys of the cement kilns at the upper end of the valley, and, using his binoculars, he could look down the entire length of the valley including the stream and much that lay beyond either shore.

The unusual observation post had been Jonathan's idea. When the teen had first suggested the idea, CC had been preoccupied with installing the new generator, and was not at all sympathetic to starting another ambitious project.

"Hey, CC," Jonathan had called airily, as he torqued down the bolts that held the generator to its new mounts, "why don't we build a sort of a treehouse in that giant oak? We could use it as an observation post."

CC's response was as airy as Jonathan's question had seemed, and completely negative. "Hey, Jonathan. How about not?" Softening his tone, he said, "We've got too many things to do right now to become involved in a dangerous project like that."

Jonathan didn't argue. Instead he cheerfully helped CC finish the electrical power project. When it was time to test the generator out, CC had him open the sluiceway. The big water wheel began to turn, he put the generator in gear, and when the electricity began to flow, and the test lamp lit, they raised their hands in praise to God.

During the days that followed, CC thought nothing more about Jonathan's impractical idea. And after Rachel, Elizabeth, and McCord had come upon the scene, they were all busy with their assigned responsibilities. In addition, they all had their individual hobbies, and since it was winter, few questions were raised about what people did with their free time.

Jonathan had been generous with his own time, operating the saw and other shop tools to help everyone assemble needed furniture, such as benches, tables, and bookcases. Nothing seemed amiss, and CC barely took note of the unusually large pile of sawdust and wood scraps near the radial arm saw.

It was about a month after CC's initial rejection of the idea of a crow's nest, and they were all sitting around the table talking after supper, when Jonathan handed CC a piece of paper.

"What's this?" he asked.

"Take a look," Jonathan said, a mischievous smile on his face.

CC was impressed with the quality of the drawing he was handed. Obviously the teen had some skill as an artist. When he realized what he was looking at, however, he almost brusquely handed it back to the boy, but then realized he didn't want to hurt his feelings, especially not in front of the others. "This is a nicely executed drawing," he said. It was a rendering of the big oak that soared above the meadow and the wood beyond.

Jonathan's face lost some of its glow when CC added, "We won't be doing anything with this tree, of course, but you're welcome to explain what you had in mind."

"Well, I wasn't thinking of a kid's treehouse or a place to play," Jonathan began. "This is a sort of crow's nest for when we think we especially need to keep an eye on the valley." He looked at CC hoping to get some encouragement, but his mentor's face reflected nothing more than casual interest in what might be considered a whimsical idea.

Jonathan stammered, then firmed his voice, "So, it occurred to me that we should invest a little lumber and hardware in building a platform about fifty feet up in the tree."

"Well," CC observed, "at first blush, that means we'd have to hang some sort of ladder up the side of the tree. It sounds a dangerous thing, and as soon as any unwanted visitor saw the ladder, they'd know that there are people nearby."

"That's true," Jonathan countered, "if we went up the outside of the tree."

"And?"

"That wasn't my plan."

"No?"

"As you know, it's a hardwood, over six feet in diameter at its roots, and over four feet in diameter at fifty feet off the ground."

"I know it's a giant of a tree," CC commented in an attempt to show himself amiable, "but I had no idea it was that big."

"I used a tape measure," the boy replied proudly. "I stood on the ground and measured it at eye level. The circumference is nineteen feet, and at fifty feet, the diameter is over four feet.

"So it's a huge tree," McCord commented sourly. "So what?" He looked narrowly at Jonathan.

"And how do you calculate the diameter of a tree fifty feet above the ground," CC asked, his eyes narrowing. "Geometry?"

"It was easy. I climbed it."

"You climbed that tree," McCord laughed. "Not a chance."

"Oh, I didn't go up the outside," Jonathan replied.

"Then how did you climb it? CC persisted.

"It's hollow."

"The tree's hollow?" CC asked. "How do you know that?"

"I've been inside it."

"You what?"

"There was a small hole at the base of the tree, and when I looked into it with a flashlight, I saw that the trunk was hollow."

"That doesn't mean it's hollow all the way up, CC observed.

"That's why I crawled in."

"You crawled in? Supposed you'd gotten wedged in that hole," CC challenged. "Suppose a big piece of rotten wood fell down on your head."

"Well, I didn't get wedged," the boy answered. "And nothing fell on my head. In fact, I measured the inside, and the hole at the bottom is more than forty inches across."

"And?"

"And I subtracted the inside diameter from the outside diameter and determined that the shell is over a foot thick, and that the bark is healthy."

Jonathan was speaking carefully, obviously attempting to make his argument before being cut off. He didn't realize that McCord's earlier interruptions had worked in his favor.

"I checked for rot by chopping at the inside with a hatchet," he continued. "The core is very hard, and when I shined my light up the shaft, it was like being in a chimney. In fact, there was an updraft."

"So your idea is that we try to find a way to go up inside the tree?" It was McCord again, his tone supercilious.

The boy ignored him, and instead addressed himself to CC. He'd long since determined who was in charge.

"So I enlarged the hole at the base to make it easier to get in and out."

"I didn't notice any change," CC said. It was a question.

"I kept the site cleaned up," the boy replied evenly, "and I made a door of plywood, and stained it to look like a giant knot."

Elizabeth noticed a hint of a smile appear for an instant on CC's lips, and wasn't surprised that he didn't comment.

Jonathan's voice filled the vacuum. "It wasn't possible to get long lengths of wood on end in the trunk to build a ladder, so I just cut a bunch of 2×4s into the proper lengths to serve as ladder rungs, and angled the ends of each one to conform to the curve inside the trunk. When I had fifty of those boards, I stacked them against the tree, and began nailing them inside the trunk, going up twelve inches at a time, until I could climb all the way up inside the trunk."

"You mean you've already done this?" CC asked accusingly. "You've actually climbed up inside the tree, and this isn't something you're asking me permission to do?" CC's voice was filled with anger. He heard an appreciative snort from McCord, and realized he shouldn't be criticizing the teenager in front of the others, particularly not McCord. He examined the faces of the others in the group, and when he noticed that McCord was smiling broadly, he clamped his jaws shut, angry at himself. CC's face had turned a rosy color, and it was obvious that he was fighting to contain his temper.

It wasn't difficult for CC to envision one of the rungs that Jonathan had nailed inside the tree collapsing beneath his weight, leaving him plummeting down inside the hollow tree, maybe jamming a leg into another rung, perhaps breaking his back and hanging there alone until he died.

They were all staring at CC, wondering what he would say next, but not Elizabeth. When she pointed at CC, and began laughing, it was as though someone had released a safety valve. Suddenly everyone except Jim was laughing hysterically.

In spite of the laughter, Jonathan spoke quickly to head off what he feared was an inevitable explosion. At the same time, he became aware that he might not have been so wise in doing what he'd done. But the deed was done. His face darkened. *CC means well, and I respect him, but he is not my father! I carry my weight here! And I've bailed him out a time or two.*

He nonetheless began talking rapidly. He'd already reasoned that it's easier to apologize after you've done something than to be refused the opportunity to attempt it. It was time to apologize.

"I could only carry up a couple of boards at a time, so the higher I climbed, the longer each trip. It took several days, and my legs were sore from the climbing. Anyway, when I finally got the forty-eighth board nailed in, I found myself looking out through a knot hole that was about a foot-and-a-half high and a foot wide. I couldn't see the entrances to our caves because they were on the other side of the tree, but I could see across the valley and down its entire length." He smiled. "It's a fantastic view."

When there was no immediate comment, he hurried on. "I built a platform about four feet beneath that hole, so that when I was standing, the hole was at eye level. Then I installed a trap door in the floor so that I could get up and down. After that, I cut a second knot hole on the opposite side of the tree so that I could look down at the mouth of our caves." With more than a little pride in his voice, he concluded, "I've watched the valley for hours, and no one ever knew I was up there."

Rachel watched CC's face with some amusement. He looked like he couldn't decide whether to put the boy over his knee or hug him in pride. Finally he did neither. All he said was, "I thought you were spending all your free time ice fishing."

Troubled Woodcutter

The Upper Cave
January 24th, 9:10 a.m.

C C thoughts came back to earth, and he turned his attention from Jonathan, high in the tree, to little Sarah, whose head scarcely reached his waist. "It's a great day to split firewood," he smiled. She looked up from the snowman she was patting together, and smiled back.

Checking to make certain that he was far enough from her play area to avoid hurting her, CC picked up a short length of sawn log and leaned it against the stump he used as a chopping block. Then he tapped the sharp bit of his ax deep into the end of the short log. Lifting the log that now gripped the ax blade, he swung it back over his head, flipped the ax over so that the log was now positioned above the blade, and swung the ax head down onto the stump, with the piggybacked log trailing it. Adding a little impetus with his wrists and shoulders, he brought the handle down and around in a smooth arc until the head of the ax smashed against the chopping block. With the ax's motion abruptly arrested, the momentum of the log continued to carry it downward, causing it to cleave itself over the razor-sharp blade, the two resulting pieces flipping to the ground on opposite sides of the chopping block.

He began to hum a carol as he continued to split the logs, throwing the pieces onto a growing pile. He realized it was frivolous. They didn't really need the wood, but they all loved to sit before an open fire when they lounged around the common room of their new cottage each evening. And it was good to have the wood on hand just in case the generator should quit.

CC frequently stopped work to breathe deeply of the crisp air, rich as it was with pine resin. He stared down the valley at a herd of deer feeding on the browse beneath the trees. The stream seemed glorious as it struggled against the ice-clad boulders that sought to arrest its flow. He broadened his focus to take in the bright blue sky and the spectacular panorama of fields and trees that swept up the far side of the snow-covered valley until halted by the soaring gray cliffs that enfolded the entire valley in their outstretched arms. For a man who had little time for poetry, nature was singing a sonata.

His eyes tired of the intense light, and he lowered them. They fell upon the neat stack of cord wood he had cached beneath the shade of the overhanging cliff. He had spent days sawing the wood by hand, and splitting the logs with a maul, hoping that no one would hear the noise and come to investigate. A sense of immense personal satisfaction and well-being overtook him and the heady wine of accomplishment brought a rare smile to his lips.

He looked out across the valley and was startled by movement beneath the trees. He blinked his eyes, telling himself that they must be failing him, but the deer browsing out there confirmed that there was something alien in their midst. Their tails flashed their peculiar warning signal as they leapt high into the air before zigzagging away across the valley, leaping up and down as they raced through the trees and across the ice-bound lake. Their panic seemed to confirm CC's impression. Someone was moving near the edge of the glade.

The day had lost its warmth and beauty, and he quickly slipped back under cover, ax in hand. It was tragic how the world had repeatedly intruded on this remote little valley. *And tragic,* he grieved, *that we cannot escape from a world bent on self-destruction.* He gestured to Sarah to leave the little snowman she was sculpting and come with him to the cave. She began to remonstrate with him, but when he put his finger to his lips and she saw his look of concern, she moved quickly to obey.

His eyes again fell upon the cord of firewood he had stacked near the cliffs. It was covered with strips of bark to protect the drying wood from snow and damp. He should have stacked the firewood inside the cave, but he counted on the cold dry air to season it more quickly. Yet leaving it outside like this might prove their undoing, for it provided mute testimony of their presence in the valley. He could only hope that the typical wanderer would not be able to determine how many seasons the wood had been stacked there, nor why.

CC sent Sarah back into the caves to warn the others, and then walked out into the meadow where Jonathan could see him from his nest high in the hollow tree. He whistled to get his attention, then pointed in the direction in which he thought he'd seen someone. The boy gave an exaggerated nod to indicate that he understood. CC continued to watch as the teen returned to his viewing point with the binoculars he would use to sweep the woods beyond the meadow.

CC turned back toward the cave entrance. Once back inside by the motor home, CC would have access to the intercom that connected with Jonathan in the crow's nest. Setting up the intercoms, running the cable underground from cave to tree, and manufacturing a wood "door" that disguised the opening at its base, were more of the teenager's brilliant ideas that McCord had derided.

It could certainly pay off now, CC thought.

Yet hours later, still uncertain about what CC had seen, he canceled the special watch and called a weary Jonathan down from the tree.

Community Problems
The Motor Home
April 15th, 10 p.m.

M arch had given way to April. Chilly nights were compensated for by pleasant afternoons. What little snow remained lay in melting drifts in the shadows on the north sides of trees and rocks. The risk of laying down a telltale trail in the snow was replaced by the certainty of leaving tracks in the sucking mud.

CC lay sleepless, several strange thoughts troubling him. *Too much coffee?* he wondered. *No, not too much coffee,* he decided, *but since these concerns were somehow brought to mind, I'll assume I need to examine them. It just may be that these are little warning bells, a still small voice, intuition, or the nudging of the Holy Spirit.*

His disquiet had begun to manifest itself when everyone had been joking about this being the 15th of April, once the deadline for filing income taxes. CC had laughed when they all had tried to calculate the value of their first harvest in the valley, and how, a short time before, the various levels of government would have taken the equivalent of over half the harvest in taxes. Even now, he thought it incredible that most Americans had never understood how the hundreds of direct and hidden taxes, compounding one another, could raise the cost of a loaf of bread a dozen times, and impact the cost of a new car. The real total tax burden on working Americans had to have been nearly 70%, and for some, far more.

CC set those thoughts aside as meaningless, and even counter-productive. He had far more immediate concerns. Since the day the man he had come to think of as "GI Joe" had walked into their cave, there had been just that one other event involving unwanted visitors. With that memory fading into the background, and with no additional visits from enemy troops, CC gave something like a sigh of relief. He joined the others in welcoming the first day of beautiful weather as a harbinger of better times.

Only McCord remained unsmiling. CC hid his own remaining tension behind a stiff smile, wondering what might happen next, and never for a moment trusting McCord's sudden apologies and passionate promises to co-operate with the group.

After the incident in which McCord had brought Elizabeth's portfolio back across the valley, there'd been no more trouble from him, and as far as CC knew, neither he nor Ross had ever tried to recross the valley to return to their cave. CC had not found it necessary to threaten them further, nor to take any steps to restrain them. In fact, he'd become very impressed with Elizabeth — her hard work, cheerful spirit, and creative ideas.

McCord was another matter. While he talked a good story, he was slow to help with any task, and did as little real work as possible. To McCord, a hundred words spoken were obviously more desirable than one minute of actual labor. To his credit, he had avoided any additional confrontations. Everyone seemed content with their present life-style, and neither words nor actions provided any indication that either he or Elizabeth had any plans beyond staying here indefinitely.

As tensions had eased, CC again focused his attention on the danger represented by outsiders. He was particularly concerned about the man he'd seen enter the cave during the winter, and insisted that anyone moving about outside the caves stay well within the natural screen that the woods provided. He was fully aware that too many restrictions would bring rebellion. They all needed to get out of the caves regularly to enjoy some fresh air and sunlight, but he could not shake the anxiety he felt.

Whether it was an intuition painfully purchased during his unknown past, or paranoia arising out of their recent unhappy experiences, its cause didn't matter to him. He was suspicious of their good fortune and unable to let his guard down. In spite of how well things were going, CC couldn't shake this vague disquiet, and on more than one occasion he wondered what Jim had in that backpack he'd taken so much trouble to secrete. He'd not seen the pack since the morning that McCord had pushed it out of sight behind his chair. *Why didn't I force his hand right then?* he wondered for the hundredth time.

CC thought back through the events of that turbulent morning. *Elizabeth had been unstrapping her portfolio from McCord's backpack when I walked up on them,* he recalled, *but she seemed far less concerned with the contents of his bag than McCord was with the contents of her portfolio. And she made no comment when he hid his own pack away. Are they,* he wondered, *involved in some conspiracy? And is their squabbling merely an act designed to deflect any suspicion? Apart from Ross, was I was the only one to notice McCord's suspicious actions?*

Later that same day, he had guided Elizabeth through a labyrinth of underground tunnels until they'd reached the heart of the mountain. Together they had hidden the portfolio containing the state papers in a remote cavity where there was no danger of spring flooding. He was not sure whether she could find her way back through the twisted pathway of tunnels they'd followed, but she didn't seem unduly concerned. In fact, she'd seemed to have trusted him.

I wonder if that portfolio is still where we put it, or if she went back and moved it, or if someone else has found it. It would be worth checking out, he realized.

Unholy Wars

More Ross vs McCord?
The Dining Room
April 15th, 6:40 p.m.

B efore the unexpected arrival of Rachel, Elizabeth, and Jim, CC had read the Bible to Jonathan and Sarah every evening. Following the arrival of the three adults, the practice became more difficult because of the housing arrangements.

Both the motor home and the cottage were comfortably warm because CC had hooked up the electric heaters he'd brought with him when he first came to the valley.

After CC partitioned the larger bedroom in the cottage, the women stayed in the motor home, with Rachel and Elizabeth sharing the rear bedroom, and Sarah sleeping on the bunk above the driver's compartment.

The meals were generally prepared and eaten in the cottage where the men also lived, but some mornings the women preferred eating their breakfasts in the motor home.

Each of the three men had one of the three bedrooms to himself, rooms a little larger than monk's cells, but having the advantage of privacy. But the carpentry took several days, and in the meantime they had to presume on the women's good natures by preparing and eating meals in the motor home, leaving early so that the women could prepare for bed.

The male/female dormitory setup made it difficult for CC to continue the Bible readings, especially because the women didn't like the men invading their privacy in the evenings. So once the construction was completed, they all began to gather around the wood stove in the cottage each evening.

On the face of it, it wasn't difficult to understand CC's latching on to the Bible. They had very little to entertain them during their free time. There were no newspapers, magazines, Internet, or TV. They had only the hundred odd books he'd gathered on the way out of Deep River Junction, and most of those were non-fiction volumes that he had selected because they might promote his survival. Chess and checkers were popular, as were card games like Rummy and Hearts.

The only radio broadcasts consisted of on-again, off-again programming from three competing stations, one operated by renegade Americans working for the Chinese, another by the Russians, and the third transmitting Jihadist propaganda, all sandwiched between threats and empty promises. Because the broadcasts were basically useless, they soon tired of them. The stations CC had listened to on the truck radio while making his escape a year earlier had emanated from distant cities and were no longer on the air.

When Jonathan first arrived in the valley, and had initially spotted CC reading the Bible, he asked him to read aloud to him. CC was annoyed, simply wanting some personal time to himself. Then, suddenly ashamed, he'd invited Jonathan to sit down with him at the table. Sarah immediately perched herself on the bench seat between the two of them, her hands folded neatly in her lap.

The Bible reading became a regular event until the night they brought Rachel home and discovered that Ross and Mc-Cord had invaded their little world. That Christmas night, Sarah assumed that they would all gather to hear CC read, and when it appeared that he'd forgotten, her voice rose above the various conversations. Jim left the motor home until CC had finished the evening's reading.

About a week later, after a hard day's work doing carpentry in the cottage, CC sat in a corner of the room staring sightless into space. Suddenly Rachel's voice caught his attention.

"CC. Sarah's been asking you a question."

He turned a questioning gaze on the seven-year-old.

"Aren't you going to read the Bible to us tonight, CC?"

CC offered her a brief, pained smile, then looked around the small living space of the motor home to gauge the response to her innocent question. He finally answered, "Sure, why not?"

When Jonathan asked him what he planned to read, CC replied, "How about the book of *John?*"

While he riffled through his Bible to find the place, Mc-Cord started for the door. As he pushed his way out, he turned and pointed an accusing finger at CC.

"We took decades to get this superstitious nonsense out of the schools and public places," he snapped. "And, it was only a year ago that we finally brought the churches under government control and began arresting those who were preaching these anti-social doctrines." Shaking his fist at CC, he said, "My God! Can't you see that you're damaging these children's minds with this nonsense?" He almost tripped as he stormed out the door and down the steps to the cave floor, slamming the door behind him.

Sarah was in tears. Elizabeth looked up from her place on the chair where she had been pretending to ignore what had been going on around her. Now, with a mischievous grin on her face, she offered a remarkably good imitation of McCord. "My God! Can't you see that you're damaging these children's minds with this nonsense?"

Rachel laughed. "He does seem a bit confused, doesn't he?"

"Indeed," Elizabeth laughed. "He invokes the name of the same God whose very existence he denies. "'My God,'" she laughed. "He's a parody of a pathetic and confused Hamlet."

Jonathan, who, a year before, had been studying Shakespeare in school, laughed heartily in agreement.

Rachel stood, placing one hand on her hip, holding the other palm up, and with a bewildered look on her face, paraphrased Hamlet's soliloquy. "To BE-lieve, or not to BE-lieve: that is the question," and then both she and Elizabeth began laughing hysterically.

McCord, standing unseen outside the motor home, was in a blind rage over being mocked by the others.

Elizabeth, having enjoyed her little joke on McCord, and still laughing, very deliberately picked up her gardening book, just as she would every night for the next few weeks. It became an effective shield between herself and those studying the Bible. But just before she opened its cover, she gazed over at CC and noticed that he wasn't laughing. He looked, in fact, unspeakably sad.

"Is it true?" he asked.

Caught by the tremor in his voice, Rachel asked, "Is what true?"

"What McCord said. Before the war, did the churches somehow come under government control?"

"Why, yes," Rachel stammered. "It all happened a few days before the war began."

"And the pastors?"

"If they indicated that they would persist in preaching the Word of God, they were immediately fined and imprisoned. In the case of several notable leaders, it was reported that radicals attacked and murdered them."

"And those pastors who did accept government control?"

"Well, it wasn't just Christian pastors who were controlled, but Jewish leaders too. And not just pastors and rabbis, but radio and TV personalities, missionaries, and virtually anyone who was considered a leader. Those who were 'politically correct' displaced those who had been faithful to God."

"I don't understand."

"Under the administration's interpretation of the law, they jailed those whom they considered the bad guys, and began turning over their ministries to men and women who would preach the politically correct party line."

"That's it? The Christians just rolled over?"

"Oh, no! Some preachers and laymen called for the organization of house churches, others actually took up arms against the armed Homeland Security and IRS agents who were sent to take over their churches."

CC winced. One of his too familiar wracking headaches had seized him. CC had come to realize that these always beset him when he was unconsciously attempting to suppress memories from his past.

As she heard them speaking, Elizabeth was gripped with confusion as well. At the time these things occurred, she hadn't been opposed to government control of the churches, but she now realized that her thinking was inconsistent with her present determination to promote liberty by protecting the American state papers. She suddenly felt that she needed to justify herself.

"I don't think most Americans favored it, but the anti-Christians in government were in control." Then she admitted, "Once I favored the idea myself, but now I realize that, whether I agreed with their beliefs or not, Christians and Jews were the only religious groups that were persecuted. Now I see that they had a right to air their views, and any effort to stifle them was a blow against everyone's freedom."

CC stared at her, his face impassive. It wasn't necessary for him to speak to make her realize how crippled her reasoning sounded, even now. He simply commented, "If all are not free, none are free."

Sarah, who among the entire group was the most sensitive to his moods, and also the one most outspoken in dealing with those moods, interrupted them.

"C'mon, CC! You promised to read us the book of *John*."

He looked at her for a moment, then exhaled deeply as he seemed to come back from a place far away. "Ah, yes," he smiled. He looked down at the book laying open on his lap, and it seemed to take him a moment to focus, to realize he'd already turned to the correct page.

He picked up the Bible, and read, "He who believes in the Son has eternal life; but he who does not obey the Son will not see life, but the wrath of God abides on him."

The verse was filled with power and potential and terror, but his voice was unaccountably lifeless and devoid of power. *Yes, that's the right word,* Elizabeth thought, *lifeless.* Elizabeth had established the habit of sitting across the room, turning the pages of her gardening book, and pretending not to listen. She attempted to hide it, but she was deeply touched by these daily readings. This one in particular actually frightened her.

The wrath of God? Am I living under God's wrath because I've neglected God's remedy for my sin?

Now she stared sightless at the gardening book that was laying upside down in her lap, and her thoughts turned to CC. She rubbed her eyes roughly, wondering at the unexplained tears.

Unlike those other nights when he has read aloud, his recitation tonight seems lifeless, though the words he is reading are alive with fire.

Rachel sensed it too. For she had come to love CC's reading of God's Word. While he rarely dramatized the text, he often altered his voice to fit the characters, and revealed himself to be an unusually compelling reader. He had a natural gift for pronouncing and placing the proper emphasis on each word so that the characters and events seemed to come alive to his hearers.

Rachel had quickly become absorbed in the readings, and admitted to herself that she was often gripped by the memories of her family and their faith. She knew her Bible well. Ordinarily, she would have initially ignored the content and evaluated the reader, but when CC read, she immediately become thoroughly engaged.

I've never heard the Bible read like this. It's as though the action is really taking place before us, and there is nothing artificial about it. What's more, I understand much better the words he is reading.

Elizabeth too realized that she actually looked forward to eavesdropping on his Bible readings. Things grew more interesting as these readings grew into little Bible studies, with CC offering very cogent answers to the questions asked of him. Then prayer was added.

McCord never said another word about religion, but he was notably absent when they all gathered around the Bible.

And from that first night on, it was the same group at the table, with Elizabeth sitting apart on the swivel chair, a book in her hands, but ever so often flicking her eyes toward CC as he read something that caught her attention. After a few weeks, Elizabeth still sat apart on the chair, but she no longer made a pretense of reading a book. Her eyes became riveted on CC, and though she never participated in the discussions, nor even opened her mouth to utter a single word, if anyone had looked at her, they would know that she was avidly involved in everything being discussed.

Depression
The Upper Cave

C C had been suffering increasing depression of late, and it was becoming difficult to hide it from the children. He knew that it was caused in part by his amnesia. He couldn't help but wonder, *Am I married? And do I have children?* Somehow he felt certain that he had been both a husband and a father, but there was no way to answer the pivotal question, *Have any of them survived?*

He told himself he ought to be able to handle it, but he couldn't shake the feeling of emptiness. And here he was with two good women who clearly took an interest in him, but, like him, were constrained by the same concerns and, at least in Rachel's case, by her obedience to God's Word.

Prior to the arrival of the adults, CC had become almost manic about his amnesia, and persisted in interrogating the children to see if they'd failed to tell him anything that might offer a clue to his identity. Even now he suspected someone here might be holding something back, especially Jim, but none could or would contribute anything. Neither Jim, Rachel nor Elizabeth had evidently moved in the same circles, and all denied having heard of anyone with the initials, CC.

Sarah, of course, was too young to know anything about him, and her grandmother's deathbed statement, praising God for CC's sudden appearance in the caverns, and his availability to care for her granddaughter, did not register with the child. Jonathan had told CC that his voice sounded familiar, but he couldn't remember in what context, though, at CC's insistence, he promised to continue thinking about it. The truth was, they all had suffered severe trauma, and they might all have memory problems.

Occasionally hints of a former life would flash across CC's mind like sparks in the wind, and like sparks, would as quickly be extinguished. They would leave him dazzled, and yet oddly result in a more confounding darkness. After these experiences, he sometimes found himself weeping tears of frustration because of his inability to recall or interpret even the simplest vision.

It was this frustration, coupled with an intrinsic determination to conquer every obstacle, that had driven him to examine the medical journals he'd packed with the supplies. He studied the chapters dealing with amnesia,   pouring over the pages, searching for clues to the cause and cure for his memory loss. Then he'd grown uncertain and even frightened of where his investigations would lead him, and he'd put the books away.

He was sometimes afraid he would learn who he was, and sometimes afraid he wouldn't. He was frightened by what he might learn about himself, but took heart that the books he'd read warned against such fear. He learned that the anxiety he suffered could actually prolong a self-induced or self-supported amnesia, but he was helpless to shake himself free.

And he was alternately encouraged and frightened to discover that he would probably have more frequent and intense glimpses into his past. He was sometimes pleased that there might ultimately be a cure for him, but he was alternately disconcerted because the book said it might take years — or even the rest of his life — to realize it.

He hoped he'd been a hero, and feared he'd been a hellion. Some nights, just before he fell asleep or before he had come fully awake, he'd see a brief vision of someone flashing before his mind's eye. He'd try to squeeze his thoughts down to concentrate on the vision, but his conscious efforts caused it to dissipate like mist in the morning sun.

It was not these brief visions he feared so much, but the ghosts that visited him in the dark hours of sleep when weird glimpses of what might have been his former life always terminated in the same dread manner. A car he was driving was skidding sideways across an ice-covered road. He would anticipate a crash, but nothing would happen. He'd just keep sliding and sliding, in a fear-filled, stomach-wrenching sort of movement from which he'd finally awaken, nauseous and terrified.

If he didn't wake up screaming, then he might get a further glimpse of the scene; the snow-encrusted windshield, the glare of a cat's eye reflector on the side of the highway moving inexorably toward him, the screaming hopeless careen of the vehicle, a sickening crunch as it ripped through a guard rail, the hurtling, tumbling chaos as it rolled down the embankment, and then ... nothing.

He'd awaken with the acrid taste of vomit in his mouth, his body soaked in perspiration, his breath coming in great heaving gasps, and the horrible certainty that he was reliving reality. He would ask himself, *"Why did it happen? Was I alone? How did I survive?"* And he'd fight to bring himself back to his new reality, the reality that he must survive. For while the past was important to him, it would remain indiscoverable if he couldn't survive in the present.

The Hot Tub
The Upper Cave
April 30th, 8 a.m.

As he relaxed alone in their newly installed hot tub, CC pondered the blessings of God on their little company of six. While one or two might not recognize God's hand upon their lives, it was difficult to imagine how any of them could have escaped death, let alone made their way to this remote and hidden valley to find themselves well-fed and secure. It defied the imagination. It was characteristic of him that it never occurred to him to take credit for any of the blessings the others shared with him.

A visit to the hot tub had become a regular practice for him, a therapeutic matter after his fall through the trees a year earlier, and he tried to soak in the turbulent hot water once or twice a week. This was Saturday, so he'd arisen early in order to get a head start on his day.

He was sitting up, looking through the polyethylene window that sealed the mouth of the upper cave, when he thought he saw someone running among the trees on the far edge the meadow. The polyethylene window made images appear distorted and fuzzy, but he imagined the movements to be furtive and suspicious, and became concerned when the person he was watching appeared to be hiding behind a large tree.

CC tensed for a moment, almost ready to climb out of the tub, then began laughing at himself. *It must be Jonathan,* he concluded, *playing hide-and-seek with Sarah.* He realized that he was wound tighter than an antique watch, but the alternative to his innocent interpretation could only mean disaster. So he forcibly turned his thoughts from possible catastrophe to an overblown frustration with the children.

Sometimes, he thought, *those kids act very foolishly.* Then he remembered that they had been very faithful to keep within his safety guidelines, staying near the cave entrance and within the confines of the meadow. He realized that he would have to speak to Jonathan again. Everyone had been instructed to avoid exiting the mountain from any cave but the main tunnel almost directly below, and it was obvious that just now they must have used another tunnel.

He lay back in the tub and closed his eyes, hoping that the roiling water would soak away the muscle tension. Instead, the stress increased with the entry of an unexpected visitor.

"Oh, I'm sorry. I didn't know anyone was here."

He really hadn't needed to open his eyes to identify the speaker. Elizabeth had come into the greenhouse area, a robe loosely wrapped about her. She looked as startled as he felt.

"That's OK. I was just about ready to get out anyway."

"Oh, no. I don't want to disturb you."

"You're not. Really. I've percolated long enough."

"You're sure?"

She went over and sat down on the edge of the hot tub, looking toward the window.

"Elizabeth?"

"Yes?" She turned to look at him, the intensity of her gaze somehow unsettling. Some long-buried feelings stirred within him. She was certainly a beautiful woman.

"Would you do me a favor?"

"What's that?"

"Go down to the storeroom and get me a towel."

"Oh, that's not necessary," she said with an impish twist to her lips. "I've got several right here."

He smiled his thanks, with no more sincerity than she was expressing. She sat there a moment longer, continuing to gaze at him.

She laughed at him.

"What's so funny?"

"You're so shy!"

He found himself disconcerted by the thoughts that flooded his mind, and he concluded that the look she was giving him had to be more comedic than lascivious. Apart from that, he was somehow certain that he was married and would therefore not so much as look at another woman. And even if he weren't married, he wasn't ready to court anyone.

Court anyone? That sounds like something out of the last century! What's the matter with me? She's made no overt suggestions. It's just my overactive imagination.

She brought him back to reality with her next words. Smiling widely, she said, "I'm just teasing you. And you look so uncomfortable that you remind me of a little boy."

"Well, would you mind going away while this little boy gets out of the water?"

She laughed mischievously. "What would you say if I got in with you?"

"I'd ask you how Jim would feel about it."

"Who cares what Jim thinks?" She frowned. "We have never had a relationship. In fact, I've never had a relationship of that kind with anyone, and won't until I find the right man." *And, she thought, I'm not sure that Jim likes girls anyway.* Aloud she added, "Besides, I was only teasing."

"I was hoping that was the case," CC replied. "I think more highly of you for that."

Her eyes took on a hurt look, and with that the magic was gone from the moment.

She turned and walked toward the polyethylene window. "You realize that you might be the last decent man on earth."

"I certainly hope not!" He paused, thinking back over earlier conversations. "What about that big man who helped you escape?"

"You mean the guy I hit with the chunk of firewood?"

CC's laugh was almost a snort. "Come to think of it, that was probably not the best way to start a romance."

Lips tight, she moved on to the mouth of the cave and stood before the plastic greenhouse wall where she gazed out across the valley. "You can get out now," she told him, her voice very controlled.

"Without a chaperone in the room?" he asked with a laugh, but his attempt to restore the easy conversation of the moment before was futile.

"Sure. I won't turn around," she replied. Then, obviously putting aside her hurt, she said in a throaty voice, "Honest, I won't." She giggled. Then, a moment later, "I really won't."

Was it a promise or regret he heard in her voice. *Relationships are always so difficult,* he thought. He'd given little thought to his past life, afraid of what he might discover. To his credit, he believed that a man who has made wedding vows has a sacred responsibility, "until death do us part." Months before, when Rachel had wistfully inquired about what he remembered of the quality of his marriage, he had answered, "I have no idea, but if a man's marriage isn't wonderful, then he needs to work harder at it."

He caught up a towel and, holding it like a curtain between himself and Elizabeth, he stood and wrapped it around his waist. Then he climbed up out of the tub. Just as he started down the steps to the cave floor, she turned around. He started to blush, but realized she wasn't really looking at him. There was something else in her eyes. Fear? Terror? Then she said the unimaginable.

"There are soldiers down there!"

He leaped down, his wet feet slapping hard on the cave floor, one hand somehow gripping the wet towel about his waist, almost throwing himself off balance. Slipping on the wet surface, he ran between the hydroponic vegetable beds, no longer concerned about his modesty.

Stepping to her side, he could make out two men at the edge of the woods, both wearing combat fatigues. They were almost invisible among the trees. It hadn't been Jonathan and Sarah playing games after all, he realized.

Oh God, he thought, *someone has found our hideaway.* CC could only hope that everyone was inside, and that these troops hadn't yet located the secret entrance to their caverns.

With every expectation of being obeyed, he said in a low voice, "Elizabeth, get down to the cottage. Tell them what you've seen. Then, get yourself dressed." He ran back toward the door. "Have Jim and Jonathan guard the entrance. You and Rachel get Sarah and start gathering the emergency packs. Make sure everyone has a gun. Get Sarah that little 22-caliber that Jonathan taught her to shoot," he added. "I'll be right down." Then, as an afterthought, "Make sure everyone has their hiking boots on, and has a complete set of winter clothing in their packs."

She was suddenly all business, icy calm, hesitating only an instant to make certain she'd understood everything he'd said.

"Got it?" he pressed.

"Yes, of course," she replied calmly. "I'm probably a little in shock, but I've got it." Then she abbreviated his orders.

"Jim and Jonathan to guard the tunnel entrances, Rachel, Sarah and me to gather packs and weapons." She was all business now, and he remembered the stories of her time in the vault below the art museum. His smile of encouragement was little more than a grimace.

Then she was gone, and he was pulling on his clothes without bothering to dry off.

Up a Tree
View from The Upper Cave
April 30th, 8:45 a.m.

C C caught up the binoculars that were hanging by a strap next to the plastic window, and began searching the woods below. It took him a moment to focus the lenses, and he had difficulty steadying them. There was now only one man in sight. He was moving from tree to tree, making his way carefully across the small clearing between the woods and Jonathan's giant oak.

Oh, no! Is Jonathan up in the crow's nest? CC focused the glasses on the base of the tree, then tracked up the trunk until the binoculars were centered on the hole the teen had cut through this side of the trunk. The openings he cut or reshaped made it possible for the boy to see not only the valley, but the cliffs and caves behind him. His heart sank when he saw Jonathan's face.

He was looking out across the meadow toward the cliff and staring straight at CC. Jonathan held his hand in front of his face, and wiggled his fingers in a playful "hello." CC pointed down, and Jonathan fixed a wry smile on his face before he shrugged his shoulders as though to say, "What can I do?" Then he held a walkie talkie up in front of the hole and waved it slowly back and forth. CC shook his head in an emphatic "No!"

Then Jonathan pulled the bud from his ear, shook it, and pressed it back in. So, the boy had the presence of mind to make certain he could hear without being heard. *Why am I surprised?* Then CC shrugged his shoulders to indicate that he didn't know what Jonathan should do either. He pointed at the teen, wiggled his index finger in a come-to me gesture, and again shrugged his shoulders to indicate he didn't know when or how.

"Please, God," he whispered, "Let this kid have the sense to stay hidden until he can get safely back into the cavern." The boy pointed down, shook his head "No," and then held both hands up, palm out. He'd stay where he was for the time being, and hopefully climb down the inside of the hollow tree to join the others if and when he was able.

In the meantime, the soldier walking toward the tree had reached its base. He'd been moving with the casual indifference of someone who believed that he had nothing to fear.

While CC's eyes remained fixed on the intruder, his thoughts turned toward the now dubious future of his little community. He realized that their best hope, indeed their only hope, lay in escape. Only a fool would risk almost certain capture or death in a gun fight against professional soldiers. Besides, if his little company's presence were discovered, the enemy would just keep coming and coming until they finally captured or killed all of them.

He lowered the binoculars and rubbed his eyes. When he opened them, movement on the periphery drew his attention back to the scene unfolding below. A big man in camouflage garb had stepped out of some heavy undergrowth and now appeared to be stalking the soldier who was approaching Jonathan's tree. CC didn't know where the other of the first two men had gone, but for some reason he didn't believe that the two he was now looking at were working together.

Fortunately, neither of the men below could easily spot CC's cave, hidden as it was by a thick tangle of vines and branches. He had the advantage of looking down through the brush at them. But the plastic he's stretched across the entrance to keep out the cold made everything blurry. Frustrated, he pulled out his pocket knife and cut a long slit through both layers of the polyethylene wall. Folding his knife, he dropped it back into his pocket, then lifted the field glasses again, giving him a far better view through the opening he'd made.

His eyes registered shock. The second man was the guy who'd come up the valley on skis earlier in the winter, and had mimicked shooting him through the artificial wall in the cave. His camouflage uniform was a different pattern from that worn by the man he was following. Something very strange was going on.

If this man had brought these others here, why does it look like he's stalking one of them? Maybe they're searching for him, and not for us. No, that's wishful thinking. Hope springs eternal, he thought in irony. *They might be hunting me!*

Then dejection set in. *It doesn't really matter. One way or the other, they've found us.*

When his attention returned to the first soldier, CC was stunned to see that he had not only taken an interest in Jonathan's oak, but he had knelt to look into the cavity at the bottom. While CC watched helplessly, he leaned his rifle against the tree, then slipped his head into the opening, twisted his shoulders, and dug his heels into the dirt, pushing himself in a position to look up inside the trunk. He certainly couldn't miss seeing the ladder rungs that ran up the inside of the tree. The soldier slipped back out of the hole, grabbed his rifle, and pushed the muzzle into the cavity he'd just vacated.

Oh, Lord, he's going to shoot Jonathan! CC turned to see whether anyone might have left a weapon in the cave near the hot tub, but he was sure that it was a forlorn hope. *It was a foolish and costly oversight on my part,* he thought.

Turning back toward the tree, he again cupped the binoculars to his eyes. The soldier was smiling as he began to slide his upper body back into the base of the hollow tree. He gave the illusion that he was being swallowed, with just his hips and legs now sticking out of the trunk.

At any second CC expected to hear a muffled discharge, but he was helpless to turn away. With the binoculars, it was as though he were standing right behind the man, looking over his shoulder. His imagination had followed the man's movements as he rolled onto his back. He could imagine him aiming up inside the tree, and tightening his finger on the trigger.

CC knew the gunman couldn't see the boy. All he might be able to see in the shadows would be the bottom of the trap door that formed a platform on which Jonathan was standing, but the treads nailed to the inside of the tree were a dead giveaway. He'd probably take a couple of chance shots, hoping to hit something...someone, but that's all it would take.

CC spun the focus knob so that binoculars took in a larger field. He was surprised to see that the other man had entered the picture, the man he'd begun to think of as G.I. Joe. He was definitely stalking the fellow who had crawled into the tree. Moving very quickly, he removed a knife from a sheath on his ankle, then knelt beside where the man's hips and legs protruded from the tree. The knife was now hidden from CC's sight, but he saw the big man's shoulders shift as he leaned forward to reach into the hollow of the tree. The legs of the soldier kicked violently for a moment, and when he finally lay still, the big man withdrew his arms from inside the tree, stood to his feet, reached down, took hold of the soldier's ankles, and dragged his limp body out of the cavity.

Then the big man gripped the handle of a knife that protruded from the man's chest, yanked it free, and wiped the blade on his victim's shirt. Again kneeling, he looked around the meadow and into the trees to make certain he'd remained unseen. Then he craned his neck back, stared up the height of the tree, and, amazingly, waved what looked like an all-clear. Bending down, he stood between the dead man's feet, again grabbed his ankles, and began dragging the body away.

At that same instant, the intercom buzzed. In the confines of the cave the noise was frightening. CC jumped, and wondered whether he was wrong in thinking that he'd seen the big man turn his head to look in his direction. CC ran for the intercom, hoping he was wrong, that the sound hadn't reached the ears of the man below. It was Jim calling, wanting to be filled in. CC told him about what appeared to be a manhunt unfolding outside the caverns and warned him not to use the intercom again.

"Do you think we have to get out of here?" McCord asked.

"I think we'd better head back into the caverns and try to avoid any contact." CC hesitated. "If, for some reason, they overlook our hidden home, maybe we will be able to return. But at least we'll be in a position to try to get away."

"Maybe we should just give ourselves up."

CC wasn't in a mood for arguing. "I'll tell you what, Jim. You give us enough time to get away, and then you to feel free to surrender. Okay?"

"It was just a thought."

"One more thing; whatever you do, avoid shooting. And don't let them see you."

"Why?"

"If we don't confront them, they won't be sure how long we've been gone, and it might give us a better chance to get away. Okay?"

"Yeah, okay. One thing's sure, we're no match for trained mercenaries."

CC ripped the wires from the back of the intercom, then ran back to look out the window. Their visitor of last winter was now on his knees, knife clasped in his hand, watching the movements of a second soldier who was crossing the meadow and approaching the mouth of the cave. This one was clearly not at ease, and kept looking from side to side as though trying to locate someone, probably his late associate.

The big man spun around and slipped beside a boulder, hiding himself from the second soldier, but still within CC's field of vision. CC was surprised when the big man laid down, his body suddenly appeared truncated, and then simply disappeared. It took CC a moment to realize that G.I. Joe had slid into a hole in the ground, dropping from sight.

"Curiouser and curiouser," CC quoted the fictional Alice. "And he's found his own rabbit hole."

It was uncanny. And unsettling. The guy had simply disappeared. *It must be another entrance to the caverns,* he reasoned. CC couldn't believe that the guy had known it was there. He hoped not, for that would imply that the man he'd named G.I. Joe probably knew a lot more about Hidden Valley than he did. Perhaps it's just a pothole that he stumbled onto by luck. Then he had second thoughts. *This guy seems too wily to be caught any place where he wouldn't have assured himself of a bolt hole out.*

It didn't matter to CC. All that mattered was that he had to gather their little company, leave their wealth of food and supplies behind, and somehow safely escape in hope that they might live another day.

Begin reading it now,

Book Four,

The Chronicles of CC

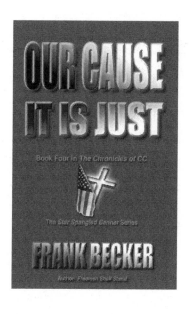

From "Our Cause It Is Just"

Eviction Day

April 30th, 9 a.m.

C C moved quickly down the cave past the hot tub. *Well,* he thought, *if I have to run again, at least I've had one last hot bath.*

He jogged down the sloped tunnel toward the lower cavern, and found the group waiting at the door to the cottage storeroom. Jonathan was there, which was a surprise, but CC realized that he'd probably seen the signal from the big man in the meadow, and had immediately taken the opportunity to climb down the tree. Any explanation of how he got to the cave without the other man seeing him would have to wait. CC just hoped the guy wouldn't be able to follow the boy, even though he'd made it clear by saving Jonathan that he wasn't an immediate threat.

"CC," he said, loud and demanding.

"I know."

"You know about the man? There I was, way up in the crow's nest, and this guy below me starts laughing and shouting that he knows I'm there and that he's going to kill me."

This was obviously news to the others because the boy instantly had everyone's attention.

"I could see him through the cracks in the trap door beneath my feet. He was pointing his rifle up at me, but then someone reached in, stabbed him with a knife, and dragged him back out of the tree."

"Yes, I saw that happen."

"Did you hear what he hollered up to me."

"He spoke to you?"

"Yes. He told to me to climb down quickly, but to stay hidden inside the tree. He said, 'Wait there until the coast is clear, then run to your cave.'"

CC didn't know how to process that. Was this guy somehow on their side, or was he feeling sorry for the kid that he'd found hiding up in the tree? It was something else he didn't have time to think about at the moment. He took one last look around. Even though he'd built it, it still seemed incongruous to him to see a cottage built inside a cave. He frowned. *It's been a good home*, he thought with deep regret.

He turned to Jonathan. "Have you shut down everything mechanical?"

Jonathan nodded in the affirmative.

"Okay. C'mon," he ordered. And turning away from the entry tunnel, he led them toward the cottage.

"Wait," Jonathan cried. "I have something to show you." He held out a crumpled page of newspaper.

"We don't have time to read old newspapers, Jonathan." CC brushed the paper aside, and turned back toward the tunnel.

Jonathan caught at his arm. "You'd better look at this one," he insisted. "Over here," and he led CC away from the others.

"Very well, show me," he demanded impatiently.

Jonathan pointed his flashlight at a picture that headed a brief article. It was a photo of some jewelry. In the half-light, CC found himself squinting to focus. He realized that it was a picture of a necklace, a necklace that looked familiar. In fact, if memory served, it was remarkably similar to the one that Elizabeth was wearing the night they'd found her in the motor home, the necklace that had been conspicuously absent from her neck ever since. CC was about to hand the paper back, but Jonathan insisted.

"Read the article. It's short."

Almost beside himself with impatience, CC grabbed the paper and scanned the words. He read it twice through before he understood.

"Where'd you get this," he asked.

"It was used for packing material in a carton of canned goods."

"O.K. Don't say anything to anyone about this."

"Right."

Everyone looked bewildered at the exchange. Why was CC taking time to chat with Jonathan when all their lives might be at stake? He crumbled the paper and stuffed it in his pocket, shrugged into one of the emergency packs that had been prepared weeks before, threw a canteen over one shoulder, grabbed his rifle, took a final look around the cave, and surprised everyone but Jonathan and Sarah by leading them into the living room of their little cottage.

They all quickly followed, and Jonathan carefully closed the door behind them. "Leave it unlocked," CC ordered. To forestall their questions, CC explained. "We don't want anyone thinking there is anything special about this little building. If we lock it, they may think we have something to hide."

CC opened a closet, slid the hanging clothes aside, and lifted a cunningly designed trapdoor in the floor.

He heard exclamations of surprise from McCord and the women. The dog slipped around him, looked down the long stairway, then skittered around and slipped back into the bedroom. Jonathan caught him by the collar.

"It's okay, boy. I'll help you down."

Jonathan led the way, holding the dog, and one by one, the others moved gingerly after him, climbing down the steep stairway, nervously gripping the railings until they reached the ledge above the dam.

CC had let them all precede him. He knelt on the top tread of the stairs, and reached up to slide the clothes on the bar above his head until they were evenly spaced across its length. Then he tucked some loose clothes in the gap between the wall and the hinged trap door so that when he dropped it down into place, the garments would spread out and help hide it during a casual search. *We need as much time as we can get*, he reasoned.

With the panel dropped back down in place, he reached up and slid a barrel bolt, making it far more difficult for anyone in the cottage above to raise the trap door.

When he reached the bottom of the staircase, he found that Jonathan was preparing to lead the others up the tunnel that lay alongside the underground river. McCord and Ross seemed dazzled by the lights glaring off the surface of the water, and certainly a bit amazed at the existence of this underground dam and water wheel.

CC crossed the dam and went down the stone stairway to the equipment below. By the time he reached the bottom, Jonathan had instructed all of them to turn on their flashlights. CC hit a switch, the lights in the area around the dam turned a dull orange and then went dark, leaving everyone temporarily blinded, and placing anyone who might try to follow at a distinct disadvantage. As their eyes began to adjust to the darkness, their flashlight beams seemed to make a pitiful glow in the vastness of the dark cavern.

CC joined them at the top of the dam, and they moved upstream along the ledge on the left side of the underground river, then climbed over a boulder to enter a narrow low-ceilinged tunnel. This smaller tunnel had been created by the flow of water, while the larger tunnel that bordered the river had been enlarged and squared by those who had removed limestone from the mountain. CC led them around a turn so they were well out of sight of the main tunnel.

Then he insisted they all take time for something to eat while he checked everyone's gear. "It's an old axiom for soldiers," he told them. "Eat, sleep, and take care of personal needs whenever you get the chance." So, in spite of the fact that they were excited and certainly a bit frightened, they all tried to eat something.

With the exception of Sarah, they were all despondent. Even for Jonathan, war had lost any possible charm. He had already been thoroughly disillusioned by death, disease, hunger, and grief. And now it was coming home to all of them that they were being forced to vacate one of the most wonderful places in the world they could imagine. In spite of any differences they might feel toward one another, none of them wanted to lose this shelter.

Nothing more had been said to mar their fellowship since the night they'd begun the Bible readings, and, for now at least, everyone seemed to be working together. *It's amazing,* CC thought, *what a little common adversity can do to bind people together. But we need to face facts. Matters are now out of our control.* He studied each of them, hopelessness evident in their dejected stares, and even Sarah was beginning to reflect their despair.

Strangely enough, he was able to sleep for a few hours, but when he awoke he was beside himself with anxiety. He felt that he had to do something, to take some action. *I can't just sit here doing nothing!*

"I'm going to take a look around," he suddenly announced. "Wait here until I return, and try to rest while you can." He'd already sent Jim back to the junction of the tunnels so that he could keep an eye on the area around the dam. Without drawing attention to himself, Jonathan had followed Jim, staying out of sight, but monitoring his activities. He simply didn't trust the man.

CC moved in the opposite direction, and when out of sight, took the tunnel that would lead to Sennett's underground barn. "Whatever happens," CC had warned them, "we must not get bottled up inside this mountain." Apart from himself, only Sarah and Jonathan were familiar with the alternate escape route, and he had told them to keep it to themselves, not knowing whom they could trust.

Also from Frank Becker

For those of you concerned about the future of the Church and your place in it, and for you who are concerned with emergency preparedness, both of these books are available in paper and as e-books.

 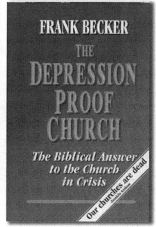

You Can Triumph Over Terror

Special Agent Frank Gil (Retired) FECR PD; featured on COPS, Metro-Dade Special Response Team (SWAT) wrote: "Frank's book should be required reading. By preparing, you increase your chances of survival, facilitate our ability to assist you, and reduce your own stress and anxiety."

The late John Sipos, Broadcast Journalist and host of "hOURTampa Bay," commented, "If you apply the ideas in this book...you and your family will radically improve your prospects for survival."

The Depression Proof Church

Here's what Paige Patterson — past president of the Southern Baptist Convention, and president of America's largest seminary — wrote about The Depression Proof Church: "Frank Becker...has clearly enunciated the one essential, namely, a return to the church of the New Testament."

And Dr. John Kenzy — who co-founded the Teen Challenge Bible Institute with David Wilkerson — called The Depression Proof Church "Compelling and timely," and said that it "exposes revelation from God."

Senator Stephen R. Wise, PhD, called it "hard hitting," "inspiring a return to biblical practices that have been forsaken in a lust for ever larger churches."

And the Jacksonville Theological Seminary created a course called, The Depression Proof Church, for students seminary students as well as undergraduates.

Follow CC at

www.FrankBecker.com

Made in the USA
Charleston, SC
31 August 2016